NOELA
&
THAT MAN IN RIO

ALSO BY MURIEL MADDOX

Captain from Corfu

Love and Betrayal

Llantarnam

NOELA
&
THAT MAN IN RIO

❧ NOELA ❧
&
THAT MAN IN RIO

Two Novellas by
Muriel Maddox

SUNSTONE
PRESS

The characters in these stories are fictitious.
Any similarity to real persons, living or dead,
is coincidental and not intended by the author.

Sunstone books may be purchased for educational, business, or sales promotional use. For information please write: Special Markets Department, Sunstone Press, P.O. Box 2321, Santa Fe, New Mexico 87504-2321.

Library of Congress Cataloging-in-Publication Data:
Maddox, Muriel,
   Noela; & That man in Rio: two novellas / by Muriel Maddox.–1st ed.
     p. cm.
ISBN: 0-86534-309-8   –ISBN 978-0-86534-567-6 (pbk. : alk. paper
   1. Rio de Janeiro (Brazil)–Fiction. 2. Switzerland–Fiction. I. Title: Noela; & That man in Rio. II. Title: Noela; and, That man in Rio. III. Maddox, Muriel, That man in Rio. IV. Title: That man in Rio. V. Title.

PS3563.A339455 N64 2000
813' .54–dc21   00-025191

Published by SUNSTONE PRESS
     Post Office Box 2321
     Santa Fe, NM 87504-2321 / USA
     (505) 988-4418 / *orders only* (800) 243-5644
     FAX (505) 988-1025
     www.sunstonepress.com

To the memory of my mother
Isabel Ramage Maddox

❧ NOELA ❧

PART ONE

October 1970

❧ 1 ❧

IT WAS THAT TIME OF YEAR when autumn lingers for a moment, gold and scarlet, with swans gliding across Lac Léman and the smell of woodsmoke in the air.

The man stood on the balcony of the Hotel des Trois Couronnes. He was tall and lean, in his late forties, with blond hair slightly tinged with gray and eyes that were blue and deep set. Above his left eye and disappearing into his hair line was a long jagged scar, faded now with the years, that gave his face an air of mystery and kept him from being too handsome.

Church bells were ringing in Vevey and the sky was pale rose above the snow-capped Alps. Below, on the promenade around the lake, an old man was walking a dog. Children's laughter drifted up. A white seagull fluttered by and perched on the black wrought-iron railing.

"What time is it, darling?" Liz called, her voice heavy with sleep.

Paul Sanderson walked back into the bedroom. The room had pale green walls, a burgundy carpet, and floral chintz draperies. There was a lace runner on the bureau and a vase of pink rosebuds sent by the hotel manager. Paul glanced at his leather travel alarm clock on the night table.

"Seven-thirty," he said.

Liz yawned under the puffy yellow quilt and turned over in bed. "I love Vevey," she said. "Wasn't it lucky that the hotel in Montreux was closed for the winter? We never would have discovered this."

"Come look at the view from the balcony." He handed Liz her robe. "It was too dark to see anything last night."

"Listen. Church bells." She sat up. "I'd forgotten it was Sunday."

"That's the nice thing about a vacation. You lose all sense of time."

"We should get away more often. At least once a year. And I don't mean Palm Springs." She fastened her robe and brushed her hair out of her eyes. "Let some of the other lawyers in the firm take your cases."

He did not answer.

Liz walked to the balcony. "How beautiful!" She threw out her arms and took a deep breath. "Isn't this Swiss air marvelous? If only we could bottle some and take it back to Los Angeles!"

Paul laughed and kissed her on the forehead.

"Look," Liz said, pointing across the lake. "See that sweet little town nestled at the foot of those mountains? Isn't that the French side?"

"Yes, I think so. The border is somewhere along there."

The border, he thought with a start, and suddenly he felt himself breaking out in a cold sweat. How many years ago was it? He had not realized they were so close to—what was the name of the town? He had blocked it from his memory, and now, there it was. Again. Across the lake. He lit a cigarette and his hands were trembling. The border. Were there guards there now?

"Let's get dressed and go down to breakfast," he said.

Liz was staring at him.

"What's the matter?" she asked.

"Nothing."

I have forgotten, he thought. It all happened a long time

ago. The war. Twenty-six years. He stared across the lake.
Now it seemed like yesterday. How curious to find that
nothing is ever completely erased from your memory, it is
always there, lurking in the dark, waiting to destroy the
present.

Liz was taking out a tweed skirt and a black sweater.
Noela had worn a black sweater. Noela. Was she still in that
village after all these years? And the priest. . . .

"We'd better call the house tonight," Liz said. "I'm
worried about the children. They haven't written any letters
since we've been gone. I can't understand it."

"You know how teenagers are," he said.

Steve and he had been tangling a lot lately. He would
never have dared speak back that way to his own father.
Maybe it wouldn't be a bad idea if the draft did take Steve,
and they would if he didn't keep his grades up. He'd have to
register in March. And Jennifer, at sixteen, thinking she knew
all the answers. . . .

"What's the time difference between Switzerland and
California?" Liz asked.

"Eight hours." He thought a minute. "It's nearly
midnight there. Saturday."

"Then if we call early this evening it will be Sunday
morning at home. They'll just be getting up. That will be a
good time to get them." Liz disappeared into the bathroom.

He lit another cigarette and sat down on the bed. He
had tried to talk to Steve, to sound him out on various
subjects, but there seemed to be a wall between them. When
Steve listened it was with an amused tolerance. They
disagreed on almost everything. And his friends had the same
problems, and worse, with their sons. At least Steve wasn't on
drugs, as far as he knew, or did you ever know about your
own children?

"Your generation has it too easy, that's the trouble," he

had told Steve one evening. "You all have your own cars, nice homes, you don't have to struggle for anything. We had the Depression, a war—"

"Okay, cool it, Dad. Besides, you were never poor. Grandfather has a lot of money."

Yes, he had to admit that was true. But he was on a strict allowance, he had to take a summer job, he didn't just loaf around during vacations the way Steve and his friends did. He saved the money for his own car. Well, half of it, and his father put up the rest. He had always addressed his father as "sir." Most of Steve's friends didn't even stand up when an adult entered the room.

"I don't believe in war," Steve said. "I don't want to fight in Vietnam. Do you want me to go to Vietnam?"

The answers had seemed so simple once. Right and wrong were much clearer.

"Your war was different, Dad," Steve said. "I guess. But what did it prove?"

He had lost control of himself then. "For your generation," he shouted, "men died by the millions, that you could live in peace, not slavery! Where would all of you be if Hitler had won?"

These young people today with their long hair and their peace signs disrupting college campuses with riots—what right had they to judge anyone? It was easy to judge, to find fault with the generation that had preceded you. Had he been as harsh on his parents' generation? He did not think so. He had thought them old-fashioned, sometimes stuffy, with their emphasis on manners. . . .

"The shower's all yours, darling." Liz opened the bathroom door.

"Oh, fine."

"I wonder if there's a hairdresser in the hotel?" Liz scowled at her reflection in the mirror above the sink. "I need to have my streaks done again."

"You look all right. And besides, there wouldn't be one open on Sunday."

"Spoken just like a husband," she laughed. She picked up a brush. "I still can't get over running into Felicia last night after all these years. I must say she looks great." Liz smoothed out a wrinkle over her forehead. "We came out the same year in New York, so that makes her forty. I wonder if she's been taking those treatments with that doctor, what's his name, in Vevey? Darling, are you listening?"

"Yes, you wonder if Felicia's been taking treatments from Doctor What's-His-Name."

"You know the one I mean." Liz came out of the bathroom. "The Duchess of Windsor and Charlie Chaplin go to him. He gives injections from the fetus of unborn lambs or something. I'm willing to bet that Felicia's been to him."

"Why don't you ask her? By the way, what happened to the Austrian baron?"

"Oh, she divorced him several years ago. It turned out he had a title, but no money. And also a boyfriend. I must say, Felicia's always had the darnedest taste in men. The last time I saw her she was going around with some alcoholic actor she was trying to reform, and there've been two other husbands in the interim. Helmut was her fourth husband."

"Well, I must have done something wrong. I still have the same wife after all these years."

"And just you try and get away!" Liz gave him a playful swack as he passed.

Paul turned on the shower full force and stepped into it. Liz was saying something but he could not hear her.

The town across the lake. How ironic that he should have come back after so long, as if directed by some unknown force. For he knew now that he must go there and find out what had happened to them, and to her.

Noela.

The scent of apple blossoms and newly-cut grass. He did not even have a picture of her, only a memory grown dim, faded, of large amber eyes, hair that was like wheat with sunbeams through it, a voice that had music and laughter.

He was happy with Liz. They had a good life together, except for the problems with the children, but all parents had those same problems today. He was a successful lawyer, they were members of the Los Angeles Country Club, the Beach Club, they had a beautiful Colonial home in Brentwood, he was able to combine pleasure and business on a three-week trip like this to London, Paris, Rome, and a few days in Switzerland. Why, then, was there an emptiness in his life, a lack of purpose?

And guilt nagged him like a shadow, an unpaid debt.

He turned off the shower and grabbed a towel from the rack. The towels had three gold crowns embroidered on them.

"Doctor Niehans, that's his name," he heard Liz say.

"Who?"

"You know, that doctor."

He opened the bathroom door. "Oh, yes," he said. Liz was all dressed, her face made up, her frosted dark hair tied back with a pink chiffon scarf. She was a handsome woman, she had kept her figure through dieting and golf, and even in a pink tweed skirt and black jersey sweater she looked chic. He was always proud of the way she dressed and the way she entertained his friends. If their love-making had become routine after twenty years of marriage, well, that was to be expected. At least he wasn't carrying on with a young secretary like some of the men he knew. "You don't need Doctor Niehans, darling," he said.

"Every woman gets to the point in life where she needs something," Liz said.

What did she mean by that? He glanced at her, but her face revealed nothing.

"You mean a new husband every few years like your friend the baroness?" he kidded.

"Oh, Felicia goes to extremes. You don't like her, do you?"

"Why do you think that?"

"It's just something I feel."

"I don't really know her. We just exchanged a few words in the dining room last night."

"Well, I promised Felicia I'd call her this morning and we'd get together and have lunch or something. Maybe you'd rather do something else. It will be boring for you—just girl talk."

"If you really want to get rid of me, I can take a steamer around the lake." He pulled on his trousers and zipped them. "I was thinking of doing that anyway."

"I don't want to get rid of you, darling." Liz kissed him.

"You and Felicia have a nice lunch and get caught up on all the gossip. I'll join you for cocktails." He took out a cashmere sport jacket and brushed it off.

"Are you sure you don't mind?"

"Quite sure."

"Felicia's leaving for Marbella tomorrow morning, so it will be the only chance I'll have to see her."

Why did she keep pressing the point? He knotted his tie. "Are you ready?" he asked, trying to keep the annoyance out of his voice. It was a habit that Liz had developed lately, repeating things several times as if she needed assurance.

"Yes. Do you have the key?"

He looked around the room. The key was on a table by the window and had a large brass crown attached with the number. He put it in his pocket and there was a large bulge.

"It would be hard to walk off with this thing," he said. "It weighs a ton."

Liz opened the door. Shoes were lined up in front of the different rooms. A rosy-cheeked maid in a striped blue and white uniform walked by carrying towels.

"*Bonjour, m'sieu-dame,*" she said, smiling broadly.

"*Bonjour.*"

"Now which way is the elevator?" Liz said. "I'm all turned around." The maid was watching them, eager to get in the room, since most of the other guests still seemed to be asleep. "*L'ascenseur?*"

"*Là-bas.*" The maid pointed.

"*Merci,*" Paul said.

It was a small self-service elevator with a red carpet, gold antique mirror and chandelier. A sign in French warned that the capacity was six persons. Paul pushed a button and the elevator started down. "I hope I pushed the right one," he said.

The dining room was empty except for a boy busy with a vacuum cleaner. The maître d'hôtel quickly appeared and led them to an adjoining room looking out on a terrace.

"We serve breakfast here," he said.

At the next table there was an older couple speaking German. He had a fat red face and she was aristocratic-looking in tweed and pearls. He had noticed them at dinner the evening before. It gave him a strange feeling to hear German, but then they could be Swiss from Zurich or somewhere.

"Isn't this pretty?" Liz said. "We can see the lake. I suppose they serve breakfast on the terrace when it's warmer."

The waiter poured coffee into Meissen cups and brought croissants and jam.

"Could you tell me the name of that town directly across the lake?" Liz asked him.

"That is Saint-Gingolph, Madame," he said. "It is in France."

Saint-Gingolph, Paul thought. Of course, that was it. The name reverberated in his head. The rushing stream, the sound of cowbells, the scent of apple blossoms. The Germans. He felt dizzy. He gulped some coffee quickly and it scalded his throat. Saint-Gingolph. He looked out to the terrace, across the lake, towards the snow-capped mountains. There it was. The town. Saint-Gingolph. He spread jam on a croissant, raspberry, there had been tiny raspberries in the woods, it was May. . . .

I am not guilty. He had defended a young man in court recently who had spoken those words.

"Paul?"

Dimly, he heard Liz's voice. Her face had a worried frown. "Is anything the matter?"

"No," he said.

It seemed as if all the threads that bound him to the past were there once more, tangled like the game he used to play at childhood parties, only then when you unwound the threads there was a prize at the end. What was there now? Something he preferred not to find? Yet he had started and he must continue, slowly unwinding, in and out, round corners, up the staircase to the secret room, opening doors. . . .

"What are you thinking about, darling?" Liz asked. "You look so serious."

"Nothing," he said. He smiled at her. "Just something at the office I've got to take care of as soon as I get back."

The waiter poured more coffee. The German-speaking couple were getting up from their table. The man looked vaguely familiar and Paul had the impression that he had seen him before. But where? The man looked at him with a curious expression as he passed and Paul noticed that he had one glass eye.

"May I have the key?" Liz asked. "I think I'll go on back to the room."

He handed it to her. "I'll be up in a few minutes. I want to check with the concierge about something."

He would find out about the lake steamer to Saint-Gingolph. Again he heard the rushing stream, the cowbells. The sound became stronger. I am not the person I was then, I have changed. Nothing remains the same. Nothing.

He lit another cigarette and stared out across the lake.

❧ 2 ❧

PAUL WAITED ON THE covered pier for the lake steamer. Next to him an elderly couple was speaking French. He had white hair and a mustache and twinkling blue eyes, she wore a purple velvet coat with a fox collar and her hair was dyed a bright orange, like a figure in a Toulouse-Lautrec painting. Swans glided across the water and the trees were shades of bronze and crimson.

In the distance he could see the white steamer coming from the direction of Lausanne. The lake was calm with just enough breeze for the sailboats. A seagull dipped down, then flew off again.

A stout woman in a gray tailored suit and felt hat with a small boy joined them, then two college-age boys with long hair and a girl in blue jeans and suede jacket. They were speaking English and one of the boys reminded him of Steve. Probably students, he thought, going to one of the Swiss universities.

The small boy pointed excitedly to the steamer and jumped up and down, speaking French rapidly. His mother was taking some coins out of her purse.

An old man in dark pants, a sweater and a navy beret appeared and stood next to the wooden gangplank.

It would not be long now, Paul thought.

The sun was shining brightly and on the snow-capped mountains and high up he could see a tiny green train crossing a bridge. It looked almost like a toy. It reminded him of the train set he once had with little Swiss houses and a paper maché tunnel like a mountain with a stream on the side. He used to play with it by the hour. How he had loved that boyhood train set!

When Steve was born he waited for the day when he would ask Santa Claus for a train set. Steve never asked. He wanted a car racing set instead. Trains were a thing of the past, they meant nothing to the young anymore.

In fact, it was hard to figure out just what did mean anything to the young of today. Maybe the only generation we can really understand, Paul thought sadly, is our own. Those who walked at the same time in the paths we trod. We shared an era they can never know nor even comprehend.

The steamer was pulling alongside the pier; two men with long poles hooked the edge, while the old man in the beret pushed the gangplank out for the passengers to board. Paul looked around. Apparently you bought your ticket on the boat. He followed the others and saw a ticket booth just inside.

The steamer was crowded. He went up the stairs and looked for a place to sit on the upper deck. There were tables inside for coffee and drinks but he decided to sit outside where he could see better.

The steamer stopped at Montreux, passed the Château of Chillon, stopped again at Villeneuve. They were getting closer now, there was only Le Bouveret and then Saint-Gingolph. He felt chilly, though the sun was shining brightly.

"Dieu te protège, mon fils."

The curé, Father Romelin. It was all coming back. He could almost see his face again, the pale face with blue eyes that glowed with a spiritual light yet had a twinkle in them.

The steamer was turning the bend. Paul walked forward to the bow and his eyes followed the road along the lake, small stucco houses with gaily painted wooden shutters, a blue café, snow-capped mountains rising steeply in back. His heart was beating more rapidly, he had trouble getting his breath.

And then he saw the yellow sign above the pier.

SAINT-GINGOLPH.

The dock was on the Swiss side of town. He looked up and he could see the railroad tracks, and farther to the right, on the French side, the church tower with the clock. The curé would be an old man now, Paul thought, for he was middle-aged then. Possibly he had retired and a younger priest had taken his place. He would soon know.

Passengers were starting to get off. He heard a couple in front of him saying that they always came to Saint-Gingolph to buy cognac because it was much cheaper than on the other side of the lake.

Swiss customs men and French police were standing on the bridge over the stream that marked the border. They were stopping cars and checking passports but they did not stop the passengers from the lake steamer.

Inside the Café de la Navigation he saw several old men sitting at tables. Next to it was a shop selling postcards and souvenirs. He walked on. A *laiterie* advertising butter from Denmark, a *boucherie-charcuterie* with sausages hanging in the window. An old woman in black passed, glancing at the tourists.

Noela was nineteen then, now she would be forty-five. Married, probably, as he was, with several children. It was unlikely that he would recognize her if she passed him in the street, a middle-aged housewife, plump, no doubt, carrying a loaf of French bread under her arm. She might not recognize him either, but he did not think he had changed that much.

He turned off the main street with its shops and took the narrow road leading up the hill towards the church. He walked under an arch with the railroad tracks passing overhead. He could hear the rushing stream. There was a brown stucco house with a steep red tile roof and an old woman was rocking back and forth on the balcony. She looked at him with curiosity. Next to it was a green stucco house with white lace curtains in the windows and pots of geraniums.

He heard steps behind him and turned. No one. His imagination was playing tricks on him.

Suddenly he came upon the church in the small square.

Like the houses around it, it was of tan stucco with a steep red tile roof and a bell tower. Over the main door was a simple white cross and on the side the tri-color of France and a plaque with names. Paul looked at the statue beside the church, a fallen soldier clutching the flag.

Were they the lucky ones, he wondered, those fallen heroes, who had not lived to see what the world had become?

He thought back to the war, when just to survive was all important, when it seemed that if only we won the war everything would be all right, all the problems of the world would be solved. And now, he thought, the world is in a complete mess. For what did so many brave men die? To uphold ideals that are now out of date? Or will the things that we once believed in come back?

Woodsmoke was coming from the chimney across the square, birds were singing, he could hear the stream rushing down the mountainside. There were rosebushes planted near the statue and someone had recently left a pot of mauve chrysanthemums. Mother of Derivez, Leon? Widow of Cachat, Jules?

TOMBES POUR LA DEFENSE DE LA PATRIE.

Paul pushed open the door of the church. It was empty. The last Mass had been two hours ago. Slowly he walked down the aisle and sat on one of the brown wooden benches.

He closed his eyes.

It seemed he could feel a hand touch his shoulder gently, hear the curé's voice.

I always knew that you would come back one day to Saint-Gingolph, my son. I knew you had not forgotten. . . .

PART TWO

May 1944

✤ 3 ✤

"WAKE UP, NOELA!"

She heard her mother's voice calling from downstairs and she threw back the blue-patterned quilt and jumped out of bed. The white blossoms from the apple tree almost covered her window, their sweet scent filled the room and gave her a sense of giddy intoxication. Outside she could hear the cowbells ringing. Dawn was just breaking over Lac Léman, and the mountains were still capped with snow, though it was early May. By her bed lay a novel of Colette with a marker where she had read late into the night.

What good was it, she thought, to be nineteen and to feel spring surging through her, with all the young men gone off to fight, or else, like her brother Raoul, working as captives for the Germans? She would grow old and never know love, the kind Colette wrote about.

She pulled off her flannel nightgown and started to dress. Her clothes were simple, suited to a girl who had grown up on a farm, who had never been farther away from Saint-Gingolph than to take the lake steamer to Montreux and Geneva. How she would love to see Paris, the Paris that Colette wrote about, to buy a pretty dress, to see the Louvre, the Arc de Triomphe, the opera! Dreams. Dreams she would never know. The Germans were in Paris, the Germans were everywhere, even in Saint-Gingolph.

She pulled on coarse black stockings, wondering how her legs would look in black net hose. Those were vain thoughts, the nuns at school would have punished her for thinking such things. I don't care, she thought, I am only young once! She reached out the window and picked a white blossom. She tucked it in her hair and waltzed around the room. Who was there to dance with? The only men left in Saint-Gingolph were old men. They smiled at her when she passed, when their wives weren't looking. There was old Monsieur Toutain, the baker, with the tall thin wife, her face pinched and bitter, her hands red and coarse. She was like one of those apples fallen on the ground in late autumn, brown, with all the juice gone.

What good was it to be young and pretty? It was wasted now. For so long she had been skinny and plain, with large amber eyes, sallow skin, and hair that was an ordinary shade of brown worn in braids. Her legs were like a bird's, without shape, always skinned at the knees from climbing trees. Vanity is not becoming, the nuns told her. She had thought of becoming a nun at one time, there was a nun she admired very much and she tried to imitate her.

The feeling had passed. Now she read novels the nuns would not approve of, and sometimes she felt that even the Abbé Romelin looked at her with disapproval when she skipped along the village streets humming.

"Noela! What are you doing?" Her mother's voice again.

Her mother was getting impatient. Her grandfather would already be up and putting logs on the fire. It was amazing how much he could do when he was half blind from cataracts. "I can still see well enough to shoot the *boches*," he said. He had fought along the Marne in the First World War and been wounded twice.

She could smell the woodsmoke now coming out of the chimney. Thank heavens there was still plenty of wood, but if the war lasted much longer they would have to be careful.

Food was scarce, the Germans had taken everything. They waited and prayed for the invasion, there were all kinds of rumors that it would be soon, but no one really knew. Five years of war, five years out of her life that would never come back. It seemed endless.

She buttoned her blue cotton print dress and put on a black sweater. It was cool in the early morning, there was still dew on the grass. Birds were chirping. She fingered the tiny gold cross on a chain round her neck. She never took it off. It has been given her by her father on her fifth birthday, which was also Christmas. The following August he was drowned when his boat overturned in a sudden thunderstorm on the lake.

Her mother had coffee and rolls on the kitchen table. They had not had butter in a long time.

Her grandfather was turning the pages of his bible. She went over and kissed him and his gray mustache tickled her cheek.

"You look very pretty this morning, *ma petite*," he said.

"She is vain enough without compliments, Papa," her mother said.

"Ah, Germaine, who else is there to tell her? What kind of a life is it for a young girl in Saint-Gingolph these days? There are no young men around to dance with her, to court her. All we think of is survival, but she. . . ." He threw out his arms in a hopeless gesture.

Noela looked at her mother. From pictures of her she could see that she had been pretty once. No traces of it remained now, and she was barely forty. She was plump, her hair was pulled back in a bun, she dressed in drab, dark clothes like an old woman.

I do not want to be like that, Noela thought, I do not want ever to be old.

She sipped her coffee. The cup had a crack in it. At

confession she would have to confess to impure, frivolous thoughts. That she wanted to dance, to have compliments, to have a man make love to her.

"She reads these cheap novels half the night," her mother said. "Putting all kinds of ideas into her head."

Germaine Fornay had put love out of her life when her husband died. Bernard Fornay. His grave was in the cemetery on the hill overlooking the lake, marked by a simple white tombstone with the dates and *PRIEZ POUR LUI*. She went often to his grave to replace the flowers and pray.

"Why did he have to go to Nyon that day?" Germaine frequently said, her voice tinged with resentment against the man she had once loved who had left her with all these burdens. "If only he had listened to me. . . ."

The past could not be changed. It was over. Bernard Fornay, beloved husband of Germaine Fornay, had gone to Nyon that day and been drowned. *Priez pour lui.* Grief prolonged became not grief but self-pity.

Should she feel guilty because she barely remembered her father? Noela wondered. Was that why her mother kept talking about him, so that she, Noela, would not forget that she once had a father? A father, who according to what she had been able to find out, had been unhappy in Saint-Gingolph and was always looking for excuses to get away. Was there another woman he had hoped to see in Nyon? No one would ever know.

I am like my father, Noela thought, filled with restless longings, wanting to see the world. Will nothing ever happen to me?

Raoul, her brother, had been content in Saint-Gingolph. He wanted to be a farmer. The Germans had taken him along with the other young men of the village to work in their factories. That was the second year of the war. They had heard nothing from him since.

"Here, my child." Her grandfather handed her the worn bible and pointed to the passage he had chosen. Each day he opened the bible at random and selected a paragraph. "Read this."

"In Him was life; and the life was the light of men. And the light shineth in the darkness. . . ."

She heard herself reading the words but her thoughts were far away. Day after day dawned with monotonous regularity, she milked the cows, gathered the eggs, then went into town to try to find enough food. The Germans had taken their pigs, so they had not had ham or sausage in a long time and only ersatz coffee. Soup was the main meal, made with vegetables from their garden, and bread.

She put down the bible. Her grandfather's face had a contented expression, he derived so much comfort from its words. She wished she could. It is because he is old, he has nothing else, she thought. But I—I have not lived yet. I want more than words!

Her grandfather was staring at her. "Yes, *ma petite*. I know."

She was startled. Sometimes she thought her grandfather saw more than he pretended.

"The war will not last forever. It only seems like forever because you are young and time passes slowly. When you are old it goes very fast." He smiled. "Too fast, sometimes."

How could life ever go too fast? She wanted to reach out to it, gather its flowers, crush them to her, till their scent overpowered her, to feel, to live, not to just exist from day to day.

She heard the cowbells, the chimes in the village church. She must stop dreaming and get on with her chores.

"Bonjour, monsieur le curé."

André Romelin smiled. He liked to look at pretty

women, it was something that being a priest had not cured him of, and there were all too few in Saint-Gingolph. Then, thinking of the church and his duties, his face became more serious.

"*Bonjour, Noela. Ça va?*"

"*Oui, ça va.*" She looked at the rose he was holding. "What a beautiful rose, Father. It still has dew on it. You must have just picked it."

"Yes, my roses are doing very well this spring. The rain has helped them."

Every morning he picked a fresh rose from his garden and took it to one of his parishioners who was sick. Today it was Madame Bertin on the Swiss side of the town. Saint-Gingolph was divided, half French, half Swiss, though his church and the larger part of the village was in France.

"If I get sick will you bring me a rose as beautiful, Father?"

He laughed. "You are too healthy. Stay that way, my child. It is good to be young."

André Romelin was forty-five, but often he felt much older. For ten years he had been the curé of Saint-Gingolph. He knew all the families, every one by name, he had seen them grow up, he had baptized them, married them, heard their final confessions, given them absolution at the end. The strands of their lives were entwined with his. "The Shepherd of Saint-Gingolph," they called him. God had chosen him, not to know the personal love of the flesh, but to know the true spiritual love of the soul, to help others on their path through life.

Every morning at early Mass he said a special prayer.

"Show me Your will today, O Father, use me as You will. I listen for Your voice."

The war had brought more troubles than ever and he prayed constantly for strength to be equal to all the burdens.

He was a small man and not robust and Doctor Jeunot had warned him many times about his heart. His heart would last as long as God had work for him to do, and that was many years yet, he told himself.

"How is your grandfather today, Noela?"

"Pretty well. Sometimes his arthritis bothers him."

"I will stop by and see him later."

At the end of the street where the bridge crossed the stream he noticed the German guards patrolling. He lowered his voice.

"Still no word from Raoul?"

"No, Father."

"We must not give up hope."

"My mother lights a candle for him every morning at Mass."

"Yes, I know. Your mother is a good woman. God will answer her prayers."

She did not reply.

"You must believe, my child."

"I try to, Father."

"It is not easy. These are difficult times. That is the reason our faith must be even stronger."

The German guard was checking the identity papers of an old woman dressed in black carrying a market basket from which protruded a loaf of French bread. He made her take everything out of the basket and put it on the ground. Then, finally satisfied, he let her pass to the Swiss side of the village.

"We must keep going," André Romelin said. "It is like my roses. Every winter they seem to die, the bushes are brown and bare. But they are only sleeping, waiting. In spring they burst forth again in all their beauty."

The bells in the church steeple chimed the hour.

"I must be on my way to Madame Bertin's," he said.

"Good day, Father."

"God bless you, my child."

He walked on. What a beautiful morning it was! The apple trees were covered with white blossoms, birds were singing, swans glided across the lake. In front of the stucco houses with their gaily painted shutters and lace curtains, red geraniums trailed from window boxes and a tawny kitten was curled up in the sunshine next to a log planted with pansies.

"*Bonjour, monsieur le curé!*" a voice called.

He looked up and saw Marie Charbonnier at an upstairs window shaking out her mop. A rug was hanging over the balcony to air. Nearby her twin daughters, Dominique and Sylvie, were playing hopscotch.

"*Bonjour, monsieur le curé,*" they echoed in unison.

André Romelin smiled and waved. "*Bonjour, mes enfants.*"

It was the small children and the old ones who fared better these days, he thought. The war did not change their lives so much. But for the ones in between, like Noela . . . he shook his head. The carefree days of their youth were stolen forever, they vanished like shadows, never to return.

A few years ago she had talked to him about becoming a nun. She would never be a nun, that one. There was a wild streak in her, a rebellion.

He was approaching the stone bridge that marked the border. There were flowering yellow forsythia bushes on both banks of the stream, and the water, filled with melting snow from the mountains, tumbled over the rocks.

He listened. There was another sound, barely heard over the rushing stream. The engine drone of a plane. He strained to hear it. The plane was in trouble.

The German guards on the bridge looked up at the sky. They had heard it too and knew it was not one of theirs. The German Air Force was reduced now to defending their cities from Allied bombing runs, so it must be American or British.

"*Halt!*"

One of the guards was new and asked him to show his identity card before crossing the bridge.

"It is all right, Horst," the other one said. "It is the curé."

The first guard was looking suspiciously at the rose.

Does he think I am concealing a message in its petals? André wondered. He must be careful. He had been lucky thus far. Because he was a priest and his parishioners were on both sides of the town, he had never been searched at the border. He could come and go as he chose. As far as he knew, no one suspected him. It was important that he keep it that way.

He crossed the bridge and started up the road to Madame Bertin's house.

And then he heard it again. The plane. Yes, definitely it was in trouble.

If it has to come down let it be on the Swiss side, André Romelin prayed silently. These airmen fell out of the sky, defenseless, like naked baby birds from a nest, and he was running out of safe places to hide them. Everywhere there were informers and it was hard to know whom to trust anymore. Each village had its Judas.

Even Saint-Gingolph.

❧ 4 ❧

PAUL SANDERSON HEARD
the sputtering of his engine and he looked at the dials and
levers on his instrument panel and saw that the red fuel-
warning lamp was on.

Damn! he thought. He had plenty of gas. Flak from his
anti-aircraft batteries over Stuttgart must have ruptured his
fuel line. He would never make it back to the fighter
squadron base at Foggia. It was impossible to make a safe
landing now. There was only one thing to do and that was to
bail out.

His helmet felt tight and he was sweating. Below he
could see the snow-covered Alps and the blue lake of
Geneva, Lac Léman on his map. Somewhere down there was
the line that marked the border between France and
Switzerland. He saw tiny white houses and trees dotting the
landscape. There wouldn't be much time.

He was rapidly losing control of the plane. He felt the
tube leading to his oxygen supply, the parachute strapped to
his back. His heavy boots seemed weighted with lead, frozen
to the rudder. His hands in the stiff leather gloves gripped
the wheel. He would have to open the escape hatch quickly,
the minute he disconnected the oxygen supply.

He looked out the window. On the other side of the
lake he saw a tiny green train crossing a mountain bridge
over a waterfall. Suddenly the Christmas he was six years old
flashed through his mind, when Santa Claus brought him a

train set complete with a paper maché tunnel and small Swiss chalets. Everything seemed unreal, none of this was really happening to him but to someone else. He was floating, he had all the time in the world.

Jump now!

Quickly he ripped the oxygen mask from his face and released the catch of the escape hatch. He pushed. It wouldn't budge. He looked at the altimeter. The plane was descending rapidly. He pushed harder. Veins stood out on his forehead. There was a strong smell of gas and he felt himself growing dizzy. Suddenly, a blast of icy air. The hatch was open. He climbed out on the fuselage and crawled forward along the surface of the wing.

The wind tugged at his helmet and whipped his flying suit against his body. His scarf blew off.

Puffs of smoke were coming from the engine. In a few minutes the plane would be on fire. All his consciousness was concentrated on getting free of the burning plane, he no longer felt fear, only the knowledge that he must jump quickly or be drawn into the swirling vortex where death waited with arms outstretched.

He jumped. He felt himself dropping, twisting in the air, and then he pulled the ripcord and released his parachute.

Like the Japanese paper flowers you put in water, the white nylon of his parachute unfolded. Suspended like a puppet on strings, he swung back and forth, drifting earthwards. Cold air rushed past him, he saw jagged mountain peaks with snow and for a moment it seemed as if he was going to land on one of them, then the wind caught him again and carried him along.

Below were tiny white houses and flowering trees and a waterfall tumbling over rocks. Now the earth was rising to meet him, faster and faster, he tried to brace himself, but it was no use. He felt himself hitting the hard ground and then he was being dragged by his canopy over rocks. A tree branch scraped his forehead and there was a sharp pain and blood running down his face. The parachute was caught, tangled in vines. He tugged at it. He must get himself free quickly and bury the parachute. If he was in enemy territory, and the chances were good that he was, they would be looking for him. He reached in his pocket for his knife and cut himself loose.

Suddenly nausea and dizziness swept him. He tried to stand but he was too weak. There was a strong scent of apple blossoms and the distant sound of cowbells, and then only the damp green moss against his face.

Noela took her purchases out of her market basket and put them on the oilcloth-covered table. Cheese, coffee, a loaf of bread. She handed her grandfather the small package of tobacco for his pipe.

"This is all the ration board would give me," she said. "I tried to get more, but—"

"It is better than nothing. Thank you, *ma petite*." Henri Fornay took a pigskin pouch out of the pocket of his overalls and carefully emptied the precious tobacco into it. "I shall enjoy a smoke after supper tonight."

Steam was rising from the copper pot on back of the stove and Noela could smell vegetables cooking for the soup. The daily comforts of life, so hard to come by now, had become luxuries. Often she would make up imaginary meals of the things that were no longer available. Flaky brioches and croissants instead of the bread that tasted as if it was made from bran and sawdust, delicious Gruyère cheese instead of this gray slab of rubber, little pastries.

She had almost forgotten what they tasted like.

Her reverie was interrupted by her grandfather's voice talking about General de Gaulle. They had listened to him on the BBC broadcast last evening, huddled around the radio they kept hidden in the cellar so that the Germans would not find it. They must hold on and not give up hope, de Gaulle had told them. The hour of deliverance was near. France would be saved.

"Ah, yes, it is fine for him to talk," her mother said bitterly. "He is safe in England. He does not have a son in a German labor camp."

"Germaine, he is doing everything he can. And I would not call London exactly safe. We do not have bombings every night—"

"But they do not have Germans in their towns, on their very soil. And French girls go out with them, this I cannot understand."

Noela said nothing.

"Your school friend, Josette, I hear, is one," her mother continued.

"I do not know, *maman*." She had seen Josette, a plump girl with dark braids who worked in the florist shop near the church, flirting with the German guards.

"Disgraceful!"

"I saw the curé outside the bakery," Noela said, anxious to change the subject. "He said he would stop by later."

"The Abbé Romelin is a good man," her mother said. "I do not know what the village would do without him. He keeps us all going." She got up wearily from the table and checked the pot of vegetable peelings simmering on the stove. "To think that before the war we used to throw these away. Or else give them to the pigs. Now we are glad to eat them ourselves."

Had her mother always complained this much? Noela wondered. She could not remember. Before the war seemed like another world, unreal, something she had read about in a book.

"I think I'll take a walk in the woods and see if I can find some raspberries for supper," she said.

She would take a book with her and some bread and cheese. It would be lovely and quiet in the woods with only the songs of birds and the rustling of the trees. She would gather some wildflowers. . . .

"Be careful. The Germans—"

"Yes, *maman.*"

She felt guilty wanting to get out of the house all the time. Was that the way her father had felt? Sometimes, lying in her bed at night, she would try to recall his face, his voice, and it was like reaching through a mist to find nothing there.

"Take your sweater, Noela. It is damp in the woods."

"Yes, *maman.*"

In the woods she felt at home, only there, never frightened, but safe, sheltered by the trees, one with nature. She was more aware of God there than in church, she could hear the earth breathe, feel the pulse of life.

Again, she felt the restless churning within her, that seemed to grow more intense day by day.

She wrapped a small piece of cheese and some bread in a napkin and picked up her sweater from the back of the kitchen chair.

"I will be back soon," she said.

André Romelin started down the steps from Madame Bertin's house and then he thought of the plane he had heard earlier. He listened. There was no sound. They were so young, some of these pilots sent off to war, to bomb strange cities that were only names on a map to them, targets, yet below were living people, doomed to die for crimes others had committed. In war it was always the innocent who suffered, not the guilty. No wonder people lost faith.

And would this be the last war? Would the world finally

learn to live in peace?

He saw the guards in their green uniforms patrolling the bridge. The Enemy. Yet they came from homes too where mothers had loved them and fathers had dreams for their futures.

André Romelin reached down to pat a stray cat. Life was a continual puzzle, an eternal challenge of one's beliefs.

He thought of his own family in Dijon. His mother had been a religious woman who loved music, who taught him to play the piano. A saint, really. His father—André's face darkened. He had spent many hours on his knees asking God to forgive his thoughts about his father, Maurice Romelin, a manufacturer of leather goods, a successful businessman, yet brutal and insensitive. He had taunted him because he was not good at sports, because he read too much, because he did not fight back when the town bully attacked him on his way home from school. His father was angry, shouted when André told him he wanted to become a priest.

"I tell you, the boy is not normal!" he roared at his mother. She had defended him.

He had two older sisters, but he was the only son and expected to carry on his father's business, *Romelin et Fils*.

So he left Dijon and only returned for his mother's funeral.

When he was young there was a girl, a pure beautiful love, but he was too shy to tell her of his feelings and so she had married someone else.

Life had other plans for him. It had directed him here to Saint-Gingolph to take the place of the old curé who had died, and he had not regretted it. This was his parish, his home.

Huguette. The name came back to him from another spring, before he became a priest, when he was only a young man hopelessly in love. He walked faster, feeling the gravel crunching beneath his feet and the fresh smell of newly-cut grass. He passed the school, waved to the children playing in the yard in their bright blue smocks. A fluffy gray-and-white cat was sitting on a red wheelbarrow next to a woodshed.

Another woodshed, his father, the word "coward" flung out into the evening air, his mother in tears, pleading.

Those years . . . those fateful years that twine round us like morning glory vines, those childhood years when the impressions of the world are formed . . . pressed like flowers under glass in our memory.

A priest was supposed to have no personal memories, only to serve God. That he did, to the best of his ability. But was not a priest also human, with human faults and weaknesses?

He passed the *Café de la Navigation*, the *Boucherie-Charcuterie*, remembering when there used to be fat sausages hanging in the window. He had always liked good food, it was one of the weaknesses he had to struggle against, but now God had removed that temptation. He had stopped accepting dinner invitations to the homes of his parishioners because he discovered they were using up a month's ration coupons to serve him a decent meal. On his rounds he would accept only a cup of tea or on rare occasions a glass of wine and a biscuit. His cassock hung on him a lot more loosely these days.

He crossed the street and turned left at the arch that went under the railroad tracks. No passenger trains ran any more, the only trains were on the Swiss side of the lake. The Germans used the rails now to transport supplies.

He started up the hill and came to the square where his church stood. The square was planted with flowers and surrounded by houses of tan stucco with red tile roofs. Behind the weathered shutters and lace curtains life went on, laundry was hung from the wrought-iron balconies, flowers were planted in window boxes, smoke rose from the steep chimneys, children were born, old people died.

How little we know what a human life really is, he thought. Even our own.

He heard the rushing stream coming from the mountain behind the church, bees buzzing, birds singing.

A life is created like a mosaic, piece by piece, of different thoughts and experiences, and it is only when you look at the whole, not at just one occurrence, that the picture becomes clear. The whole of a man's life was what was important, not just one episode, one mistake.

André Romelin pushed open the heavy door of the church. Dipping his fingers in the holy water, he made the sign of the cross and walked down the aisle between the rows of simple brown benches with their kneeling rails. On the altar were calla lilies from the Sunday Mass and six tall white candles. He looked up at the figure of Jesus on the cross and beyond to the stained glass window, the only one in the church, for stained glass was expensive and his parish was poor.

He crossed himself and knelt, his black cassock trailing on the floor, and just then something caught his eye that filled him with horror. Bright red blood splattered on the black marble communion table. He looked closer, wiped his hand across it. His hand was clean, there was nothing there. Was it only his imagination then? But he had seen blood, he was sure.

I am getting tired, Father, he thought. He could not remember when he had last had a vacation. Years.

He could hear the stream through the walls of the quiet church. He closed his eyes. Just a few brief prayers, a few moments of meditation, and he would be on his way again.

❧ 5 ❧

THIS WAS HER SPECIAL place, this bower high in the mountains, it was where she had come since earliest childhood when she wanted to be alone. Above her head the leaves formed a lacy green canopy and far below she could see Lac Léman sparkling in the sunlight, barely visible through the branches of the trees.

Noela ate her bread and cheese and then opened a slim volume of poems by Paul Verlaine and started to read aloud.

"Souvenir, souvenir, que me veux-tu? L'automne
Faisait voler la grive à travers l'air atone. . . ."

Memory, memory, what do you want of me? Autumn drives the thrush down the languid air. . . .

How beautiful the words were, like music. She reached in her basket for a raspberry, then continued to read.

"Nous étions seul à seul et marchions en revant. . . ."

And how romantic!

We were walking in a dream and we were alone. . . .

Suddenly she stopped and listened. Was that a faint moan coming from the woods or was it only her imagination?

She looked around but she could see nothing.

Then she heard it again, a human voice over the singing of the birds, mingling with them, yet apart, like a cry for help.

She closed her book and stood up.

"Help!"

This time there was no mistaking it. It was someone

calling for help. Cautiously, she started towards the place from where the voice came. Then she stopped. What if this was a trap? She knew that members of the Maquis were hiding in the woods and the Germans were looking for them. She must be careful.

Through the trees she thought she could see something white, like a torn sheet hanging in the branches. She walked on, her heart beating faster. . . .

Then she saw the man.

He was lying on the ground, his ankle twisted under him, and blood ran down his face from a cut above his eye.

"*Mon Dieu!*" she gasped.

He was young and blond and very handsome and he was wearing a flying suit. She remembered the plane she had heard earlier and she realized suddenly that the white sheet she had seen was a parachute, tangled in the trees. He must be a pilot and either British or American.

He was looking up at her.

"*Parlez-vous anglais, mademoiselle?*"

"A little." She knelt down beside him. "You are an American?"

"Yes. Where am I?"

"This is Saint-Gingolph. It is in France."

"That's what I was afraid of."

"It is on the Swiss border, but still it is France. The Germans must not find you."

"Are there many around?"

"Not many. But enough."

She took her handkerchief from her skirt pocket and folded it into a bandage, then she put it over the cut to stop the bleeding.

He winced.

"I am sorry. You have much pain?"

He pointed to his ankle. "I don't know whether it's

broken or if it's just a bad sprain." He tried to grin. "But it sure hurts."

She unlaced his boot. The ankle was badly bruised and starting to swell.

"Can you walk at all?"

"I don't know."

She held out her hand to him and he made an attempt to stand but the pain was too great. Noela shook her head. "I do not think you can walk very far on it. I must go and get help." She noticed his expression. "Do not worry," she said quickly. "I am not a collaborator."

"I was not thinking that."

"You can trust me. My name is Noela. Noela Fornay. I live down there." She pointed. "At the bottom of the hill."

"Noël means Christmas."

"Yes. They called me that because it is on Christmas that I am born."

"My name is Paul."

"You are a pilot?"

"Yes."

"What happened to your airplane?"

"It caught fire and I had to bail out."

Suddenly she remembered what led her to him. "Your parachute—I must get rid of it."

"I think it's caught on some branches."

"Do you have a knife?"

He reached in his pocket and handed it to her.

"There is a cave nearby where I used to play with my brother. I can hide the parachute there."

Noela walked over to the place where Paul's parachute was caught in the lower branches of a tree. She cut the ropes and tugged and pulled until it came free. Then she tried to roll it up as best she could. She had no idea that a parachute could be so heavy.

Paul lay on his side watching her. "Do you think you can manage it?"

"Yes." She was out of breath. "I have it now." She was glad the cave was not far. She carried the parachute to the cave and covered it with leaves. Then she came back and picked up her basket.

"It is well hidden," she said. "No one will be able to find it."

"Good. Thank you very much."

"You will be all right until I return?"

Paul looked up at her and grinned.

"Sure," he said. "I'm not going anywhere."

André Romelin sat at his piano playing a Brahms waltz while his cat lay curled up at his feet. Music was one of the few pleasures left him, but he had little time for it these days. This particular waltz was one his mother had taught him. How long ago that seemed, those years of his childhood in the old house in Dijon. He remembered a yellow canary hopping about in a cage near the piano, singing as his mother played, and how the rays of the morning sun through the window made the canary look a pure gold. Those were the happy times, the mornings after his father left for work and his sisters were in school, and his mother seemed like a light-hearted girl playing the piano.

There was a knock at the front door.

The cat meowed and arched her back. He heard the door knocker again over the music and he stopped and got up. His housekeeper, an elderly widow who came several days a week to clean and prepare his meals, was getting deaf and would not hear it.

He was surprised to see Noela Fornay standing on his doorstep. She was carrying a market basket and had a worried expression. He held out his hand.

"Noela, my child, come in. Is there something the matter? Your grandfather—"

"No, Father, he is all right. But there is something I must ask you."

He led her into the living room and indicated the sofa by the fireplace. "Please sit down."

Noela looked at the upright piano against the wall. It was the one good piece in the sparsely-furnished room and had been left to him by the family of a parishioner.

"That was a Brahms waltz you were playing, wasn't it, Father?"

"Yes, the A-flat. It is one of my favorites."

"Sister Celeste used to play it for us at school."

He smiled. "I can remember when you wanted to become a nun." He sat down in an armchair facing her. "Not so very long ago." He paused. "But that is not what you have come to see me about."

"No, Father."

The cat jumped up in his lap and he stroked her, waiting for Noela to speak. She seemed uncomfortable and was twisting her hands nervously.

"Yes, my child? What is it?"

She did not reply.

"It must be something very serious."

"It is."

He leaned forward. "You know that you can talk to me about anything."

"I know that, Father. And I mean to come to Mass more often, really I do, it is just that lately—"

"It is what lies in the heart that counts."

"Father, I need your help. I don't want to involve you, but I don't know where else to turn." She took a deep breath. "There is a man. . . ."

So that was it, what he had feared after all. He tried to

keep his face expressionless. But who was the man? The young ones had all gone off or been taken away. Was it one of the middle-aged men of the village, someone's husband who had taken advantage of her youth and innocence?

"My child, do not be afraid. God does not judge—"

"He is a flier, an American." Noela stopped and her cheeks flushed, as if she suddenly realized what he had been thinking. "He is wounded," she said.

André remembered the plane he had heard earlier, the plane that seemed to be in trouble.

"The Germans must not find him," she continued. "I thought—"

"That I could help?"

Did everyone in the village know that he had been helping Allied fliers to escape? And now, another one. He must be very careful or there would be reprisals, not only against him, which did not frighten him, but others, innocent ones would be rounded up and shot.

"He is wounded, you say?"

"Yes, Father. He hurt his ankle when he parachuted from his airplane. And he has a bad cut on the head."

"And where is he now, this flier?"

"In the woods. I went to pick raspberries—"

"Is it near where the Germans are patrolling?"

"No, the other direction. Up on the hill above the road that goes to Meillerie."

André got up and walked over to the window. Two tame blackbirds were hopping about on his lawn, then they both flew off. He turned. Noela was watching him.

"He cannot walk without help," she said. "If I could get him to my house—Raoul's room is empty—he could stay there until he is better."

"And then?"

"Then?" She stopped. Clearly, she had not thought that

far ahead. "Why . . . there must be some way to get him across the border."

"It is not quite that simple." He looked at her. "You realize the penalty if the Germans find out?"

"I am not afraid."

"And what about your family? Your mother, your grandfather? You would endanger them also."

"But, Father, I cannot just leave him there in the woods to die—or be captured. And that is the same thing."

"You are sure he is not a German in disguise? They have been known to do things like that before."

"I am sure, Father. As sure as one can be of anything today." She reached for her basket and stood up. "But if you think—"

"Sit down, Noela," he said gently. "I was only testing you. It is just that we must be very careful. You understand?"

She nodded. "Thank you, Father. I knew you would help."

"Tell your mother and your grandfather. No one else. And they must not speak to anyone."

"I understand."

"It is a terrible thing that in France these days one does not know whom to trust. Even in a village like Saint-Gingolph." A sadness came over him for a moment to think of Frenchmen betraying Frenchmen. It was something he had found hard to accept, but nevertheless, it was a fact of the war. "Now," he said, "let us consider the situation. It would be dangerous to try to bring him down before dark. Do you think he will be safe where he is until then?"

"Yes, Father, I believe so. I can take him some food and perhaps get him as far as the cave."

"Good. Then I will come by your house after supper. In the meantime, speak to your family."

"Yes, Father. I am going home now."

"There must be nothing unusual for anyone to suspect."

"I know."

"Do not be afraid," he said. "God will help us."

❧ 6 ❧

"BUT IN RAOUL'S ROOM!" Germaine exclaimed, her knitting needles clicking as she rocked back and forth.

"It is empty, *maman*," Noela said.

"How well I know it is empty! *Sales boches*!"

"Then you do not mind?"

"A stranger sleeping in my son's room? Of course I mind." Germaine put down her knitting and looked over at Henri for his reaction. His eyes were half-closed and he was molding his tobacco pouch with his fingers. "Papa, say something."

The old man sighed wearily. "Germaine, he is a soldier. We must do all we can."

"For me the war ended the day they took my son away."

"Please, *maman*," Noela said.

Germaine did not intend to give in that easily. "And how long must we hide him here?"

"Only a few days. Until Father Romelin can get him across the Swiss border." Noela threw her arms around her mother's neck and kissed her. "Thank you, *maman*! I will get some food now to take to him."

Germaine shook her head. "It is crazy. If anyone in the village finds out. . . ."

But her words dangled in the empty air. Noela had already run from the room.

❧

That French girl is sure taking a long time getting help, Paul thought, looking at his watch. She should have been back long before now. And just because she's pretty and was born on Christmas is no proof that she isn't a collaborator and won't turn me over to the Germans. It's been done before. A lot of these French girls have German lovers. Maybe that's the "help" she's getting.

Noela. Even the name could be phony.

No, she seemed genuine. And she had an air of innocence about her. She wasn't the type. . . .

Are you kidding? he asked himself. They're the most dangerous kind, those innocent-looking ones.

And here he was, a sitting duck, just waiting for them to pick him up.

Name, rank and serial number, that's all you were supposed to say. But would he be equal to the torture?

By now the rest of the squadron would be back at the base at Foggia.

"What happened to Sanderson?"

"Crashed, sir. His plane got hit by flak and we saw it on fire."

The inevitable telegram to his family in Santa Barbara. "THE WAR DEPARTMENT REGRETS TO INFORM YOU. . . ."

His mother fainting when she opened it. He remembered how hysterical she had been when he fell from his bike at twelve and broke his collarbone. The impact of the fall onto the cement driveway had knocked him out for a short time and his mother thought he had a fractured skull. His dad would take the news better, or at least he wouldn't show it so much. But still, an only son. . . .

Look here, stop writing your obituary, he told himself. They haven't got you yet. Not by a long shot.

He looked around. It might be a good idea to conceal himself behind those bushes though, and not be just lying out here in the open in case a German patrol came by.

Slowly he inched himself along the ground. His ankle was hurting like hell now, the pain seemed to go all through his body and he was starting to feel faint again, but he kept going. It had been early morning since he'd had anything to eat. He kept crawling until finally he was hidden from view behind a clump of bushes.

Now there was nothing he could do but wait. . . .

"Bonjour, mademoiselle."

Noela jumped at the sound of the guttural voice speaking French, and turning quickly, she recognized the young German guard she had seen with Josette. She clutched her basket more tightly and tried to appear calm.

"I hope I did not startle you." He was smiling. "It is a beautiful day, is it not, Mademoiselle?"

She looked at him coolly, the plump rosy cheeks, the cropped blond hair, the green Nazi uniform that she hated.

"I come from a small town too," he said. "Dinkelsbühl. Now the lilacs will be blooming everywhere." He paused. "Would you like to have a glass of beer with me, Mademoiselle?"

"Thank you, no."

"You are not very friendly. I cannot understand. We are not beasts, we Germans. We come as friends."

She decided it was unwise to anger him. "I have chores I must do."

"I see. Perhaps another time?" He waited for the response that did not come. "You are very pretty, Mademoiselle. I will see you again. Good day." He clicked his heels and walked off in the opposite direction.

A shadow of fear crossed Noela's face. I must be

careful, she thought.

She turned off the main road and started up the hill. A black crow cawed and flew through the sky, a pale eggshell blue above meadows carpeted with wildflowers. A chipmunk ran across her path. Several times she stopped and looked behind her to be sure she was not being followed. She quickened her steps. Now there were no more houses or woodsheds, only dense woods. She passed the sign on a tree that read: *RESERVE DE CHASE*. She could see the lake far below and the air was clear and sweet. Just a bit farther now. She hoped that the American was all right. She had not intended to be gone so long, but it had taken her more time than she planned.

At last!

But this was the place and he wasn't here.

She looked around and felt a cold fear. What could have happened to him?

"Paul?" she called softly.

She heard a rustling behind the bushes.

"Over here." It was his voice.

She sighed in relief. "When I did not see you at first I was afraid that. . . ." She did not finish the sentence.

"I thought this would be safer."

"Yes, you were right." She knelt beside him on the ground and opened her basket. "I brought you some food." She took out bread, cheese, a bottle of wine, and some raspberries.

"It looks great." He started to eat. "Were you able to get help?"

"Yes, the curé. We have to wait for darkness and then Father Romelin will come back with me. We can hide you in my house until he finds a way to get you over the border. You can stay in my brother's room." Paul looked at her. "He is in a German labor camp—or somewhere. We have not seen him since the second year of the war when they took all the young men of the village.”

“I'm sorry.”

“Raoul is about your size. You can wear some of his clothes.”

“You are taking a big risk to help me. I want you to know I appreciate it.”

Noela smiled. “It is all right. I am happy if I can help.” She looked over her shoulder. “I must go now, but as soon as it is dark, I will be back with Father Romelin.”

The shadows lengthened and the darkness of the trees became deeper. Behind the shutters of the houses lights were starting to go on and in the distance a dog barked.

At a table outside the café Josette and Horst, the young German guard, were drinking beer and laughing. They seemed oblivious of the disgusted glances of the few French patrons, old men in workclothes with berets.

Suddenly something caught Horst's interest and he put down his beer mug and looked down the street. André Romelin was approaching on his bicycle.

“Your priest is carrying a red rose with him tonight. I wonder where he is going?” Horst said. “It is the opposite direction from the church.”

“He is probably making a call on someone who is sick.” Josette appeared uncomfortable and turned her head slightly as the curé passed.

“Now you will have to confess to being friendly with the enemy.” Horst's lip twisted in a queer sort of smile.

“I do not care. What harm is there for me to have a beer with you?”

“There are some in this village who think it is treason. Who treat us like dirt. What have we done? Only our duty.”

Two old men at another table were glaring coldly at

Josette and the German officer. One had an arm missing, a memento of the First World War.

"I think I had better get home now," Josette said nervously, standing up. "Thank you for the beer."

"But it is early yet."

"It is starting to get dark and my grandmother will be waiting for me."

"Very well." Horst stood up and clicked his heels. His voice was thick and he was somewhat unsteady on his feet. As soon as Josette had left he downed the rest of his beer and then snapped his fingers arrogantly towards the owner of the café.

"Another beer," he said.

André continued on his way. It had disturbed him seeing Josette sitting with the German. She was an orphan who lived with her grandmother, who worked in the florist shop next to the church. He had given her her first communion. No doubt she was lonely, but still it was a poor excuse. He must not judge her until he heard her confession, he reminded himself, but with so many brave young men of the village gone because of the Germans. . . .

Raoul Fornay was one. It was almost four years now since the Germans had taken him and there had been no word whether he was dead or alive.

Suddenly he felt discouraged. If only there could be peace and brotherly love everywhere. Was this too much to hope for? It seemed that fighting was part of freedom, it was a fact of history. War followed war, with brief periods of peace in between.

He turned up the path to the Fornay farm. An owl hooted in a tree and another answered. He listened. They seemed to be saying a name. Huguette, Huguette. It was an absurd thought, he told himself, I have forgotten long ago.

He was a priest, for many years he had been a priest and she was married and had children. His sister had written him the news as if to say: See, she wasn't for you. He had also heard that she was not happy. Would things have turned out differently if he had declared his love? And if she had loved him in return? No matter. It was twenty years too late. The pattern of his life was set and so was hers. He had given his life to God and she belonged to another.

He got off his bicycle and leaned it up against the wall of the Fornay house. Then he took the red rose from the container attached to the handlebars. If anyone should pass by it was important that everything appear as normal as possible.

He knocked on the door and waited.

He knocked again. Two eyes peered through the slats of the shutters and then he heard the heavy bolt on the door sliding back. Before the war, André recalled, no one in Saint-Gingolph bothered to lock their doors, they welcomed visitors. Now, a knock on the door filled them with dread.

Germaine Fornay opened the door.

"Good evening, Germaine."

"Good evening, Father. Please come in." She closed the door behind him and latched it. "Have you had supper?"

"Yes, thank you. I have already eaten."

He noticed Germaine's look of relief, which she tried to conceal. She led him to the kitchen where Noela and Henri were seated at the table. Noela jumped up to greet him.

"Please sit down, Father," Germaine said. "We are just having our coffee."

She took the coffeepot from the stove and poured him a cup while Noela got a small vase for the rose.

André pulled up a chair beside Henri. "And how is the arthritis, Henri? Any better?"

Henri shrugged. "It comes and goes. I am used to it now."

"Grandpapa says the pain is worse when it rains," said Noela, placing the rose in the center of the table.

"Yes, I am better than a barometer." Henri chuckled. "I can always tell when it is going to rain."

Noela leaned over to smell the rose.

"Such luck you have with your roses, Father," Germaine exclaimed. "What a beautiful red this one is!"

"And the scent is very sweet. It was the favorite rose of my mother."

The church chimes were heard in the distance.

André looked at the clock on the kitchen wall. "It is time now," he said.

❧ 7 ❧

THE STARS CAME OUT AND the night air grew colder. Paul shivered and rubbed his hands together trying to keep the circulation going through his body. The waiting seemed endless. Had something gone wrong? He tried not to think about that possibility. His leg felt numb from the knee down. He shifted his weight and attempted to put pressure on his ankle. There were sudden shooting pains.

If he did try to go somewhere, where would he go? In which direction? He would be likely to walk into a German patrol and that would be the end of it. If they had seen his plane go down they were surely looking for him.

There were a few sounds from the village below. He heard bells striking in a church tower and the hooting of owls, then a dog barked. He looked up at the sky. When he used to fly over these towns and villages on his way to a bombing target they were just places on a map, tiny dots, and he had never thought about the people living in them. It was better when you were a pilot not to personalize things.

And now, here he was, in enemy-occupied France, dependent on those very people for his survival. It was a strange feeling.

Before the war he had given some thought to his future and what he wanted out of life, but he had not worried about it that much. He remembered filling out college application forms for Yale, where his father went and where his own son, if he ever had one, would go. They wanted to know your goal in life. Who really knew at eighteen? Then he had only been interested in girls and having a good time. Like most children of wealthy parents, he never thought much about money. It was something that was just there.

But one thing he knew for sure, he didn't want to die yet. At twenty-two he still had a hell of a lot of living left to do.

He raised the wine bottle to his lips and drained it.

Suddenly he heard the sound of footsteps and a twig breaking along the path, then a man and a woman's voice speaking softly in French.

"He's right over here, Father."

It was Noela and the priest was with her. He seemed a rather slight man of medium height, not the stocky peasant priest he had expected, and Paul wondered how the two of them would be able to carry him down the mountain.

"This is Father Romelin," Noela said.

Paul held out his hand and started to say his name but the priest quickly interrupted.

"Names are not necessary. The less we know about each other, the better. It is safer that way, my son." As he spoke he took one side and Noela the other and they pulled him to his feet. "Now lean on us," he said.

"It is all right, I am quite strong," Noela said.

"We will manage," said Father Romelin. "But there is no time to waste."

In the kitchen Germaine and Henri waited. Germaine got up and poured herself another cup of coffee while Henri puffed on his pipe.

"There is nothing like a good pipe," Henri said. He reflected a moment. "Well, at least when one is my age."

Germaine looked at him sharply, then at the door.

"They should be back by now."

"All in good time." Henri drew in on his pipe. "When you have lived through two wars you learn to take things more calmly."

"One war was enough for me," Germaine said. "And this one is not yet over." She started to pace back and forth, then stopped and listened. There was no sound.

She opened the shutters a crack and peered out. Three figures were coming through the cow pasture, the one in the middle limping on one foot and being half-carried. She was glad that there was not a full moon.

"They are here," Germaine said. She thought of the turned-down bed in the other room. "If only it were Raoul coming home," she said.

Henri tapped his pipe and did not reply. He was seventy, he had seen two wars, his only son drowned, his grandson taken away by the Germans. For more than ten years he had been a widower. Often he found his daughter-in-law a trial, but after so long he was used to her ways. And besides, he had nowhere else to go.

"If only we knew where he was. . . ."

Germaine left her sentence unfinished and opened the back door. As they came closer she could see that the American flier was very handsome. No wonder Noela was so eager to help. She hoped that her daughter would not get any silly romantic ideas about him. Noela had inherited her father's sentimentality and not her own practicality. She lived in a dream world that did not exist.

"*Bonsoir*," Germaine said stiffly. "Come in."

"This is my mother," Noela said.

"*Bonsoir, madame.*"

"And my grandfather."

The old man nodded and smiled at Paul.

"My mother and my grandfather, they do not speak

much English," Noela explained, as she and Father Romelin helped Paul to Raoul's room, which was on the first floor just by the stairs. Noela took a flannel nightshirt from the bureau drawer and handed it to Paul.

"I will bring you some coffee," Noela said, leaving the room so that Paul could get undressed.

She went down the hall to the kitchen. So far, so good, she thought. He is safe now. She thought of how this morning she had awakened thinking that nothing ever happened in her life, that it would stretch on forever with no excitement, just the same old routine. That was the thing about living in a village, it was the boredom that got to you, even in a village as beautiful as Saint-Gingolph. Its boundaries were too small.

"I hope no one saw you bring him here," Germaine said.

"No, *maman*, we were very careful."

"And we must continue to be careful as long as he is here. It is very dangerous."

Noela poured the coffee. She felt alive, tingling with a strange new feeling. This morning she had danced round her room alone, dreaming of an imaginary partner, and now, out of the sky, had come a handsome American. She glanced at her mother, hoping she could not read her thoughts. Finally I am alive, she thought, alive! She spilled some of the coffee and hastily wiped it up.

In the hall she almost collided with Father Romelin.

"You are leaving, Father?"

"Yes, it is past the curfew. I must hurry."

The curfew. She had almost forgotten. Suddenly she realized how much he was risking. "Thank you for your help, Father," she said. "Thank you so much." Then impulsively she kissed him on the cheek.

He seemed flustered. "I will come back tomorrow. Goodnight, my child."

"Goodnight, Father."

I should not have done that, she thought, I have embarrassed him. It was just that tonight I feel so happy. . . .

She knocked on the door of Raoul's room before entering. It seemed strange to see Paul wearing Raoul's nightshirt in the old brown bed with the quilt tucked round him. She handed him the coffee.

"That smells good," he said.

"Do you think you will be all right now?"

"Yes, fine, thank you."

"Then I will see you in the morning. Sleep well."

"*Bonne nuit.*"

Noela smiled. "*Bonne nuit.*"

André Romelin got on his bicycle and started down the path from the Fornay house. Noela's kiss brought back memories, thoughts long put out of his mind, or so he told himself. The night air was sweet with apple blossoms and the breeze ruffled the hem of his cassock. It was a night made for all the things he had given up. It reminded him that once he was a young man filled with the desires of all normal young men. He himself had made the choice, no one else. Circumstances had helped, had shaped his decision, until it seemed he had been called by God. "The desires of the flesh are passing, the love of God is eternal." He had chosen that theme once for a sermon. There was a woman in the village, married, who had fallen in love with another man, a man who was also married and had children. He could see her now, sitting in the front pew as she listened to his sermon, her face strained, tortured. She was Italian, the only Italian in the village.

After she gave up her lover she suddenly aged, she no longer paid any attention to her appearance, constantly she fingered her rosary beads, and then she became ill and died. "I cannot live without him, Father," she had said. "No one dies of love," he told her. "You must be strong. It is only the love of God that matters."

Did he really believe that?

Most of the time he did. It was only tonight, with the scent of spring in the air, that longing rose in him for another kind of love, a love that was forbidden to him. Did the Catholic religion demand too much of its priests?

Now, he must find a way to get the young flier across the border, and soon. He must not remain long at the Fornay home. Noela was inexperienced and vulnerable, she could easily develop a crush on him and be hurt.

Yes, the sooner he got him into Switzerland, the better for all concerned. Of course if the Swiss police caught him he would be interned at Schaffhausen for the duration of the war according to international agreement, but Switzerland was not Germany and at least he would be safe there. And there was always the chance, though slim, that he could get back to his base at Foggia.

But by all means, he must be gotten out of France.

Noela sat up in bed, her arms clasped round her knees, dreaming, yet wide awake. The novel of Colette's was on her bedside table, the marker in the same place she had left it the night before.

How quickly life changed! In a moment fate stepped in and the whole world was painted with different colors.

Paul. It was such a nice name.

She leaned forward. I wonder if he has a girl at home? Or if he's married. No, she thought, he's too young.

She had heard that in America men married younger than they did in France. Here you had to be sure you could support a family, sometimes also your parents, so the men waited. Of course the girl must have a dowry, though in the villages the dowry was usually very small.

She suddenly wondered what her dowry was. She fingered the tiny gold cross at her neck. Had her father left anything? No one had ever told her.

Paul was in the room right underneath hers. Was he sleeping now? She hoped his ankle would not heal too quickly so that he could stay with them for a few weeks at least. Was that selfish of her? Then they could get to know each other and who knows what might happen?

Noela, Noela, what a dreamer you are! "Face reality," her mother would say. I don't care. I want a man to fall in love with me, to love him in return.

Those mysterious things that happened between a man and a woman she had only heard spoken of in veiled whispers. Surely it must be something wonderful to have inspired so much poetry and music.

Once her mother had said, "Men are animals." What did that mean? She had grown up around animals on the farm, seen them mating, grunting and rolling in the grass. But if that was all there was, only a physical coupling, and if people were like animals, where was the magic, the music? No, there was more to it than that, much more, there must be, something that no one could describe in words.

She thought how nice it would be to go with Paul to America, to cross the seas, to leave this village where nothing ever happened. Who was there for her here? Jacques, the butcher's son, when he came back from war? He used to dip her braids in the inkwell at school until Sister Celeste smacked his fingers with a ruler. Later he said it was because he liked her, he wanted to catch her attention. If she married Jacques she would end up working in the back of the butcher shop, wrapping bloody pieces of meat and sausage in brown paper, until she grew old and fat like her mother. It was a horrible picture.

And then there was Marcello, the cobbler's son. He was short and dark and reeked of garlic. His mother had been a pretty woman, always singing Italian songs. She missed Italy and the other women of the village didn't like her. There was some kind of a scandal about her, and then suddenly she died.

So much for the young men of the village. And even they were all gone now and who knew how many would return?

It was a woman's role to wait, to be chosen, to have no say in her destiny, and she was tired of it. She would not end up like the other women of Saint-Gingolph, her life would be different.

She tiptoed across the room and leaned on the windowsill. The air was sweet, moonlight laced the white blossoms of the apple tree.

How good it is to be young, she thought. I do not want ever to be old!

❧ 8 ❧

IN THE DREAM HE WAS
back at boarding school in Ojai, California, and he was
fifteen. The French teacher was giving him a lecture because
he had not sufficiently studied his irregular verbs and
therefore had a C instead of the A he was informed he was
capable of getting. He thought French was a bore and
preferred to spend the time on the basketball court. He also
found the French teacher, who was not French, amusing. Mr.
McKendall was a frustrated actor and loved to demonstrate
the verbs by acting them out.

Somewhere a rooster was crowing. Paul opened his eyes
and blinked. He looked round the room with the sloping
ceiling and its one window with the brown paint peeling that
looked out on an apple orchard. Directly opposite him was a
chest of drawers with a blue china pitcher and basin and in
the corner a carved oak armoire. There was a religious
picture on one wall and a worn rug beside the bed. He sat up
and rubbed his eyes. He realized he was wearing a flannel
nightshirt and he was in a French farmhouse.

He pulled back the covers and looked at his ankle. It
was still puffy and bruised but the pain was less than the
night before. He put his legs over the side of the bed and
gingerly he put his feet on the floor and tried to stand.

"Ouch!" He winced.

He would have to manage by hopping on one leg. He
hopped over to the bureau, feeling like some kind of a lame

gull with the white nightshirt flapping around his bare legs.

The pitcher had cold water in it and he poured some in the basin and splashed it on his face. He rubbed his hand across the rough stubble on his chin and wondered if Raoul had left a razor around somewhere. Maybe he would grow a beard, it would be a good disguise anyway, until he got back to the base. He just hoped Father Romelin would be able to get him across the border in a day or two at most.

He looked out the window. The sky was tinged with pink and beyond the apple trees he could see Noela milking a brown-and-white cow. Nearby another cow was eating clover and both had large cowbells around their necks.

He limped over to the chair where the priest had neatly folded his clothes and took a pack of Camels from his pants pocket. He sat on the bed and slowly inhaled the smoke. The cigarette tasted good and he only had a few left. He'd have to ration them carefully. He wondered if the rest of the family was up yet. He opened the door and he heard sounds coming from the kitchen and there was the smell of coffee.

It was awkward dressing, but he finally managed. Then he made his way up to the bathroom at the top of the stairs, the only bathroom in the house. The tub was an old-fashioned kind on claw feet, like the one he remembered from his grandparents' house in Maine, and the toilet had a tank overhead with a long chain.

Funny, he hadn't thought of that house in Maine in years. It was on a lake and they used to go there for summers when he was a boy. He had learned to swim in that cold lake when his older sister pushed him off the dock. The house had a big porch all around it with white wicker furniture and a stone fireplace in the living room where they used to toast marshmallows and his grandfather would tell them stories.

His grandparents were both dead now and the summer place in Maine had burned in a forest fire.

He pulled the chain on the tank and washed his hands. There was a glass on the sink and he rinsed his mouth. He'd have to get a toothbrush.

In the kitchen the old grandfather was seated at the table reading his bible and the mother was busy cleaning vegetables.

"*Bonjour*," Paul said.

They both looked startled to see him up so early.

"*Bonjour*," they said.

The old man smiled and pointed to the place next to him at the table. "Please sit down," he said.

Germaine went to the stove for the pot of coffee and a mug. "You are better today?" she asked.

"I think so. I slept like a log." He noticed their puzzled expressions. There was no way to translate that into French. "*J'ai bien dormi*," he said.

"*Ah, bon*," said Henri. "You speak very good French."

Suddenly Noela appeared at the kitchen door.

"Good morning," she said happily. "You are up already? We were going to let you sleep."

"I heard the rooster and decided it was time I was out of bed."

Noela clasped her hands. "It is so beautiful outside! The fields are like *un tapis de fleurs*." She searched for the right words in English. "A carpet of flowers. I wish you could see it."

"It is not safe for him to go outside," Germaine interrupted quickly. "He must stay hidden all the time. Until the curé comes for him."

"Yes, they will be reporting me missing at my base and sending a telegram to my family. I must get back as soon as possible."

Germaine looked at him sharply. "You have a wife?"

"No, no wife. I am not married. But my mother will be

very upset. She worries a lot."

"Like all mothers," Germaine said. "It is only natural." She picked up one of the cabbages, carefully inspecting the leaves as she removed them.

"Where are you from?" Henri asked.

"Santa Barbara, California."

"California!" Noela exclaimed. "I have read about it. They say it is beautiful there."

Germaine shredded the cabbage leaves and threw them into a sieve.

"Yes, it is," said Paul. "We live just outside of Santa Barbara in a place called Montecito."

Henri took the loaf of French bread and cut a piece for Paul. Then he cut a small piece for himself and dipped it in his coffee. Noela was watching Paul, hanging on to his every word. Germaine put the shredded cabbage aside and wiped her hands on her apron.

"Noela," she said, "I think you had better go to town now and get some food. We need bread and other things."

"Yes, *maman.*"

"And is there any way you could get me a toothbrush and some toothpaste?" Paul asked.

"Of course. I will stop by the *pharmacie.*"

Suddenly there was a scratching sound outside the kitchen window and they all turned.

"What is that?" Henri asked.

"I will go see." Germaine got up and went over to the window and looked out. "It is nothing. Only a neighbor's dog burying a bone. But we had better be careful." She glanced quickly at Paul.

Madame Toutain was leaning over the counter gossiping with Madame Pelletier when Noela entered the bakery with her market basket over her arm. They stopped abruptly.

"Bonjour, Noela."

"Bonjour, mesdames."

"The bread is just out of the oven." Madame Toutain held up a loaf. "See, it is still warm."

"Good. I will take two of them." Noela put the bread in her basket and paid for it, then left.

The old women's eyes followed her as she started down the street.

"She is suddenly becoming very religious, that one," said Madame Toutain. "Yesterday she and the curé were talking together for a long time outside the shop. And last evening—" she lowered her voice, "—I saw them walking together. They passed my house and they were going towards the woods."

"You are sure, Yvonne?" Madame Pelletier's false teeth made a whistling sound when she talked.

Madame Toutain was indignant. She drew herself up. "There is nothing wrong with my eyes, Monique. Even in the dark I can see."

"It was after the curfew?"

"No, before. What does it matter?"

"I cannot believe that the Abbé Romelin—"

"And why not? Priests are not all saints—they are men." She shook her bony finger in the direction of where her husband was putting dough in the oven. "And we know what men are."

Madame Pelletier put her wrinkled hand over her mouth and snickered.

Noela had been anxious to get out of the bakery to avoid any conversation with Madame Toutain and Madame Pelletier. They were both gossips and she was sure that they were now picking her apart like some choice morsel fallen in the town square. Is that what old age meant? Living vicariously on the lives of others? It was bad enough to get lines and gray hair, to have one's figure get lumpy or bony. She walked faster, almost skipping, as she continued her errands, and she was just coming out of the *pharmacie* when she saw the hated green uniform approaching. It was Horst.

"Good day, Mademoiselle."

"Good day." She started to walk on, but Horst blocked her way, his hands on his hips and an arrogant expression.

"If you were nicer to me I could perhaps do a favor for you." His eyes had a peculiar glint.

"Such as?"

"I could arrange with the ration board to let you have more tobacco. Your grandfather would like that, would he not?"

"He manages well enough." She forced a smile, not wishing to antagonize him. "But thank you."

"Any time, Mademoiselle. You have only to let me know." Horst stepped aside to let her pass.

He is becoming a nuisance, Noela thought. If only she could tell him what she really thought of him, but that would only endanger herself and others. She had never been good at concealing her feelings, even as a small child things burst out of her unbidden. . . .

She was passing the school now, a gray stucco building with a white wooden balcony, and through the large window framed in white shutters she could see children in blue smocks sitting at their desks. Beside the school was the cemetery. Noela thought that was rather ironic. In most villages it was next to the church. But it was such a pretty cemetery, well tended, with flowers on every grave and the marble and stone tombstones always polished. The dead were not forgotten in Saint-Gingolph but were close to the living.

In the far corner, next to two cypress trees and overlooking the lake, was the Fornay family plot. It was there that her father was buried, where he lay quietly now, his restless wanderings stilled forever. There were times when she missed him, she even had imaginary conversations with him, telling him her dreams and asking, "Do you approve, Papa?" He always did. That was the nice thing about imagination, you could make it turn out the way you wanted, hear the answers you wanted, instead of scolding and disapproval. The shadowy figure who was Bernard Fornay was stronger in death than he ever was in life.

A gray kitten ran under the black wrought-iron gates of the cemetery and meowed at her feet.

And then she heard another sound, a sound which brought back the war and the danger everywhere. A German jeep with two officers was going up the hill towards the church and Father Romelin's house.

André Romelin ran his hand over the front tire of his bicycle. The tire was getting very worn and he wondered how much longer it would last. He had patched it several times and thus far it had held out. He was about to get on the bicycle when he saw the jeep approaching with two German officers, ones he had not seen before. They stopped the jeep in front of his house and one got out and walked over to him.

Suddenly André recognized the silver death's heads on the black uniforms and caps. S.S., he thought. What did they want?

"Good morning, Father," the officer said pleasantly. "Can you tell me, have you seen any strangers around here?"

"No. And I know everyone in the village."

"Yes, that is what we thought. But nevertheless, an American plane has crashed somewhere in the vicinity and we want you to be on the lookout for the pilot in case he survived and is seeking refuge in one of the homes."

"You have found the wreckage of the plane?"

"Not yet, but we will."

André felt relieved. Possibly the plane had burned totally and they would think that the body had also. "I have seen no one," he said. He was sure that God would forgive his lie.

"We will not search your house this time, but we will be back. In the meantime, if you see or hear anything we expect you to report it. You know the penalty if you do not." He raised his arm. "*Heil Hitler.*"

André stared coldly at the swastika armband and said nothing.

The officer turned and strode down the path, got in the jeep, and drove off with his companion.

Yes, they'll be back all right, thought André. They had been polite but they meant business.

He got on his bicycle and started down the road.

The Germans were suspicious and there was no time to waste. He looked out across the lake towards Switzerland. A boat was out of the question now. At the beginning of the war he had gotten two British fliers across under cover of fog after hiding them in his house for two nights, but the man who had rowed them across did not want to risk it anymore. He explained that he had his family to think of and it was too dangerous.

There was no doubt about that, but some way must be found. The guards were more on the alert now because of the expected Allied invasion. Troops were massing in England, he had heard. Every day there were more rumors in the village as the people waited and hoped.

The invasion must not fail. The hopes of all Frenchmen and the salvation of the rest of the world depended on it.

God would be on their side and help them, good would triumph over evil, truth would prevail over injustice and oppression. Even in the dark days of 1940 he had never doubted that in the end Hitler would lose. There had been little to cling to then but blind faith. But was not faith believing in the heart what you could not see with the eyes?

French we are, he thought, French we will remain.

André pedaled faster. He had many things to do today.

❧ 9 ❧

DURING THE NIGHT THE rain started, the heavy drops falling like hailstones on the tile roof. In the morning the apple blossom petals lay scattered on the ground and Lac Léman was hidden by fog. The rains continued, less heavy now but a steady drizzle. Then, just as suddenly as it began, it stopped and the sun burst through the clouds. The drops on the trees and grass trembled like crystal prisms and in the woods a thrush sang.

Henri Fornay was taking his usual afternoon nap and Germaine had gone to the cemetery. Noela and Paul were sitting at the table in the kitchen, the shutters closed so that no one could see in from the outside.

Noela leaned forward. "Someday," she said, "when the war is over, I want to go to Paris, to travel—even to the United States."

Paul smiled.

"Why do you smile? My English is bad?"

"No, it is charming. And you speak it very well."

"And you . . . you will return to California . . . afterwards?"

"I suppose. I have to finish college. And then I want to go to law school. But that all seems very far away now."

Noela sighed. "Everything seems far away—after the war—before the war. It is as if I have had no other life, as if I will have no other life that is not within certain boundaries and guards with guns. . . ." She formed the shape of a box with her hands. "Like so. I envy the swans on the lake—at least they can go where they wish. No one stops them." She shrugged. "Ah, well. It is fun to dream."

"We all have dreams."

"Yes. That is what is so sad about growing old—like *maman*. She has abandoned life, she lives in the past. Since fourteen years Papa is dead, but *maman* talks as if it was only yesterday that he was drowned." She fingered the gold cross at her neck. "Papa gave me this for my fifth birthday. I wish I could remember him better."

Paul leaned towards her. "You are very sweet." He touched her hair. "And pretty."

"Do you really think so? That I am pretty?"

"Very pretty. Has no one ever told you that?"

She laughed. "Only my grandfather."

"You know, I've never met a French girl before. They're not the way I imagined."

"And how did you imagine them to be?"

Paul did not answer.

"You are disappointed?"

"No." He smiled and drew closer to her. "I like you very much."

Her face flushed. She felt a sudden desire to have him hold her in his arms, to kiss her lips, to know what it was like, all those things she had read about in books and had never experienced . . . but she did not want to appear easy. That was probably how he imagined French girls to be. And yet there was so little time.

"What are you thinking?" Paul asked.

"You know me only since two days."

"Does that make a difference?"

She hesitated. Today he was here in Saint-Gingolph, tomorrow he would be gone. The war shortened things, there was no time for games, for courtship, there was only now. He took her hand and she noticed how blue his eyes were.

Just then there was a loud cough and her grandfather came in the kitchen. She pulled back her hand and quickly jumped up. "Did you have a good nap, Grandpapa?"

"So-so." Henri rubbed the back of his neck. "Where is your mother?" He suddenly remembered. "Ah, yes, the cemetery." He turned to Paul. "Every afternoon she goes there, rain or shine. He is my son, but I mourn him here . . . ," Henri touched his heart, "and I go on living. What has happened we cannot change." He shrugged. "I think I will go out and work in the garden now that the rain has stopped."

"But your arthritis? Won't it bother you?" Noela asked.

"So I should become a vegetable?" Henri snorted. "It is better if I keep moving."

The old man left the room, holding his shoulders straighter as if to defy the passing years and the crippling that was slowly taking over his body.

Noela watched him go.

"Your grandfather is quite a remarkable guy," Paul said. "*Formidable*."

"Yes, Grandpapa has courage. He will not give in to life, no matter what happens to him." She glanced at the shuttered windows. "How I wish that we could go outside and I could show you around—it is so beautiful everywhere! The horse trough up on the hill near the barn—there is a table with benches to sit and you can see across the lake."

"I will have to come back when the war is over."

"Do you think that the invasion will come soon?"

"I hope so."

"And then France will be liberated! You cannot imagine what it is like all these years living under the Germans! Always one has fear. And the worst part is that you do not know who are the collaborators among the French." She went over to the window and looked through a crack in the shutter. "I can see my mother coming up the road." She shook her head. "Poor *maman*. She makes everything so difficult for herself. I wonder if I will be like that when. . . ." Noela looked at Paul. "How long do they wait before they let your family know that you are missing?"

"A few days."

"You are the only son?"

"Yes. I have two sisters."

Noela nodded. "I know how it is. Like Raoul."

"You haven't heard anything?"

She shook her head sadly. "Nothing. It is hard on us all, especially *maman*. He was her favorite." There was the sound of the front door opening. "Here she is now."

Germaine entered, dressed in black as usual, her purse over her arm. She looked worried.

"While I was at the cemetery I saw a German jeep go by with two officers. I have not seen them in the village before. We must be very careful. They will be looking, asking questions."

"I realize the risks you are taking to hide me," Paul said, "and I will never forget it."

"We are happy to do so," Noela said. She turned to her mother who was brushing the raindrops from her coat. "Are we not, *maman*?"

Germaine sat down wearily. She gazed straight ahead for a moment. "Of course," she said.

That evening Paul had difficulty going to sleep. The last two nights he had been so exhausted from the shock of the crash and the pain in his leg that he had quickly fallen into a heavy slumber. But now he felt restless. He tried different positions but nothing worked. Finally he decided to get out of bed and look for something to read.

He made his way to the living room as quietly as he

could and was just starting to look through the bookcase when he was aware of a figure standing in the doorway. He turned quickly to see Noela, a long robe over her nightgown and the tiny gold cross gleaming at her throat.

"I thought I heard someone walking about," she said. "It was you."

"I tried to be quiet. I'm sorry I woke you. I was just looking for something to read."

She came into the room and stood beside him.

"I was not asleep," she said. "It is starting to rain again. I love the sound of rain on the roof at night."

"So do I," Paul said.

"Do you find anything you want to read? The books, they are mostly in French, but a few are in English."

"Where did you get those?"

"We read them in school." She took down a copy of Byron's *The Prisoner of Chillon.* "I had to memorize the whole poem," she said. "It was very hard but I still know it. The castle is right across the lake, near Montreux. On the Swiss side."

"You like to read?"

"Very much." She looked at him. "You seem surprised. In a village like this there is not too much to do. Sometimes I think. . . ." She stopped.

"What?"

"There are so many things to see in the world outside and I wonder if I will ever see them. So instead I read about these things. All the places, the people. . . ."

Paul reached over and took her hand. "You are very sweet. Come, sit down. I don't really want to read. I'd rather talk to you."

"But I cannot like this. I am not dressed."

"It's all right. You look fine."

She hesitated and he tried another approach.

"Besides, I'm tired of standing. My ankle is hurting."

She was suddenly concerned. "Oh, I am sorry. It gives you much pain?"

"Not much, but I'd like to get my weight off it. Come." He led her over to the sofa near the fireplace and they sat down.

"You have a girl waiting for you at home?"

"A lot of them." Paul laughed at her serious expression. "No one special."

"But there was someone special . . . once?"

"Oh, when I was in college, yes. But we broke up."

"And what happened to her?"

"I don't know. I haven't seen her in a long time."

"I see."

French girls weren't so different from American ones after all, Paul thought. They all asked the same questions, they all wanted to make claims on you. Women wanted eternity in love. Men did not. Women wanted promises, men were frightened of them. Noela was looking at him intently.

"What are you thinking about, Paul?"

"Nothing much," he said. He leaned closer. "You are very pretty." He reached for her and kissed her. "And sweet."

He continued to kiss her. At first she resisted slightly and then her arms went around him and she kissed him back. He slipped his hand under her nightgown and caressed her breasts. He could feel her heart beating. "I want you," he said. He wanted her now, this moment, as he had wanted nothing else. He pressed his body against hers, and she was warm and soft and yielding and there was no longer any space between them. Their love-making became more and more intense. Suddenly she gave a small cry.

"Did I hurt you?" Paul asked.

"No, it is all right." She lay quietly in his arms.

"I'm sorry. I didn't know—"

She put her fingers to his lips. "I am glad you are the first."

In the distance there was the sound of church chimes.

"Soon it will be time to get up," Noela said. "I must go back to my room."

Paul kissed her. "You are very lovely," he said.

❧ 10 ❧

BOOTS, BOOTS, MARCHING
on cobblestone streets, a frightened cat runs past and the
boots continue under the arch with the railroad tracks, up the
hill, past the church and the statue of the fallen soldier of
France. A tan stucco house with a red tile roof, roses
blooming in the garden, a bicycle parked under the eaves out
of the rain. The boots stop. There is a loud knocking on the
front door, an old woman in the house across the street, her
gray hair plaited in a long braid, opens her window to see
what is going on.

"Open up!" the guttural voice commands.

The priest's house. The woman crosses herself and
closes her shutters. There is no safety anywhere.

It is not yet dawn and in his bedroom André Romelin is
kneeling in front of the prie-dieu saying his morning
devotions. The room is simply furnished. A brass bed with a
crucifix hanging over it, next to it a small night table with a
worn bible. The bible has a marker of pressed flowers from
Bethlehem which a priest who went to the same seminary
sent him from the Holy Land. On the bureau there is a faded
photograph of his mother in a silver frame and a lace runner
she had crocheted.

Today, Saturday, he will be hearing confessions. From
his dark confessional he has heard so many. Who is he to
judge them really, to mete out the punishment for their sins,
so many Hail Mary's, so many Our Father's? The catastro-

phes of life are often far easier for people to bear than the monotony of their daily lives. As village priest he knew that well.

"Open the door!"

André went to the window and looked out. A soldier in a green uniform and helmet was beating on the door with his fists. He recognized the German guard, Horst.

"Just a minute," André called. He put his bathrobe on over his nightshirt and went downstairs and unlatched the door. "It is not necessary to knock down the door," he said. "What is it I can do for you?"

Horst's eyes narrowed. "We have reason to believe that you are hiding someone. You know that is treason, punishable by death?"

"I am aware of that fact. But come in and see for yourself. There is no one else here." There was a sound from the kitchen. "Other than my cat."

Horst pushed his way in and looked around.

"If you will excuse me," André said, "I was just about to get dressed." He turned and started to go up the stairs.

"Wait here." Horst pointed to a door. "Where does that lead?"

"To the cellar. Shall I show you?"

"I can find my way."

Horst flung open the cellar door and looked down the stairs into the darkness.

"Where is the light switch?"

"The bulb is burnt out but I will bring you a candle."

"Never mind." Horst drew his revolver and went down the stairs, his boots clomping on the wooden steps. Suddenly there was an oath in German as he stumbled over something.

In a few minutes he came up carrying two bottles of wine. André noticed that they were two of his best vintage, ones he had been saving for a special occasion such as when the bishop came to visit, which he did sometimes, though he had not been lately.

"Now, the upstairs," Horst ordered.

André started ahead, but Horst shoved him aside roughly. "I will go first," he said. "That way you cannot warn anyone."

"There is no one to warn."

"We shall see."

Horst put the wine bottles on the bureau next to the picture of André's mother.

"That was a good year," he said, glancing at the labels. "In Germany we like French wines. I regret to say it but they are the best, even better than German wines."

Horst whistled a tune as he went through the armoire and drawers and looked under the bed. André watched him in silence. Rumors of concentration camps had reached Saint-Gingolph, stories so terrible that they defied the human imagination. Could it really be true that the Germans were gassing Jews in ovens, hundreds of thousands of them?

"What is in the other bedroom?" Horst asked.

"It is empty."

It was a smaller room and there was a bath in between. André, still in his nightrobe and slippers, felt chilly.

"You do not mind if I get dressed now? I have a Mass shortly."

"Go ahead, Father. You have your duties, I have mine." Horst picked up the wine bottles. "Thank you for the wine. I see you are telling the truth, there is no one here."

André felt anger rising in him and if the German did not leave soon he would forget that he was a priest. He went to the armoire where his cassock was hanging and took it out.

"However I will just give another check in the kitchen on my way out. I am very fond of *paté de foie gras*. It will go well with the wine."

André clenched his fists. "I do not have any," he said. "Nor have I for a long time. My budget does not afford it, even if it were available."

Horst ignored this remark. "Good day, Father." He went downstairs, a wine bottle under each arm, whistling a Strauss waltz.

Noela came in the kitchen wearing a scarf over her head and carrying a milk pail. Germaine was putting the kettle on the stove.

"Good morning, *maman*," Noela said happily.

"You are very bright for such a dreary morning."

"And why not? The rain makes everything so fresh and green." Do I look different after last night? she wondered. Perhaps that was what her mother noticed. Her face flushed.

Her grandfather entered carrying his pipe. Noela ran to him and kissed him on both cheeks. "Good morning, Grandpapa."

"Good morning, little one."

"Is our guest up yet?" Germaine asked. "I must be off to Mass in a few minutes."

"Do not worry, *maman*, I will fix breakfast for Paul. And Grandpapa and myself," she added hastily at Germaine's look. "You go ahead."

Just then Paul came in. "Good morning."

"Good morning," said Noela. *Bonjour, mon amour*, she thought. *Tu as bien dormi*? Her mother looked at her, then at Paul. Paul sat down at the kitchen table, avoiding looking directly at her. She went over and got the coffee from the stove and poured a cup for Paul and her grandfather and then fixed a cup for herself.

"You slept well?" Henri asked Paul.

"Yes, very well."

"I will be going now," Germaine said.

Henri took a sip of his coffee. "Light a candle for me, Germaine."

Germaine started to say something, then shrugged and left.

Noela brought the bread to the table and sat down.

"You are not Catholic?" Henri asked Paul.

"No, Episcopalian."

Henri nodded blankly, not quite sure what that meant.

"We used to sing a French Christmas carol at school," Paul said. '*Minuit Crétien.*' Do you know it?"

"How does it go?"

"Like this." Paul started to hum the melody.

"*Cantique de Noël!*" Noela exclaimed. She sang the words softly. "*Minuit Crétien, c'est l'heure solonelle—*"

"Yes, that's it," Paul said.

"We are now in May and already talking of Christmas carols," said Henri, slicing off a piece of bread with his knife.

Noela turned to Paul. "I wish you could see our church on Christmas Eve! It is so beautiful. We decorate it with pine branches and there is a *crêche* with the Virgin Mary and the Infant Jesus and the Holy Men and all the animals. . . ." She stopped suddenly, realizing that by Christmas Paul would be gone.

He stared at her. "I would like to see it."

Henri looked at them both, then cleared his throat and opened his bible. He put it in front of Noela and at random selected a passage. "Here, my child."

"But if we walk in the light, as He himself is in the light," she read, conscious of Paul's eyes on her, "we will be mutually in communion and the blood of Jesus, His Son, will purify us of all sin." She closed the bible.

Henri got up. "And now, *mes enfants*, I have some things to do." He picked up his pipe and went out.

"Ah, Grandpapa, he understands," Noela said. "Sometimes I think his eyes are not so bad. I think he sees very well."

Paul leaned over and kissed her. "I love you, Noela."

"You do not have to say it because of last night."

"I mean it. I really love you." He seemed surprised by his words.

"And I love you. If only. . . ."

"The war will end. I will come back."

"Yes, it will, won't it? I want to believe that. Oh how much I want to believe that!"

André Romelin walked quickly across the square. He was late and he had a busy Saturday ahead of him. The month of May was sacred to the Virgin Mary and every day there was a special Mass in her honor. At eleven he would hear the children's catechisms, rewarding each child afterwards with a pat on the head and the picture of a saint. Then all afternoon there were confessions to hear.

"Bless me, Father, for I have sinned. . . ."

A repetition of phrases picked out of the prayer book Examination of Conscience, mumbled to the small grille of his confessional where he sat in the dark listening. Voices recounting sins of omissions, petty foibles, wanting absolution, cleansing of the soul.

In a small village one soon recognized the voices.

He went in a side door of the church. Several old women were already there kneeling and praying, waiting for the Mass to begin. In front of the statue of the Holy Mother extra vigil lights were burning and at her feet were bouquets of flowers brought by the children of the village.

The day had barely begun and already he was tired. His cassock, patched at the elbows, hung on him like a black shadow.

Father, show me Thy will.

For a brief moment his mind went back to the seminary at Saint-Sulpice, a kind of military school for young priests, a barracks of a place with its stink of greasy soup.

Its discipline had served him well. Even so, there were times. . . .

The world, so tolerant of the faults and foibles of men, tolerated no weakness in a priest.

It was a role that weighed heavily.

In the sacristy he changed quickly to his vestments to serve the Mass.

The altar boys were lighting the candles.

On the left side of the church, in her usual pew, he saw Germaine Fornay. He must speak to Germaine after the Mass, alone, where they could not be overheard, and warn her. If his house had been searched, others would follow. There was no time to lose.

Germaine was out of breath and puffing from the walk back to the house and wisps of gray-black hair escaped from the bun pinned up hastily under her black felt hat. This morning she had not lingered after Mass to greet friends but had hurried off after Father Romelin had called her aside to speak to her. She was perspiring as she put her key in the front door.

"Noela?" She did not see her. "Noela?" she called again.

Noela was in Raoul's room making up the bed and Paul sat on a chair watching her.

"Ah, *mes enfants*, I have news and it is not good." Germaine took the pins out of her hat. She removed it and thrust the pins into the felt.

Noela smoothed the sheets. "What is it, *maman*? You look so agitated."

"And with good reason. Father Romelin wanted to speak to me after Mass. It seems that early this morning his house was searched by a German guard. The new one. The one called Horst with the fat cheeks."

Henri came in during this. He waved his arm in the air. "*Les boches! On les aura!*"

Germaine turned on him. "And with what will we get them, Papa? The war is not yet won. They are still in charge."

Noela had grown pale. I was too happy this morning, she thought. It was too much to expect that it could last. If only we could have at least a few weeks together, but now. . . .

"It is not safe for you to remain in Saint-Gingolph any longer," Germaine told Paul.

"You are right. I do not want to endanger you."

"But, *maman*, do they have any evidence that. . . ." She stopped and looked at Paul and suddenly her eyes were moist. Only three days ago you came into my life, *mon amour*, and already you are leaving. Now is turning into yesterday before my eyes and there is nothing we can do about it. It is too cruel!

"They do not need evidence," Germaine said. "They are losing the war and they must prove they are still in control."

"What does Father Romelin suggest?" Noela asked.

"He was not able to say. Only that he will be by this evening and in the meantime to be very careful."

"If I hid in the barn would that be better?" Paul asked. "Then if the house is searched they wouldn't find me and hold you responsible."

"The barn is the first place they would look," Henri said. "And how would you climb into the loft with your ankle?"

"It is much better now," Paul replied.

"No," Henri said. "It is better you stay here and be comfortable. We will take the chance."

Noela kissed him. "Thank you, Grandpapa."

She felt fear grip her insides. Soon Paul would be gone. She would see him only with the eyes of memory, waiting, praying, hoping that somewhere he was safe. And would he forget that he had ever been in a place called Saint-Gingolph, until it became like a picture postcard found in a drawer years later? The life of the village would go on, she thought, we will still be here, seasons will come and go, some will die, some marry and have children. . . .

I would like a child by him, she thought suddenly, he is the only man whose children I want to bear. I want to live beside him, share his burdens, laugh with him, grow old with him. How could everything have happened so fast? Yet that was what war did, one lived a lifetime in a few hours, knowing it might be all the life one would have before it was snatched away, perhaps forever.

She looked at Paul's profile with the bandage round his head and thought how handsome he was. Or was it because she loved him that she thought he was handsome? No, she had thought that the first time she saw him. She tried to frame the picture of him in her mind so she could keep it with her in the days ahead. Until he comes back, she told herself.

She would be here, waiting, trying to imagine where he was every minute of the day as she went about her daily chores. And would he be thinking of her or would she be just an incident in his life, the French girl in a village whose name he could no longer remember?

I would die if that happened, she thought.

If only—if only there was something to bind him to her to keep the memory of her from fading. . . .

The sun coming through the half-closed shutters made diamond patterns on the bed. Paul took Noela in his arms and buried his face in her hair. It smelled fresh, clean, like rain gently falling on country hedges.

"*Tu m'aimes?*" she asked.

"*Je t'aime.*" Do you love me? I love you. How simple are the words of love. The language does not matter. They are one and all the same.

He was in France, in a strange house with a girl he had known three days yet it seemed that he had known her forever. Tenderness mingled with passion, he kissed her hungrily and she responded with abandon.

"Paul, Paul. . . ."

It was strange how someone could say your name with a faint foreign accent and make it seem new, like music unheard before.

"Hold me close. Do not let me go. Nevaire."

"Never."

He felt he knew everything about her and yet he knew nothing.

They had no past, no future. It was all contained in this moment, in this room.

The stolen hours of love are perhaps the sweetest, the most intense, mingled with the agony of farewell.

They were lost to the world, to everything but each other. Tomorrow would come soon enough and they did not want to think about it.

They did not want to think at all, only to feel.

IT WAS LATE AFTERNOON
when André finally heard the last confession and he had
difficulty concentrating. Pictures kept forming in his mind of
hostages being rounded up and taken off, who knows where
or lined up against a wall and shot. They had done it in other
villages, young boys, children even. Usually it was for killing a
German soldier but other times for no reason at all.

He had helped a flier escape one time in a hearse, but
first there had to be a funeral so he could arrange it without
suspicion. It seemed to him that almost every plan had to be
discarded as soon as he thought of it. But there must be some
way. He pulled at the white clerical collar around his neck.
There was one possibility. . . .

He got on his bicycle. The skies were clear, the air
fragrant with lilacs. The shopkeepers were just locking up.
Before the war Madame Alphand's candy store was filled
with bonbons and lollipops. Now, with sugar so scarce, it was
almost impossible to obtain the jelly beans and chocolate
eggs that the children looked forward to at Easter time.

A memory suddenly came back to him, a scene from
his boyhood. He had saved his centimes to buy a chocolate
egg decorated with pink roses and violets. It was an Easter
present for his mother. He was walking home with it in a box
under his arm and some bigger boys grabbed it from him.
He remembered his feeling of utter desolation as he watched
them run off with his precious egg, taunting him to get it. He

started to run after them and slipped and fell in a mud puddle.

"*Bonsoir, monsieur le curé.*"

It was Yvonne Toutain. Her face had the pinched expression of someone who has just eaten a sour pickle.

"*Bonsoir, Yvonne.*"

Her husband, the baker, got drunk every Saturday night and stayed that way all weekend. He was fat and his red face was covered with tiny broken veins. Doctor Jeunot had warned him to stop drinking but it did no good. André wondered how many people really listened to their doctors— or their priests for that matter. They nodded in agreement and went on about their way the same as before, doing whatever they felt like. It was only when they became really ill that they heeded the warnings, calling for doctor and priest, begging to be saved in both body and soul.

We are all human, André thought, we want what we want without paying the price. Yet life demands a price and no one escapes.

No one.

He passed the cemetery and continued on the road to the Fornay farm.

Horst finished his beer and paid the bill, trying to ignore the hostile looks from the other patrons of the café. An unfriendly people, the French. He couldn't figure them out. No harm had been done to the village, in fact things were running in more orderly fashion than before, and outside of the shortages of food, which his family wrote him was even worse at home in Dinkelsbühl, they weren't really suffering.

So, he had searched the priest's house this morning, but that was done on orders from headquarters. The Germans were not savages, they were clean and orderly and practical, which was more than could be said about the French, he thought angrily.

He stood up and looked down the street. He was young and he felt lonely in this village filled with hatred. He wanted to be back in Dinkelsbühl sitting in a beer garden with a pretty blonde German girl. The trouble was, he had no luck with girls, at least the ones he wanted. Josette, the plump girl who worked in the florist's shop, was friendly, but the pretty one, Noela, would have nothing to do with him. It had been the same way in Germany. The girls he was interested in all had preferred someone else.

He wondered what it was that women looked for in a man. After all, he was not bad looking, he was clean and neat and he was not stupid. On the contrary, he had gotten good grades in school and he had already passed his examination for the University of Heidelberg when Hitler invaded Poland.

At first, it looked as if it would all be over quickly, but now the war had dragged on for almost five years. If only America had stayed out of it, but as usual they had to meddle in places they didn't belong. But let them try and crush the German Reich! They would find it wasn't an easy job. Still, he was worried about all the bombings, German cities being turned to rubble by British and American planes. He'd heard that the Luftwaffe was in really bad shape and that they couldn't get parts for the few planes they still had left.

He started strolling down the street. He had to be at his post at eight o'clock, so he still had some time. He looked around. There was nothing to do in this village, they did not have even a movie house. He liked to go to films and especially cabarets. How he envied the men who were posted in Paris! Here there was not even a whorehouse.

Tonight he felt the need of a woman, any woman.

He wondered where Noela was and he thought how lonely it must be for a pretty girl like that with no young men around. He wanted to go by her house on some pretext but there was not time. And he had his pride. He would like to have her come to him for some favor. Yes, that was the way to do it, then she would be grateful. He smiled in anticipation.

Now, what to get for her that she would appreciate, to get her to have at least a beer with him and then . . . who knows? If he could only convince her that he wasn't so bad after all, but just a young man who came from a village like herself and wanted companionship. In Paris there would be many things to buy: silk stockings, pretty scarves, lingerie trimmed with lace, but here in Saint-Gingolph, nothing. There were the bottles of wine he had taken from the priest's cellar—no, that wasn't a good idea and besides he intended to drink those himself.

So what was there?

An idea suddenly came to him. It was hard to get tobacco and he knew that her grandfather smoked, a filthy habit, he had never done it himself, but for those who did smoke the tobacco ration was very small. She had turned down his offer before but if he got some tobacco and left it in a package on her doorstep with a bouquet of flowers. . . .

Possibly a note? No, no note, she would guess who it was from.

He thought of how soft her skin would be, how her hair shone with gold glints where the sun touched it, she was almost as pretty as a German girl.

Then he thought of how she looked at him when he spoke to her, cold, mocking, as if she despised him. He would change that look.

He smelled lilacs. In Dinkelsbühl there was a lilac bush growing in their garden. Now it would be blooming. He felt

hungry for some good sausage and sauerkraut and he felt
hungry for a woman. He walked faster, trying to think of
other things for the moment. He had to relieve Klaus at eight
at the sentry post on the bridge. In the soft spring twilight
birds were calling to one another. He saw one sitting on the
forsythia bush near the stream looking at him with small,
black beady eyes, so close he could almost reach out and
. . . he felt a sudden desire to grab it and wring its neck. He
had done that once as a boy to a tame bird that hopped on
his hand. He couldn't remember the reason, it was just
something that came over him.

Well, it was only a bird.

He saw Klaus standing by the guard house on the
bridge. He was forty, a cabinetmaker, and had a wife and two
children in Cologne to whom he wrote letters every day.
Klaus was as homesick as he was. He was not cut out to be a
soldier, besides he was too old, but the Third Reich needed
everyone. And to think that Hitler had promised them a
quick victory!

Horst felt disloyal. They could not lose, it was not
possible. He would not allow himself to think such thoughts.

"This is the plan," said André.

They were gathered around the kitchen table. With a
pencil André drew the Fornay house, the road leading down
to the village, past the cemetery and the school, back of the
church and across the bridge that marked the border.

"You see why I did not decide to become an artist," he
remarked with a while.

"It is a fine drawing, Father," said Germaine.

"If it is clear, that is the main thing," André said. He
turned to Paul. "You will not be able to stop and ask for
directions." He pointed to the map. "You must memorize it
and then destroy it."

"I understand."

"Now," André continued, "it would be better to have a rainy night, but if we do not have rain soon . . . well, we cannot wait much longer. You are to wear one of my cassocks with my rainhood to help cover your face and ride my bicycle."

Paul nodded.

"Let us go over it again. This is the border, the River Morges, but when it comes down the mountain and empties into Lac Léman it resembles more a stream than a river." André made a circle with the pencil. "When you cross this bridge you are in Switzerland, even though it is still Saint-Gingolph."

Paul studied the map, while Noela watched him in silence. She remembered herself as a small child walking across that bridge when the gray metal railing was taller than she was and she would look through it at the rushing water below. There was just a small guard house with the Swiss customs on one side in their gray uniforms and the French customs on the other in blue uniforms. Gray for Switzerland, blue for France, that was how she always thought of them. There were only tourists going back and forth then, no Germans.

"They can shoot even when you are in Switzerland," André said, "so don't slow down until you are out of gun range."

Noela's eyes widened. Shoot. They must not shoot him. I would die too, I would want to die.

"Keep going until you come to a blue café, the Café Eugénie. There you can leave the bicycle and the cassock. The proprietor is named Gascon."

"Gascon. The Café Eugénie."

"You are to say to him, 'The canary's feathers are wet.'"

"The canary's feathers are wet," Paul repeated.

"He will answer, 'They will soon be dry.'"

"But is his ankle well enough to ride a bicycle, Father?" Noela asked. "Do you not think that Doctor Jeunot should see him first?"

"We do not want to involve more people than necessary."

"Yes, Father Romelin is right," Henri said.

"I can manage," Paul said.

"It is too bad we are not more the same height," André said. "But on a bicycle it will not show." He suddenly thought of something. "Your boots. The cassock will not cover them."

"If it is dark enough no one will see them."

"Yes, it must be a very dark night. No moon."

Soap bubbles floating in the sunlight and then vanishing without a trace. She used to blow them with a small pipe and watch her kitten try to catch them. Now what made me think of that? Noela wondered.

"There will be a new moon in a few nights," Germaine said. "It was at the time of the new moon that Bernard—"

"Germaine," Henri admonished, "let Father continue."

"We will need luck but there is no other way. A boat is out of the question," André said.

"I'll manage all right, Father."

"I'm sure you will, my son."

Remember, Noela thought, remember. She must catch every moment, gather them like flowers in an apron spun of cobwebs. How fragile are the things we really want in life! The others, things which do not matter, seem to be tougher, more durable. She tried to visualize the days ahead without Paul, her life without Paul, and it was like a room in which the lights have suddenly gone out.

When will I see him again?

Question. Questions without answers. All he is intent on now is escape, but I . . . I will remain in this village, waiting endlessly, endlessly. And now that I know what love is, how can I live without it?

"Noela." Her mother's voice startled her. "Get Father some more coffee. His cup is empty."

"No, thank you. No more."

"Or perhaps you would prefer a glass of wine, Father?"

"No, nothing, thank you, Germaine. I will be on my way in a few minutes."

Paul looked at the map Father Romelin had drawn.

"As soon as you know it by heart," André warned, "burn it."

The map of this village, of Saint-Gingolph, burn it, but keep it in your memory always, my love, do not forget the way back, the road that led you to me. Noela felt tears filling her eyes and she hoped the others did not notice. She got up quickly and poured herself a cup of coffee. Her hands were trembling and she spilled some on the stove.

"It is a chance," André said, "but I think it will work. The German mind expects everything to be in a pattern, always the same thing. They have no imagination, they do not expect surprises. So if the guard sees a priest on a bicycle on his usual routine he will not think anything of it. Especially if it is sufficiently dark and he has had a beer or two."

Henri raised his glass. "*Les boches, on les aura!*"

"*A la victoire,*" the others echoed.

Yes, victory, Noela thought. May it come soon. Very soon.

Paul lay beside her in the narrow bed.

That is all that is real, she thought, the war is not real, it is not true that he is going away, that this may be the last time we ever make love. This moment is real, now, now. . . .

She moaned softly.

Outside the trees sighed, the moon was a silver crescent,

getting smaller, and when it was the new moon Paul would be gone. They lay tangled together, breathing as one.

The hours passed and dawn started to break, a pearl cloak lined with lavender, creeping slowly over the sky, casting a pink glow on the snowy mountain tops, coming down gently over the green trees to the sleepy village.

The church bells chimed.

"Do you think it will be today?" Noela whispered.

Paul put his fingertips over her lips. "Ssh. Do not think about it."

Her eyes filled with tears and splashed on his bare shoulder. "I cannot help it."

His body was hard and muscular, she felt safe in his arms. She could not bear the thought of anyone harming him. The slow ticking of the clock was her enemy, the morning light and the hours passing. She was a woman now, not a girl, she belonged to him, to him alone, she did not want anyone else to touch her ever.

So this was what love meant, this intensity of feeling, and yet there was so much pain as well, she had not realized one could suffer so terribly at even the thought of parting. She held him closer. Do not go, my love, never, never. One more time, and then. . . .

❧ 12 ❧

HORST WRAPPED THE tobacco in a neat package. It was several months' ration for a Frenchman. For an instant the thought occurred to him that perhaps Henri Fornay would be too proud to accept it from a German. No, tobacco was tobacco and other French people were buying it on the black market. Why should he refuse a gift left on the doorstep? Noela would know where it came from and be grateful to him.

He looked at himself in the mirror over the chifferobe. You are after all not a bad-looking fellow, Horst, he told himself. Why should she continue to refuse you?

Noela. He said the name to himself. It was easier to pronounce than some French names. He had heard of girls named Noelle but not Noela. It suited her.

He could hear the couple who owned the house moving around in the kitchen. Their son had been killed early in the war, and since they now had an empty bedroom, he was billeted with them. They spoke to him only when necessary, served him his meals in silence. Sometimes they looked at him as if they would like to put poison in his food, but of course they knew that if they dared to kill a German soldier there would immediately be twenty Frenchmen rounded up and shot.

With such good organization, as compared to the French, he could not see how Germany was losing the war.

He went downstairs for his breakfast. The French couple

would not sit down at the table with him but stood looking at him with cold hatred while he ate.

This morning he was surprised to see that she had her hat on and the man was dressed in his best suit. He had forgotten that today was Sunday. Now the flower shop next to the church would be closed, but never mind, on his way to Noela's he would pick some lilacs.

The woman said something to her husband in French and they left, slamming the door behind them. Horst continued to eat his breakfast.

Then he got his package and started off. He had an hour before he had to be on duty.

There was a bright sunshine yet a fog over the lake and it was impossible to see across. He heard the sound of the gulls. The shops were all tightly shut and there were few people about.

He had always liked Sundays at home, the big Sunday dinner with pork roast and potato pancakes, sauerkraut and apple strudel, then sitting in the beer garden in the afternoon and singing German songs, watching pretty girls stroll by. . . .

There was a large lilac bush in bloom ahead and he stopped and broke off a few sprigs.

He smiled to himself. As he turned up the road to the Fornay farmhouse he started to feel more confident. After all, he reasoned, Noela must be lonely for companionship and so am I. What does it matter that she is French and I am German? The war does not change our basic needs. Human nature is human nature.

Paul unwound the bandage and flexed his ankle. It was still tender and bruised but the swelling had disappeared. He stood and leaned his weight on it. He still had to be careful, but if he did a few exercises to strengthen it that might help.

Every day that he stayed here the danger increased.

Gascon. The Café Eugénie. The canary's feathers are wet.

He now knew by heart the map that Father Romelin had drawn. He had always been good at memorizing, it had helped him through many an exam and he always crammed at the last minute. Thus far his luck had held out.

If he could just make it safely across the border into Switzerland, then he could find some way to get back to the base at Foggia. Well, maybe that wouldn't be so easy. He would have to watch out for the Swiss police or he would be interned at Schaffhausen for the duration of the war. Still that wouldn't be like being in a German prison camp, it was a castle and he'd heard that you were pretty free there, you just couldn't leave Switzerland. He wondered if the Allied invasion had started yet. No, they would have heard something over the BBC. But even then it would take many months to liberate France and then they had to march on to Berlin. He didn't envy the guys who had to land on one of those beaches and knock out German artillery under fire. There were bound to be enormous casualties. There had been a lot of speculation around the base about where the landings would actually take place, but wherever it was, he hoped they took the Germans by surprise. That was the only way they could have the advantage.

He rotated his ankle in circles, first to the left and then to the right.

Somehow, he had always thought he would come out of this war alive. But was that what everyone believed? No, there were guys who thought that their number was up before going on a mission, and usually those were the ones who didn't return.

He listened. He thought he heard footsteps outside on the path leading up to the house. It was too soon for Noela and her mother and grandfather to be back from church. Yesterday the priest's house had been searched, now had they come here? He'd better get under the bed or somewhere and hide, not that it would do much good. There wasn't really any place to hide.

He held his breath and waited. His hands were wet with perspiration and his throat felt dry.

Time hung suspended. He watched a spider crawl up the wall and disappear out of sight under the eaves.

The thin line between freedom and death.

How fragile it was!

Now he thought he heard boots retreating into the distance, or was it his imagination?

It seemed that he had been in this room forever, a fugitive, hiding, and it had only been four days. What would it be like to be confined in a cell for months, perhaps years?

The freedom of space was what he liked about flying, the soaring over mountains and towns like an eagle, looking down on the world below. Feeling the controls in your hands, one with infinity. . . .

Not this waiting like a trapped animal to be caught. Now he knew how they felt, cornered, helpless, looking desperately for an escape.

He could feel his heart pounding.

He listened again.

Whoever it was seemed to have left. But would he be back? And when?

Slowly he crawled out from under the bed. He wanted a cigarette but he'd better wait.

He sat on the bed. It seemed he knew every inch of this room far better than he had ever known any room in his life. Years later—if he had years—he would be able to recall each detail, of that he was sure. He wondered if Raoul thought about it, wherever he was, the room in which he grew up and of the house and family he might never see again.

Or was Raoul already dead?

He thought of Noela and all that had happened between them in a brief four days. There was pain at the thought of leaving her. He meant it when he told her he loved her, but what could they do about it? The future was all too uncertain. After the war. . . .

It seemed that everyone's lives were suspended on those three words.

After the war.

Then they could all pick up the pieces and go on with their normal lives. But would anyone's life ever be the same again? Could bombed cities be rebuilt the way they were before?

The dead could not be brought back nor the maimed be made whole again.

The interrupted lives, like a broken melody, would never be as they once were.

He heard a key turn in the lock and voices. The family was back from church.

The family.

He thought of them as his family, he felt closer to them in many ways than to his own blood ties, these three who less than a week ago did not even know of his existence and yet had risked their own lives and everything they held dear to hide him from the enemy. Would his own family have done the same for a stranger?

He heard them talking in the hall but he could not make out all of the French.

There was a knock on his door.

"*Entrez*," he said.

It was Noela. She came in and closed the door behind her. He noticed that her face had a worried expression. She took off the scarf tied round her head and shook her hair loose.

"Is something the matter?"

She sat down on the bed beside him. "Paul, while we were at Mass, did you hear someone at the door?"

"Yes, I thought I heard footsteps, but then they went away."

"He did not try to come in?"

"No. Why? What has happened?"

"It was one of the Germans. He left something."

"What?"

"Some tobacco, enough for several months, and also some lilacs."

He remembered the sound of boots. "But how do you know who it was?"

"I just know, that is all. He has approached me in the village several times and asked me to have a beer with him." She shuddered. "I wish nothing to do with him, yet I have tried not to anger him. That would be dangerous." She threw herself into his arms. "Oh, Paul, what are we to do? I am so afraid."

He held her, saying nothing.

"You are going away . . . and I do not know when we will see each other again." A tear rolled down her cheek.

"I will come back as soon as I can."

He buried his face in her hair. There was no telling how long the war would last. And even if the war in Europe ended soon there was still war raging in the Pacific. Japan would have to be taken, island by island.

How could he make any plans about the future? One lived from day to day and hoped to be alive tomorrow, but no one really knew.

"I am being foolish," she said. "But I cannot help it."

He held her closer. "No, you're not. But there isn't anything we can do about it."

"I know."

There was such an innocence and freshness about her, yet an intensity of feeling that made her seem older than nineteen. He wanted to protect her, to be with her always. He had never felt quite this way about any other girl and it had all happened so quickly and by chance. If he had not parachuted down into this particular village. . . .

Her arms tightened around him. "Let us try not to think about tomorrow," she whispered.

André looked at the sky. Gray rain clouds hung on the distant horizon. Tonight, he thought. It must be tonight. After what has happened we can wait no longer. From the armoire he took his other cassock, like this one carefully patched and darned, and folded it in a large piece of brown paper.

"*Dieu te protège, mon fils,*" he said softly.

The other ones had gotten safely across the border, Paul would also.

As he tied up the package his mind wandered to those others. Where were they now, those fliers who had crossed his path so briefly? There had been many and their faces were a blur now. He had never known their names, only sometimes a home town.

They had trusted him and he had been able to help. Someday, perhaps, they would remember and help someone else, and so the chain would go on, from one to another, reaching out in friendship and in love, a spiritual flow that was unending, in spite of war, in spite of death.

There was a rumble of thunder. He took out his black raincape with the hood and laid it on the bed. Now, everything was ready.

13

GERMAINE FILLED THE
bowls with cabbage soup, cut four slices of bread, and put one
beside each place. No one spoke, they ate in silence, waiting.

Noela saw Paul looking at her, his eyes tender and
gentle. We have made love for the last time, she thought and
she bit her lip to keep back the tears. Any minute Father
Romelin would be here and then Paul would be gone from
her life, her life would be as empty as it had been before—no,
worse—it would be filled with pain and longing, she would
reach out for him and call his name and he would be far
away, unhearing.

Outside it was dark with no moon, the stars hidden by
mist. The heavy drops of rain continued to beat on the roof.

"Noela, you have not touched your soup."

"I am not very hungry tonight, *maman*."

Henri looked at the clock. A dog barked and then there
was the sound of Father Romelin's bicycle on the path.
Germaine got up and looked through the shutters. "He is
here," she said. "Noela, go let Father in."

Noela opened the door. The curé looked like a black
raven in his hooded raincape, a package under his arm.

"Good evening, Father."

"It is a perfect night," he said. "Just what the good Lord
ordered. There is no one about."

"Yes, Father." Noela bolted the door and took his wet
raincape.

He peered at her. "You have a cold, my child?"

"No, Father." She could feel her eyes filling with tears and she turned away quickly. "Everyone is in the kitchen," she said.

"Ah, good. We must waste no time."

Paul came back into the kitchen wearing the cassock. It felt strange to be masquerading as a French priest and he just hoped that he looked convincing.

"It is a little short," André said, "but never mind. Now, the raincape."

Paul put it on and pulled the hood over his face.

"Very good. And you will need these Swiss francs." André handed Paul a small purse. "My bicycle is just outside the front door. *Dieu te protège, mon fils*."

Paul clasped the priest's hand. How could he ever repay these good people who were risking their lives to help him? "Father, I—" His voice broke.

"There is no need to say anything, my son. We are all fighting for the same cause. *Bon courage*."

"*Bon courage*," echoed Henri and Germaine.

Good courage. That was better than saying goodbye. He looked at Noela. Her lip was trembling and she was trying hard not to cry. He went over and put his arms around her and he felt a tear brush his cheek. "Take care of yourself," he said.

"And you too," she whispered.

He looked at them all one last time and then he opened the door and went out into the night.

Noela ran quickly up to her room and threw herself across the bed sobbing. Once again, as in her childhood, unseen hands reached out and claimed those she loved—first her father, then Raoul, and now Paul. Everything vanished, everything.

"Paul, Paul. . . ."

The sobs wrenched her body, she dug her fingernails into the pillow, she wanted to rip it apart till the room was filled with flying feathers.

"Paul, come back, do not leave me!"

The blossoms had fallen from the apple tree outside her window, they lay on the ground now, wet and heavy with rain.

How would she face tomorrow and the tomorrows after that? She was nineteen and everything had crumbled away before she had barely begun to live. This was the bed where she had dreamed of love, read about it, now she had known it and for what? She could feel Paul moving over her, his arms crushing her, the feeling of being one, completely his, an ecstasy no words could ever describe. Already she ached for his body—I cannot stand it, she thought, how do I go on, how do I live without him?

She was dimly aware of someone coming in the room. She raised her head and saw that it was her mother.

Germaine put her arms around Noela. "My poor child," she said. "I was afraid of this. But you are young, you will get over it."

She stared at her mother, a shapeless lump dressed in black, her mother who had lived without love all these years, who had substituted the love of God for a man's arms, daily Mass for words of tenderness.

"Please, *maman*, I want to be alone."

"Very well." Her mother withdrew, looking hurt. She stood at the door a moment, then she closed it and went out.

Time passed, hours, minutes, she did not know. She felt spent, exhausted. She did not have the energy to take off her clothes and put on her nightgown. Finally, she fell asleep.

In the dream she was in a small boat on the lake looking for her father. She could hear him calling, far off, far

off. . . . Yes, Papa, I am coming, hang on, do not give up, I
will save you. The water was so dark and deep. She felt
frightened. Papa, Papa, where are you? I cannot find you.
There was a wind coming up and large ripples on the lake
that suddenly turned into waves. The boat was rocking, a
large wave splashed over her and she could not breathe,
there was water in her lungs, she was being pulled down,
down. . . .

She awoke to find the room dark and the pillow over
her face. There was the sound of rain on the roof and of
water pouring down the gutter pipe. It seemed as if she had
been dreaming for a long time but she still had her clothes on
and she had slept less than an hour. She undressed and put
on her nightgown and went back to bed.

This time she dreamed that she was in church sitting in
the confessional box.

"Bless me, Father, for I have sinned."

"Yes, my child, what is your sin?"

"There is a man and I . . . we . . ."

"Yes, continue."

Suddenly she realized that it was not Father Romelin
behind the grill, the voice was guttural and spoke French
with a German accent. Where was Father Romelin? What
had happened? She got up quickly and started to leave. A
figure in a black cassock came out of the confessional box
and grabbed her. It was Horst dressed in the curé's robes.

"Why do you always try to run from me?"

But she could not run. Her feet seemed to be cemented
to the floor.

"There is nothing to be afraid of. Come."

"Let me go!" She started to scream but no sound came.
Horst was roughly dragging her to the altar when she awoke.

The rain had stopped and it was dawn.

❧

"*Bonjour, monsieur le curé,*" said Yvonne Toutain, handing him a load of bread just fresh from the oven. "You do not have your bicycle this morning."

"I need to repair one of the tires," André said. "I did not have time to fix it."

She nodded. "I noticed you were having trouble with it last night."

"Yes, the rubber is wearing thing." He wondered what else Yvonne had noticed. Could she tell in the dark and from her window that it was not he riding the bicycle back from the Fornay farm? "But I will manage. Good day, Yvonne."

He tucked the loaf of bread under his arm and left the bakery. Around lunchtime he would go to the Café Eugénie and get his bicycle and his cassock. He hoped and prayed that everything had gone all right with Paul and that there had been no problems.

"*Bonjour, monsieur le curé.*"

"*Ah, bonjour, Georges.*"

Georges Michelet was the village pharmacist and also the mayor. He seemed anxious to tell him something.

"There was a message on the Algiers radio last night," Georges said. "From my son. At least I think it was from Jean-Pierre."

Jean-Pierre Michelet had joined the Free French in Algiers right after the fall of France, before the Germans started taking "volunteers" to work in their factories.

André clasped Georges' hand. "But that is good news, *mon vieux*. What did the message say?"

"Jean-Pierre is well and happy and embraces Papa, Maman, and Simone in France. Do not despair. Courage!"

"It was Jean-Pierre's voice?"

"I could not be sure. There were a lot of crackling

sounds on the radio."

"It has been a long time."

"Yes, it is more than four years since I have seen my son." The mayor quickly wiped a tear from his eye. "I had almost given up hope."

"We must never do that."

Georges noticed for the first time that André did not have his bicycle. "You are walking today?"

"Yes, my bicycle has a bad tire."

"And it is impossible to get new ones."

"I think I can fix it somehow," André said. He looked in the direction of the bridge where two guards in green uniforms were patrolling. "Grasshoppers," the French called them behind their backs. It occurred to him again that the Germans could never really understand the French, never really penetrate their subtle psychology. "I am so happy to hear news of Jean-Pierre," he said. He shook Georges' hand. "*Bon courage.*"

André walked on, thinking of the young men of the village, all of them gone now. They were his sons too, the sons he would never have. Jean-Pierre had been an altar boy and Raoul as well. How fast they grew up and went off to war. Some were with the Free French in Algiers, others were fighting with the Maquis, blowing up bridges and derailing trains with German troops and supplies, the rest in factories in Germany or in prison camps. He prayed constantly that they would return safely.

He started up the hill towards the church. The air was fresh after the rain, drops of dew still clung to the flowers. This morning he could see clear across the lake to Switzerland.

"Noela is taking it badly," Germaine told Henri. "She has been staring out the window most of the morning, as if she hopes he will suddenly reappear."

"Well, possibly he will," Henri said. He paused. "One day."

Germaine continued chopping up onions. "I do not think so."

"But you must not tell her that, Germaine."

"And give her false hopes? So that she mopes around year after year waiting for a letter?"

"He seemed like a nice boy. And he has been gone less than a day."

Germaine wiped her hands on her apron. "Noela!" she called. "Come here."

Noela appeared looking pale and drawn. "Yes, *maman*?"

"We need some things in the village. Bread, cheese, coffee." Germaine handed her a list. "And perhaps if you run into Father Romelin he will have news."

Noela brightened. "Oh, yes, *maman*, I will go right away."

Horst was sitting at a table outside the café when he saw Noela approaching, her shopping basket over her arm. Now, surely, after the flowers and the tobacco for her grandfather, she would be more friendly. As she came closer he noticed that she seemed pale and looked as if she had been crying. He wondered why.

"Good day, Mademoiselle." He stood up and clicked his heels.

She nodded and started to pass him, saying nothing.

He moved quickly in front of her. "I hope your grandfather is enjoying the tobacco. I can get some more any time you would like. It is not necessary for you to stand in line at the ration board with the others."

She did not answer and seemed to be avoiding his gaze.

He pointed to the table. "May I offer you something to

drink? A glass of wine, a coffee?"

"No, thank you. Excuse me, but I have shopping to do."

He was getting nowhere and he felt anger rising in him. "Perhaps you have a boyfriend with the Maquis?"

There was only a cool silence. At a nearby table an old man with one arm was watching him.

"Then what harm is there to be friendly to a lonely soldier who admires you very much?"

"Please, I must go."

He stepped aside. "You will regret this, Mademoiselle." He felt pleased at his self-control. He wanted to sweep everything from the tables and then smash them, pound them into bits. He sat down and gulped the rest of his beer. He watched Noela walk down the street and go in the bakery. They would be sorry, all of them, he thought.

On the wall beside him were two canaries in a wicker cage pecking on a piece of lettuce. The proprietress had hung the cage on a hook outside to give the birds some sun. Horst stood up suddenly and opened the door of the cage. The birds hesitated, looked at each other and then at the open door and flew out. He watched them go circling up in the air timidly, then flying off. They would be lost, of course, without their safe cage. They would not know how to find food, bigger birds would attack them. He tilted back on his chair and laughed. Survival of the fittest, that was what life was all about.

He saw the one-armed Frenchman staring at him with cold hatred. So what? Let them realize who the conquerors were.

The proprietress came out of the café. She suddenly saw the empty case with the open door and threw her hands up in the air and screamed.

"*Mes oiseaux! Où sont mes oiseaux?*"

Horst took out some francs for his beer, threw them on the table, and stood up.

She turned on him. "Why?" she asked. "Why did you do it? My little birds, they were all that I had." She started to cry. "Such cruelty, and for what? I do not understand it."

"It was a close call," Gascon said, handing André his cassock and raincape, which he had wrapped up in brown paper. He shook his head. "Too close for comfort."

"But he got through all right?"

"I think so. But the Swiss police were here just before he arrived. They have been alerted by someone, so they will be watching the roads. I do not know how far he will get."

"But he cannot be turned back?"

"To the Germans? No. After all, Switzerland is neutral," Gascon said with a wink. "We cannot take sides. If he is caught he will be kept in Switzerland."

"At Schaffhausen?"

"Yes."

"It is becoming more and more difficult to get them safely out of France," André said with a sigh. He shook hands with Gascon. "I thank you again for your help, my friend."

"I am glad to do my small part, Father. Now, let me show you where your bicycle is. I have hidden it where it would be safe."

Gascon led André out to a shed in back of the café. He took a key from his pocket and unlocked the padlock.

"I did not want to risk it being stolen," he said.

André got on his bicycle. "God bless you, my friend."

"And you, Father." Gascon smiled. "*A la victoire*. May it come soon."

As André pedaled along the road by the lake he thought of how many brave and good people there were in the world. The spirit of man, that eternal flame that could not be extinguished, would prevail, in spite of all. The individual life might be shortened, but what did that matter? The human spirit would endure.

He looked up at the mountains, his beloved Alps, their peaks still covered with snow. His heart did not permit him to climb very high, but he thought how wonderful it would be to scale the heights of Mont Blanc or the Matterhorn or the Jungfrau. He could understand the enthusiasm of those young explorers who risked their lives to stand on top of a mountain peak and who were able to say, "I have made it. I have reached the top."

But there were many ways of climbing, André told himself. Each one has his individual Matterhorn to climb. The mountains were there to test us, to remind us that life was not meant to be easy. He had chosen a life of service, to God and to others. Or does life choose us, mold us, so that each of us has a role to play in His Master Blueprint?

A priest was expected to know all the answers, yet he, like everyone else, had his challenges and despairs.

But today he felt uplifted and thankful that once again he had been able to help another flier to freedom. It was a good feeling and he prayed that God would continue to send him those he could help. And soon, surely soon, there would be the long-hoped victory and peace.

He continued on his way. At the border it seemed to him that the guards looked him over more carefully than usual. No matter. His mission was accomplished. Paul was safe.

He pedaled down the main street of the village and turned under the bridge beneath the railroad tracks and started up the hill. He could see his church and then he saw something else.

A German jeep was parked in front of his house.

As he approached the house he could hear music. Someone was playing his piano. Berthe, his housekeeper, opened the door with a frightened expression and nodded in the direction of the living room.

"They are in there," she said.

A German officer sat at his piano playing Schumann's "Träumerei." Another officer sat on the couch with some official-looking papers.

The German continued to play. He had a sensitive, sad face and played well, André noticed. Very well. He finished the piece and stood up.

"You will forgive me trying out your piano, I hope," he said. "I have not had the opportunity to play in a long time."

"You play very well."

"I am rusty. And I have trouble with the pedal. My foot." He pointed. "A souvenir of Russia."

André saw that he was wearing a special boot on one foot and limped slightly when he walked.

"So, we will get down to business, Father. The wreckage of an American plane has been found in the mountains, but there was no body, so that means that the pilot escaped. You understand what I am saying, Father?"

"You think he might be here in Saint-Gingolph?"

"There is a strong possibility."

"You are welcome to search my house."

"We intend to do so. And all the other houses in the village as well."

"It will be a waste of time."

"We have plenty of time. And we will take each house, starting with yours, until we find him."

There was a loud knocking at the door.

"Open up," said the voice. "*Machen Sie schnell.*"

"Germans," Germaine said. "I was afraid of this." She went to the door and opened it. Two German officers came in and looked around. One started upstairs, the other stayed downstairs.

Henri started to get up.

"Stay where you are, Grandpa," the younger one said. "We know what we're looking for."

"And what might that be?" Germaine asked.

He opened the door to Raoul's room. "Who sleeps in this room?" He pulled back the sheets and felt the mattress.

"It is my son's room."

"And where is he now?"

"He is in Germany working in one of your factories."

"The mattress feels warm."

"Sometimes I take a nap there instead of going up the stairs to my room," said Henri.

Just then Noela came in carrying her packages. The officer quickly stepped up and took them from her. "Let me assist you, Mademoiselle." He put them down and went through everything.

"What is it you want?" Noela asked, trying to keep her voice steady.

"We have found the wreckage of an American plane and we are looking for the pilot. We have evidence that he parachuted down into this village."

"And you think he is hiding here?" Noela asked. "You are wasting your time."

"That is precisely what the curé said." The officer smiled unpleasantly. "Nevertheless, we intend to search until we find him. He will not get far."

Noela held her breath and her hand went to the gold cross at her neck.

The Germans went down to the cellar and then came up again. "Let us search the barn," said the officer who had been playing the piano. "So. . . ." He looked at them all. "As long as you are telling the truth you have nothing to fear."

Then they both went out, closing the door behind them.

"I was afraid they would find the radio in the cellar," Germaine sighed.

"It is well hidden, *maman*."

"Did you see Father Romelin?" Henri asked Noela.

"No, he was not in the village."

"I am sure everything is all right."

"But the American left not a minute too soon," said Germaine. "Suppose they had found him here? It is something I do not want to think about."

"But they did not, Germaine, that is the important thing. The good Lord was watching over him."

"And over all of us," Germaine said, crossing herself.

❧ 14 ❧

LIFE IN SAINT-GINGOLPH
went on, the waiting went on, May turned into June. Will the
invasion never come? Noela wondered, as they gathered
around the radio for the evening broadcast of the BBC news.

"Kindly listen now to a few personal messages," said the
voice from London, switching to French. "*Les sanglots longs
des violins d'automne.*"

How much longer? Thought Noela as she heard the line
from the poem by Verlaine. The long sobs of the violins of
autumn, it was beautiful but what did it have to do with
anything? It only made her sad.

She did not know that this was not just a line of poetry,
it was more, much more. All over France leaders of the
underground had been waiting for this very message. The
long-awaited invasion was about to begin.

On the evenings of the second and third of June the
same line of poetry was repeated, and then on the fourth
followed the next line of Verlaine. "*Blessent mon coeur d'une
longueur monotone.*"

The invasion was now less than forty-eight hours away.

On Monday evening, the fifth of June, there were more
personal messages than usual on the BBC. In the cellar of his

house, Georges Michelet, the mayor, listened and waited. No one knew, his wife or daughter, or even the curé, that he was with the Maquis.

"It is hot in Suez," said the announcer solemnly. "It is hot in Suez." Then he heard another message. "The dice are on the table." The messages went on. "Napoleon's hat is in the ring." He waited for the message for his area. "The carrots are cooked." That was it. He took off his earphones and quickly went upstairs.

"I have to go out," he said to his wife, "and I may not be back until very late. Do not worry."

Each member of the underground now had his role to play. They would continue until all of France was liberated.

Tuesday morning the bells were ringing in the church, not just striking the hour but playing hymns. Noela ran to the windows.

"*Maman*, Grandpapa, do you hear the chimes? Listen. The invasion! It has started!"

"At last," said Henri. "Thanks be to God!"

"Can it really be true?" Germaine asked. "Noela, go get the wireless."

Noela ran down the stairs to the cellar and brought up the small radio. They turned it on and all of them listened tensely. It was true. The Allies had landed on the Normandy beaches just before dawn.

Noela clapped her hands. "They are here, they are here!" She started to dance around the room.

Germaine wiped tears from her eyes. "Soon it will be over. My son will be home."

Henri had his ear glued to the radio. There had been many casualties. They would have to hold the beaches under German fire and then fight through every village and town on the way to the Rhine. And then on to Berlin. If only he could be with them! He wanted to be a young man again fighting to free France. He stood up and started to sing.

"*Allons enfants de la patrie—*"

"*Le jour de gloire est arrivé!*" joined in Germaine and Noela. They held hands and continued to sing the Marseillaise, tears streaming down their faces.

Everyone was gathered in the little church. Old women, children, nuns, men in workclothes, the whole village was there. André led the special Mass asking for success for the invasion and protection for the brave men involved.

"And, Father, in Thy Infinite Mercy, bring our sons back to us," he prayed.

Many women were weeping. They had waited so long, and now, finally, hope was here.

Noela suddenly felt queasy. She covered her mouth with her handkerchief and quickly left the church. No sooner had she gotten outside than she was violently sick.

Germaine got up and followed her.

"Noela, are you all right?"

"Yes, *maman*. It was just the excitement and the church was so hot and crowded."

Germaine looked suspicious. "You are sure?"

"Yes, *maman*. You go back inside for the rest of the Mass. I will wait here in the fresh air."

Noela had not told her mother that her period was almost two weeks late. She had never been late before, and now she knew the truth. She was pregnant. She was carrying Paul's child.

She felt frightened but at the same time happy. Part of him was growing inside her, there was a bond with him now that could not be broken. She knew how shocked her mother would be, her grandfather, Father Romelin when she had to confess, as she would have to. I do not care! she thought. Let them gossip about me in the village if they wish. The invasion had started, now the war will be over soon and Paul will come back.

If only there was some way she could let him know. . . .

She hoped he would not feel trapped. No, he loved her, he had said so. They would go to America together, live there, raise children, be happy. Why shouldn't they be happy? They loved each other and that was all that mattered.

People were starting to come out of church so the Mass must be finished. She saw her mother and grandfather and walked over to them.

"Are you feeling all right now, *ma petite*?"

"Yes, Grandpapa. I am fine."

"Good." He took her arm.

"You still look pale," Germaine said.

"I am all right, *maman*. Please."

She wished her mother would not fuss over her so much. If she suspected the truth . . . Noela shuddered at the thought. She could well imagine the scene, the crying, the hysterics. Well, there was no point in saying anything until she started to show and that would not be for several months at least. Somehow she thought her grandfather would understand, but perhaps not. And Father Romelin . . . in the eyes of the church she had sinned and would have to pay for it in eternal fire.

"You are looking very solemn, little one."

"I was just wondering . . . how much longer do you think the war will last, Grandpapa?"

"It is hard to tell. Six months, perhaps a year."

"A year! But the Germans are almost beaten."

"Ah, no, they are not beaten yet. There will still be fighting and they will resist to the end, of that I am sure. But we will win."

A year, she thought, a year without him, wondering all the time if he is all right, it is more than I can stand. Paul, Paul, where are you now? If only I could reach out and touch you, feel you close to me. I feel so alone. . . .

On the bridge Klaus Winkler listened to the chimes and watched the villagers leaving the church. Soon it would all be over, he thought, he could go back to being a cabinetmaker in Cologne instead of a soldier, be with his wife and children, enjoy a schnapps in the evening with friends. This stupid war that Hitler had started. . . .

He saw Horst watching him. He must be careful, guard what he said, be sure that nothing slipped out accidentally. Horst was young and eager, a good party member, he could report him for disloyalty. He wondered what he would find in Germany when he returned home. There would be hard times, of that he was certain, it would be a struggle just to survive, but he was glad that the war was finally coming to an end.

And he was sure that there were many Germans who felt the same way.

That evening Noela and her mother and grandfather sat around the radio listening to General de Gaulle broadcasting from London.

"The supreme battle is engaged," said the general, his voice filled with emotion. "It is of course the battle of France and the battle of the French people. France, submerged for four years but neither reduced nor vanquished, still stands."

"*Vive la France!*" said Henri. He took off his glasses and wiped them. There were tears in his eyes.

An appeal from Marshall Pétain followed, asking everyone to obey the orders of the government.

"Pétain—traitor!" Henri said. "I spit on him, and Vichy!"

Noela listened quietly, her thoughts far away.

Where was Paul now? She knew that he had gotten safely across into Switzerland, for Father Romelin had found his bicycle and cassock at the café. But beyond that she knew nothing. It was as if he had vanished into space. If only he could send her some message, tell her that he was all right, that he loved her, that he would come back for her. But she knew it was impossible to get a letter through to occupied France.

All she could do now was wait.

You will come back one day, my love, she whispered to herself. I know that you will come back.

❧ 15 ❧

"BUT THE DISGRACE!" Germaine exclaimed, wringing her hands. "How could you do this to me? And what will people in the village say? We will not be able to hold our heads up. Why in my day, any girl who got in trouble was thrown out of the house and never allowed to return." Germaine paused for breath. "Who in the village would marry you now? Answer me that!"

"The village is not the world, *maman*."

"No, it is not Paris where such things go on, so I am told. Where loose women carry on—"

"*Maman*, listen to me. I am not a loose woman. I love Paul and he loves me. We intend to be married after the war."

"You mean if he comes back? And in the meantime what will you do? Walk around with your stomach sticking out to here?" Germaine held her arms over an imaginary bulge. "Be the object of gossip and snickers?"

"I cannot help what people say."

"No, but you could have prevented it. How could you let something like this happen? I have told you what men think of girls who permit liberties. They have their fun with them and then—pouf—they are off to new conquests."

"*Maman*, please, are you through now? I can't take any more." Noela started to cry.

"And well you should cry. A good Catholic girl, brought up by the nuns. I cannot understand it." Germaine blew her nose loudly. "For the first time I am glad your father is not alive to see his daughter pregnant with a bastard. The disgrace!"

"I am sorry I told you," Noela said.

"Well I would have found out sooner or later. You cannot keep such a thing secret for very long. Besides, I suspected something of the sort that time you were sick at church." Germaine gathered wind, like a ship at full sail, unable to stop. "It is because of all those books you are always reading. By that immoral woman—" She paused, trying to remember the name. "Colette, that's the one," she finished triumphantly.

"She is a great writer, *maman*."

Germaine ignored this. "You are like your father, a dreamer, impractical. He would never listen to me. To the very end he would never listen to me! If he had, he might be alive today."

Now I understand why Papa wanted to get away, Noela thought. Did *maman* always nag him this way? How did he stand it? Or was he able to close his ears? If only I could get away somewhere, anywhere. Suddenly she had an idea.

"Perhaps I could go and stay with Aunt Lucile in Arles," Noela suggested.

"Your father's sister? And let all of them know what disgrace we have fallen into? Never!"

Henri came into the room. "Germaine, what is all the shouting for? I was trying to nap and—" He saw Noela crying. "What is going on?"

"Let your granddaughter tell you." Germaine folded her arms across her chest. "I have said enough."

Henri looked from one to the other.

"You do not have to put the dots on the i's," he said. "I can guess what it is."

No one said anything.

"So, it is not the first time such a thing has happened and it will not be the last."

"It is the first time in my family," Germaine said.

"Have you no feelings for what Noela is going through?"

"But what about my feelings? I had hoped that she would marry someone in the village. Jean-Pierre Michelet, perhaps, when he came back from the war—"

"Germaine, today young people fall in love. It is not like it was when you were young and the families arranged the marriages."

Germaine bristled. "Bernard loved me."

"I am not saying he did not. It is just that you cannot plan people's lives. They want to have a choice in who they marry and perhaps it is a better system than the old one, who knows?"

Noela looked up through her tears. "Thank you, Grandpapa. I knew you would understand."

"We will do what we can to help you, *ma petite*." He glared at Germaine. "Both your mother and myself."

"But what will we tell people?" Germaine asked.

"We will worry about that when the time arrives," Henri said. "And now, I think I will go out and work in the garden until supper. Noela, would you like to come with me?"

"Yes, Grandpapa."

They went out together.

"Your mother will be all right," Henri said. "It is just a shock to her, but in time she will get used to the idea and be happy about having a grandchild."

"I hope so."

"Trust me. You will see." He patted her hand.

"But if she does not? I feel so alone, Grandpapa. And so frightened."

"There is nothing to be frightened of. We are a family and we will stick together. Now, let us see a smile. Ah, surely you can do better than that? Good, that is more like it."

"I do not know what I would do without you, Grandpapa. Paul said you were *formidable*."

The old man smiled. "He did, eh?" He thought a minute. "Well, I have managed to survive. That is what is important, not to give in to life, no matter what she does to you. You understand?"

"Yes, Grandpapa, I think so."

"Good. Now let us go work in the garden. There is much to do."

The fighting continued along the Normandy Coast. There were massive Allied air raids on Caen, the town was in flames and the populace was forced to flee.

"They are dropping bombs on French towns and killing French civilians," Germaine said angrily.

"Unfortunately there is no other way to get the Germans out," Henri said. "We are lucky that it is so peaceful here and that we are not in the path of the fighting. There have been no guns fired on Saint-Gingolph, no bombs dropped."

"Yes," said Noela. "I feel sorry for the people in those towns in Normandy."

Isigny was liberated by the Americans, then Caretan. But on the thirteenth of June, as British troops entered Troarn, the first V-1 flying bomb fell on London. Hitler had a new and terrible weapon.

Horst was in a good mood as he walked to his sentry post. He had known all along that Hitler would pull them through. It was just a matter of time now before London would cease to exist. He smiled. England would be forced to surrender, the British would be on their knees begging for peace on any terms.

Continually the bombs rained down on London,

dropping out of the sky with no warning. The death and destruction was enormous, but Britain did not crumble.

In France the Allied armies pushed on. Forty thousand Germans defending the Cherbourg Peninsula were isolated by American divisions. More French towns were liberated.

And then on July twentieth there was startling news. A group of German generals had tried to assassinate Hitler.

But Hitler was not to die yet. By nightfall those responsible for the plot had been rounded up and shot.

The war raged on.

"You will speak now," the Gestapo officer said, taking Josette's left hand and shoving the fingers into the open space between the hinges and the wall. "We know you are a courier for the Resistance. We want the names of the others."

Her eyes widened in fear. She had seen the twisted and scarred fingers of those who had been subjected to the door torture. Another member of the Resistance had his fingernails pulled out one by one to get him to reveal names. He had not talked and then they killed him.

"This is your last chance."

She shook her head and clenched her teeth. Suddenly she let out a piercing scream as the door was slammed shut breaking and crushing her fingers. Still, she did not speak. Open and shut, open and shut, the door continued, blood gushed forth, the pain was unendurable. Finally she blacked out.

But it was only a brief respite. The Germans brought her to with water and started all over again. No one could hear her screams in the cellar, there was no escape. How long could she hold out?

"Now we will take care of the other hand. Unless of course you prefer to be cooperative." There was a pause. "No? Very well."

The fingers of her right hand were shoved in the door crack. "The curé is one of them, is he not?"

She shook her head.

The officer slapped her in the face. "Answer me, you French pig!"

How long was this going to go on? She could not take much more. . . .

The door closed on her fingers, there was a crunching sound of bones breaking and blood ran from her hand onto the floor. "Stop!" she cried. "I'll tell you what you want to know. Only stop. I can't stand any more!"

André had just finished serving the last Mass. He was in the sacristy about to remove his vestments when two German officers marched in and grabbed him roughly. The younger one shoved a pistol in his ribs.

"So you won't try to escape, Father," he said sarcastically.

"Escape? I don't understand. What is it you want?"

"You, Abbé André Romelin, are guilty of hiding Allied airmen and helping them to get across the border. As you well know, that is treason, the punishment death."

So it was here, the moment he had been expecting at any time. He had been found out.

They bound his hands behind him and dragged him out of the church to the square and stood him in front of a cypress tree. There were more soldiers there with rifles.

"Do you have a last request, Father?"

"I do not get a trial?"

"For what? Are you afraid of dying?"

"No," he said calmly.

Death he was familiar with. His duties as a priest included preparing men to face death, calmly and bravely, in faith, but now that death awaited him with almost certainty, he found he was not yet ready and it shocked him. It was not that he was afraid. He believed in the hereafter and Life Eternal. But it seemed to him that his tasks here on earth were not yet finished. He felt that he had done very little. There was still more, so much more.

Or did all men facing death feel that? No, he had seen men and women in pain, after months and sometimes years of suffering, beg for release. They were glad to go, to have an end to pain.

The people of his parish were gathering.

"Not Father Romelin!" a woman cried. "Not our curé!"

Fernand, the postman, walked up to the soldiers. "Take me in Father Romelin's place," he said.

Bless you, *mon vieux*, André thought.

"Get out of the way, old man!" They shoved Fernand roughly aside, so that he stumbled and almost fell.

The soldiers raised their rifles.

A woman screamed and burst into sobs. Others bowed their heads and started to pray.

He had given the Last Sacrament to many, but he himself would not have it. No priest would hear his final confession, give him absolution. How much had he accomplished of what he set out to do in life? He had tried to do his best, to help others, and that was all that any man could do.

He looked out across the square, past the red-roofed stucco houses to Lac Léman shimmering in the July sunlight and then up at the mountains, his beloved Alps. He was seeing it all for the last time.

"Unto you, O Father, I commit my soul. Forgive—"

The shots rang out and he sank to the ground.

PART THREE

October 1970

❧ 16 ❧

PAUL DID NOT KNOW HOW
long he had been kneeling in the empty church when he
heard a heavy door open and close and the sound of
footsteps on the mosaic floor.

He looked up and saw a priest in a black cassock,
plump with white hair, walking towards the altar. Could it be
the same curé? he wondered. No, it was not possible after all
this time. The priest had his back to him so that Paul could
not see his face, but he was of a much heavier build than the
frail curé he remembered.

Slowly Paul got up and started to walk down the aisle.

The priest turned.

"Can I help you?" he asked.

"Excuse me for bothering you, Father." His French was
rusty, but it was rapidly coming back. "But could you tell
me—were you the curé here during the war?"

A smile spread over the priest's face. "You are an
American?"

"Yes, Father."

"That was Father Romelin of whom you speak. I did
not have the honor of knowing him." He held out his hand. "I
am Father Barthelemy."

"My name is Paul Sanderson," he said, shaking the curé's
hand. "I suppose I didn't really expect to find Father Romelin
still here after all these years. You see, he saved my life during
the war, and it is a bit late, but I wanted to thank him."

"You were one of his fliers?"

"Yes. How did you know?"

Father Barthelemy smiled. "It was not difficult to guess."

"I meant to come back before this." Again he felt guilty. "But something always prevented me." What a lame excuse that sounds like, he thought, as he said the words. I could have come back. I should have. "I suppose that Father Romelin retired a long time ago?"

"He did not exactly retire."

"You mean that he is dead?"

"Yes."

So it was too late to thank him, far too late.

"We have a plaque honoring Father Romelin. Perhaps you would like to see it?"

The curé led Paul over to the stairway leading up to the choir balcony. On the wall beside it was a marble plaque. He saw Abbé Romelin's name and the date of his death, July 23, 1944. With a shock Paul realized that it was only two months after he left.

"Father Romelin was a very courageous man," the curé said. "He saved many lives."

"How did he die?" Paul asked.

"The Germans shot him—" Here Father Barthelemy hesitated. "For helping Allied fliers. He saved more than a hundred," he added quickly.

And what about Noela and her family? Had they also been killed for helping him? He felt a sudden chill go through him.

"It was on a Sunday that it happened," Father Barthelemy continued. "Someone informed the Germans that Father Romelin had been hiding Allied airmen and helping them escape across the border—"

"Someone in Saint-Gingolph?"

"Yes, a young girl who worked in the florist's shop near

the church. The Germans came to the church after the last Mass and dragged him to the square and shot him. Then they accused the people of hiding members of the Maquis in their homes and demanded that they be turned over or they would take hostages and burn the village." He stopped.

"And then?"

"So then the Germans took six children as hostages and shot them in front of the schoolhouse. After that they set fire to the village."

"All of the houses were burned?"

"No, some escaped. And the church did not burn."

"There was a family, the Fornay family. Could you tell me what happened to them?"

"Ah, yes, the Fornays."

"They hid me in their home. There was a mother and a daughter and a grandfather."

"The Fornays are still in the same farmhouse. It was away from the other houses and did not burn."

"They are all there?"

"The mother is and the son, Raoul, and his family."

So Raoul came back from the war, Paul thought, Raoul, whose room he slept in, whose clothes he wore during that week in May so long ago. "Of course the grandfather would be dead by now?"

"Yes, since many years."

"And the daughter?" Paul felt his heart beating faster. "She has probably married and moved away. Her name is Noela."

"Noela Fornay?"

"Yes. Do you know what happened to her?"

Father Barthelemy seemed reluctant to speak. Finally he said, "She is dead."

Noela dead. No matter what he had pictured, he had not thought that. It was not possible that Noela was dead, she who was so vibrant, so full of life. He was almost afraid to ask the next question.

"Was she shot, too?"

"No." Father Barthelemy was looking at him strangely. "I heard that she died in childbirth."

"When was that?"

"I am not sure of the date. She is buried in the cemetery. Would you like to see her grave?"

Had she married someone else after he left? Or could it have been his child she had died having?

Scenes returned, watercolors washed with memories. Noela holding him and saying, "Paul, do not leave me. Nevaire." Her accent when she spoke English, the way she smiled, all the things he had loved about her. . . .

"I will take you there if you would like," the curé said.

Paul nodded. He did not trust himself to speak.

Father Barthelemy touched his arm gently. "Come, my son."

He walked along beside the priest, through the streets of memory, groping his way. Then it had been dark, a moonless night with rain obscuring everything. He had trouble managing the bicycle with his ankle, twice he had lost his way. And then there were the German guards. One had chased him and he thought he wasn't going to make it, but he did. Gascon was there at the café. Gascon . . . all the names were coming back after so long. He had left Father Romelin's cassock and raincape and bicycle with him and started walking around the lake in the direction of Montreux. . . .

He was young then, idealistic, full of hope for the future. Like so many others he had thought that if only the war would end, if only peace would come, life could be normal once more. But what is normal? Is there ever a time when the world revolves on an even keel, when there are no problems?

They were passing a large, gray stucco building with a white balcony and a few trailing geraniums.

"This is our schoolhouse," Father Barthelemy said.

It was a cheerful-looking school with large windows and white shutters. Was this the school Noela had attended? Paul wondered. Near the entrance was a flagpole and he noticed a large stone slab set in the ground with an inscription. He translated the words: HERE, ON JULY 23, 1944, FELL SIX FRENCH HOSTAGES. STOP, CITIZEN. TO THEM YOU OWE YOUR LIBERTY AND THAT OF YOUR CHILDREN. He turned to Father Barthelemy. "Was this where. . . ?"

"Yes, this was the spot where they shot the hostages. The oldest boy was fourteen, the youngest only ten. Mere children." Father Barthelemy shook his head. "How could they do it? I do not understand. And now, in Vietnam, the same thing again." Hastily he corrected himself. "I do not mean the same thing exactly, but another war, innocent civilians suffering, their villages burned. And for what?"

Steve already had his draft number, if he was called he would have to fight in Vietnam, or else run away to Canada, the way many young men were doing. Be a draft dodger. In my day, Paul thought, that was one of the worst things you could call a man. It meant that you were less than a man, a coward. "I don't believe in war," he heard Steve say. "I don't want to fight in Vietnam. We never should have been there in the first place."

There were no easy answers, no simple solutions.

Before he left Los Angeles a friend of his, a top surgeon, had gone to his office one Sunday with a gun, put a note on the door not to open it but to call the police, and blown his brains out. His nurse opened the door Monday morning and found him. Everyone was shocked. He was in good health, married with two children, well-liked and respected, he had everything. Why had he done it? No one could figure it out. Were there no more challenges left for him, no mountains to climb? Had life become stale, without purpose?

And am I, too, at the same crossroads? Paul wondered.

"This is the cemetery," Father Barthelemy said, pushing open the black wrought-iron gates.

They started walking along the white gravel paths. Everywhere there were flowers, some of them ceramic, and many of the marble and stone tombs had photographs.

"The Fornay family plot is in the far corner overlooking the lake," said Father Barthelemy.

A woman in black was putting flowers on a grave and a family was standing quietly by another tomb with many names engraved on it. Father Barthelemy nodded to them and moved on. Then he stopped.

"Here is Father Romelin's grave," he said.

There was a simple white cross with another raised cross on top and a rosebush planted next to it. The tombstone read merely: ABBE ROMELIN, SHOT 1944. In front of the grave was a white plaque with his name and the words: VICTIM OF GERMAN BARBARISM, JULY 23, 1944. There followed a quotation from the Book of John about the good shepherd who gave his life for his flock.

"And here are the graves of the children the Germans shot as hostages that same day." Father Barthelemy pointed to six graves with small white crosses. "It is fitting that they are buried next to Father Romelin," he said. "May they rest in eternal peace."

They continued along the path and came to some cypress trees.

"It is here that the Fornay family is buried," he said.

There was the grave of Bernard Fornay and next to it that of Noela's grandparents, Henri and Claudine Fornay. Then Paul saw a small marble tombstone with a photograph in a gold frame and engraved below: NOELA MARIE FORNAY, 1925-1945. In the photograph she looked very serious in a white, high-necked dress with the gold cross that she always wore. It was probably her high-school graduation picture, Paul thought. He stared at the photograph. The amber eyes seemed to look out at him, full of trust.

He turned around. Father Barthelemy was standing to one side watching him.

"You said, Father, that she died in childbirth?"

"Yes."

He saw no grave for the baby. And Noela had not married, for the name Fornay was on her tombstone.

"What happened to the baby?"

"Ah, the baby." Father Barthelemy's round face beamed. "The baby is now a beautiful young lady. Anne-Marie is twenty-five years old."

Anne-Marie. His daughter. For she must be his, his and Noela's. "Does she live here?" he asked.

"No, Anne-Marie lives in the Midi."

"The south of France?"

"Yes, in Saint Paul de Vence. Do you know it?"

"I have heard of it."

"It is not far from Nice."

Paul remembered reading about the old walled town perched up in the hills, popular with artists and tourists.

"Sometimes Anne-Marie comes home for a visit. She was here last Christmas with the family."

Anne-Marie. It was a pretty name. He wondered what she was like and what she had been told about her father. I was looking for answers, Paul thought, and my search has brought me more questions, for he knew now that he must find her. He must go to Saint Paul de Vence.

"Would you like to go by the Fornay farmhouse?" asked Father Barthelemy.

"Yes, I would. But, Father, I am taking your time. You must have many other things to do this Sunday afternoon."

"That is all right. I will show you the way. Or perhaps you remember it?"

"No. It was night when I left and it has been so many years."

"Then come with me."

So many years. And why did I not come back? he asked himself. In the beginning he had intended to, but as time passed that world receded farther and farther away. He finished college and went on to law school, he met Liz, he got married.

And what good would it have done if I had come back? he rationalized. Noela was dead, Father Romelin was dead.

But I did not know that. I did not know it until today.

Father Barthelemy closed the gates to the cemetery.

"Where is your home in America?" he asked.

"I live in Los Angeles."

"Ah, yes. Disneyland."

Paul smiled. "And where are you from, Father?"

"I come from Arles, in Provence. I have been the curé here for twelve years. Before that I served in Avignon."

They started walking along the road by the lake. An old man with gray hair and a wooden leg was riding a bicycle. Father Barthelemy greeted him as he passed.

"I guess you know everyone in the village, Father," Paul said.

"Yes, just about. But then, you see, it is not a very large village."

They turned off on to another road. Queen Anne's lace grew alongside and a tiny lavender flower that Paul did not recognize. There were walls of dark stone covered with green moss, fruit orchards and red apples on the ground, wood stacked next to barns filled with hay. Three black-and-white kittens were curled up on a wooden plank enjoying the sunshine while nearby the mother cat was licking herself.

Two boys of about eight, one carrying a soccer ball under one arm, came running down the road laughing.

How simple and uncomplicated life seemed here, Paul thought, the way he remembered his boyhood summers in Maine. He smelled woodsmoke, heard birds singing and cowbells. Then suddenly the sound of a plane overhead broke the spell. We could not go back to the way things were before, but must progress always destroy beauty? Soon would there be no places where the air was not polluted, no lakes where the water was not dirty?

"We are almost at the Fornays'," Father Barthelemy said. "There are the orchards."

Paul saw a tall ladder leaning against one of the trees and a farmer in blue overalls was filling a basket with apples.

"That is Raoul Fornay," the curé said. He waved to him.

Raoul waved back and stared at the stranger.

"You did not meet him before?" Father Barthelemy asked.

"No. Raoul was in Germany then working in one of their factories or someplace. I stayed in his room."

"Yes, the Germans took many 'volunteers' from the village. Some came back. Raoul was one of the lucky ones."

As they came closer, Raoul started to climb down the ladder. He was heavy-set with brown eyes and dark hair that was streaked with gray.

"Raoul, I would like you to meet someone," the curé said, indicating Paul. "He will tell you about himself."

Raoul wiped his hands on his overalls before extending one. "Please excuse me. I am not very clean. I have been working in the orchard most of the day."

Paul shook his hand. "I am Paul Sanderson." He hesitated, waiting for his reaction. Raoul showed no recognition. "I was here during the war. Your family was good enough to hide me and I slept in your room."

"Ah, yes. Now I remember. The American flier. Yes, I heard about you."

Paul wondered what he had heard. The voice had a touch of animosity.

"Yes," Raoul repeated, continuing to stare at him.

"We would like to call on your mother," Father Barthelemy said quickly. "Is she at home?"

"Yes. *Maman* is in the house with Danielle."

"Good. We will see you later."

They started to walk towards the house.

"I will go in with you," the curé said, "and then I must be on my way. You will have no trouble finding your direction back?"

"No, Father. And I want to thank you for taking your time. You have been very kind."

"I am glad if I can help."

❧ 17 ❧

"I WONDER WHO THAT IS with the curé?" Danielle remarked, looking out the kitchen window above the sink where she was peeling apples. "I have never seen him before."

Germaine was kneading pastry dough. "What does he look like?" she asked her daughter-in-law.

"Tall and blond. Not young, but not old. Nicely dressed. Were you expecting someone?"

"No." Germaine went over to the window and looked at the two figures walking up the path. There was something familiar about the man with Father Barthelemy.

"Do you recognize him?" Danielle asked.

"I'm not sure."

"He's not French," Danielle said. "He looks like he could be an American."

Germaine rinsed her hands and took off her apron. "I'll go let them in," she said.

When the door opened Paul recognized the woman in black immediately. He was surprised to see that Germaine did not appear much older than she had twenty-six years earlier, except that her hair was now completely gray. But then at forty Germaine Fornay had seemed sixty, so there was not the sudden aging that one usually finds in women one has not seen for a long time.

"I have brought someone to see you," Father Barthelemy said.

"Please come in." Germaine looked at Paul quizzically. "So you have come back," she said finally. "I must say that I did not expect to see you again."

"It has been a very long time."

A woman joined them whom Paul judged to be in her late thirties or early forties, pretty with dark hair, tending on the plump side.

"This is Danielle, my son's wife."

"How do you do?" Paul said. "I just met Raoul in the orchard."

Danielle smiled at him.

"I must be going now," Father Barthelemy said.

Germaine looked disappointed. "You cannot stay, Father?"

"No, unfortunately." He turned to Paul. "If there is anything else I can do, you know where to find me."

Paul shook hands with the curé. "I cannot thank you enough, Father, for your help."

"It is nothing. God bless you, my son, and may you find what you are searching for."

And with a cheery wave of his hand to them all he went out the door.

"I will finish up in the kitchen," Danielle said.

Germaine and Paul walked into the living room.

The old farmhouse looked much the same as he remembered, Paul thought. There was the same sofa where he and Noela had made love the first time on that rainy night when he couldn't sleep and had wandered in looking for a book. . . .

"Please sit down," Germaine said. "Will you have a glass of wine?"

"Yes, thank you."

When Germaine left he got up and looked around the room. On a table was a stiffly-posed wedding picture of

Germaine and Bernard. Already Bernard looked as if he would like to escape. There was another photograph of Noela and Raoul as children, wearing old-fashioned bathing suits and standing near the lake.

Suddenly two teenage boys ran in the room.

"*Oh, pardon, monsieur,*" they said quickly, seeing Paul.

At that moment Germaine returned with two glasses of red wine.

"These are my grandsons, Christian and Yves," she said proudly. "Raoul's sons."

"*Enchanté,*" Paul said, shaking hands with each of them. "*Je m'appelle Paul Sanderson.*"

"Oh, we speak English," the older one said. "We learn it at school."

They were dressed in corduroy trousers and sweaters and their hair was short. Paul could not help thinking how much neater they looked than Steve and most of his friends.

"I am very glad to have met you, sir," Christian said.

"I, also," said Yves.

"Those are fine-looking boys," Paul said. "How old are they?"

"Christian has seventeen years and Yves fifteen."

Christian is only a year younger than Steve, Paul thought, and yet he appeared more mature. And certainly he was more polite.

"Next year Christian goes to the university," Germaine said. Again there was a note of pride in her voice. "The Sorbonne."

There was silence for a few minutes as if they were both avoiding the subject, and then Paul said, "Tell me about Noela."

❧ 18 ❧

"IT WAS THE WINTER AFTER you left," Germaine continued, "the last winter of the war. But such a winter! I have not seen one like it before or since. The cold was enough to freeze your very bones." She shivered, remembering. "And food was scarce, but somehow we managed."

Paul remembered that winter. It was when the Germans broke through the Allied lines during the Battle of the Bulge. His college roommate had been killed in it the week before Christmas. He was a first lieutenant in the infantry, a nice guy with a good sense of humor and big plans for the future, a girl waiting for him at home. . . .

"The baby was due the middle of February." She stopped and looked at him accusingly. "Today it is different when young girls think nothing of having a baby without a husband, but in those days and especially in a small village, well, you can imagine what it was like for Noela."

Yes, he could imagine. He did not answer. What could he say?

"The waters broke and the baby started to come a month early. It was in the middle of the night. We tried to get Doctor Jeunot, but by the time he got here it was all over." Germaine wiped tears from her eyes. "It seems like yesterday when I talk about it. I cannot believe it has been so many years." She took out a handkerchief and blew her nose.

"We put the baby close to the fire to keep her warm.

She was so tiny that we did not think she would survive but she was a strong little thing. Anne-Marie." Germaine smiled. "She was a joy to me during all those lonely years. An extraordinary child."

"Do you have some pictures of her?"

"Yes, of course. I will get them."

Germaine came back with a photograph album. There was Anne-Marie as a baby with large, solemn eyes and a tuft of fair hair. Anne-Marie at five holding a kitten. Anne-Marie in her school uniform, books under her arm. Anne-Marie in her first communion dress.

Paul noticed how much she resembled him, far more than did Jennifer, who took after Liz's family.

"She was a pretty, happy little girl," Germaine said. "Blonde with blue eyes. But it was not always easy for her. The children in the village taunted her for not having a father. They called her *bâtarde*."

Paul winced. "What did you tell her about her father?"

"Only that he was an American and that he was dead."

Of course, Paul thought, that is what Germaine would have said. It was a much simpler explanation than the truth.

"We did not think that you were ever coming back."

"Is that what Noela believed?"

"No, she was waiting for you. Until the very end. She was sure that you would return."

"I wrote her a letter. I gave it to one of the guards at Schaffhausen. Did she never get it?"

"No. She heard nothing. There was no word from you."

"But—"

"You see," Germaine interrupted, "I remember the First World War. I was young then and there were girls also who had affairs with American soldiers. Some of them became pregnant." She shrugged. "It is an old story."

"But it was not like that. I really loved Noela."

"Perhaps."

She does not believe me, Paul thought, and why should she? "When the war ended they shipped us back. My father wanted me to go to law school."

"And a girl from a French village did not fit into the picture?"

"No, it was not that." But it had been, partly, and as the years passed Saint-Gingolph faded from his memory, it seemed unreal, like something that had happened in another world to someone else. And now Noela was dead, but out of that love there was a daughter. A life he did not know existed, breathed, laughed, wept, because of him. She was his child as much as Steve and Jennifer were his children and he must find her.

"I would like to see Anne-Marie," he said.

"What for after all this time?"

"Because she is my daughter. And I did not know anything about her until today. How could I have known?"

"I suppose there was no way."

"Would you give me her address? I am told she lives in Saint Paul de Vence."

Germaine looked suspicious. "Who told you that?" she asked sharply.

"Father Barthelemy."

"I see."

"Perhaps there is some way I could help her. I would like to. Surely you can understand that?"

"Very well. I will give you her address. But I cannot assure you that she will be glad to see you."

"I realize that."

Germaine took a piece of paper and wrote down an address. "This is where Anne-Marie works," she said.

"Thank you." He put it in his wallet. "And I would appreciate it if you would say nothing to Anne-Marie about me. I would like my visit to be a surprise. A pleasant one, I hope."

Germaine said nothing.

"I know it is not easy for you to see me again, to dredge up all these memories that are painful for you. You must hate me for everything that happened and I cannot blame you."

"I do not hate you."

"I hope not. Because I really loved Noela. You must believe that. And now I will be going." He held out his hand. "*Au revoir, madame.*"

Germaine clasped his hand and he saw tears in her eyes. "*Au revoir, Paul.*"

It was not until he started walking down the path from the house that it struck him. Germaine had never before called him by his first name.

19

THE NEXT LAKE STEAMER
back to Vevey did not leave for almost an hour. Paul sat
down at a table outside a café and ordered a cognac. He felt
drained, as if he had stirred up emotions long dead and
talked with ghosts in rooms that had been locked for years.
Slowly he sipped the pale amber liquid and tried to collect
his thoughts.

He had looked for answers and found some of them. He
knew now that no man stands alone. Life is a chain and we
are all part of it. Our lives touch others and change them
forever, often without our knowing it.

He would find Anne-Marie, help her in whatever way
he could. And Father Romelin—he would make a generous
donation in his name to his church. He would contact Father
Barthelemy as soon as he returned home. A new stained glass
window, a scholarship for some needy student? There were
many things. It was only a small gesture, but it was a start.

The landscape of life passed in the street before him.
All of it was there, he observed, in different stages.

A woman called, "Natalie!" to a toddler who ran ahead
of her, a young couple strolled by, their arms around each
other, a bent old man with a white mustache and wearing a
shabby suit and cap sat down at the next table, clasped his
gnarled hands over his stomach, and stared out into space.

One day would he also sit like that waiting for time to
slowly pass? It was not a pleasant thought.

But it is not time that passes, it is we who pass through time, leaving behind fragments of ourselves in people's lives. Nothing remains the same. We try to cling to moments of happiness, but we are swept on by a swift current. Those we love vanish and others take their place. Do people change or do we? Dawn turns to sunset, spring to winter, dreams fade, and suddenly we are old. Only memories remain.

There is no easy path in life and there is not meant to be.

A large bee flew by and lit on a red geranium nearby. He heard laughter from inside the café and a voice shouted, "*Voilà, bonne chance!*"

An old woman in a brown coat with a scarf over her head approached, a long loaf of French bread protruding from her handbag. Then from the opposite direction came an old man and the woman smiled at him and gave a little kick with her foot as if dancing a jig.

"*Ça va?*" she asked.

"*Ça va, oui,*" he replied and gave a kick in return, and then each continued on their separate ways.

That is the answer, Paul thought, watching them. Life goes on, the human spirit goes on, no war can destroy it, no dictator can ever enslave it, conquer it completely.

A boy on a motor scooter came roaring down the street. He recognized some of the tourists from the lake steamer walking back towards the pier carrying packages. He looked at his watch. It was time to leave.

He emptied his glass and paid the check.

Liz's voice was bordering on hysteria.

"But why do you have to look her up?" she asked. "She's managed without you all these years."

"You don't understand, do you?"

"No, I don't. I believe in letting sleeping dogs lie. Why

stir up the past?"

How had he expected her to understand? To want to see a daughter borne by another woman long ago, a woman he had loved before he met her.

"But it has nothing to do with you," he said. "I knew her before you came into my life. In fact, if Noela and her family had not hidden me in their house I would not be alive today. You would never have known me."

There was silence. After a while she said more calmly, "It can only cause trouble. Can't you see that? If Anne-Marie had known about you she would have tried to find you. Obviously she didn't. And now there will be demands, she will want money."

He started to say something but she interrupted.

"What about Steve and Jennifer? Have you thought of the effect this news would have on them? To discover that you have an illegitimate daughter in France—"

"I don't think it would bother them. The young these days don't think anything of such things."

"Well it bothers me!"

He tried again. "You should understand that I have an obligation, a debt that I can never repay."

"Then why try?"

It was impossible to reason with her, Paul thought.

"I wish we'd never come to this place!"

"But we did," he said quietly.

It was getting dark and lights were going on around the lake. Paul walked out on the balcony and lit a cigarette. Cars passed below and there was the sound of music from a café. In the bedroom he could hear Liz crying. He should have said nothing, just made some excuse about business and gone to Saint Paul de Vence on his own. Yes, far better. Why had he been fool enough to think Liz would understand and not be jealous, even though it had happened before he met her.

It just showed how little he really knew about women.

"I think I'd like a drink," came Liz's muffled voice. "A strong one."

"I'll order something." He came back in the room and picked up the phone. "Two double Scotches and water," he said. "Room 316."

"And we have to call the children tonight. Or had you forgotten?"

That was below the belt. "No, I hadn't forgotten. I'll place the call now."

"You aren't going to say anything to them about—?"

"No, of course not." Not now, he thought. He gave the overseas operator the number of the house. "And make it collect," he said.

❦ 20 ❦

AS THE TAXI WOUND UP through the hills from Nice he could see the old walled town in the distance.

"You have been to Saint Paul de Vence before, Monsieur?" the cab driver asked.

"No," Paul replied. "It is the first time."

"It is a very beautiful town. Many tourists come here. Not so many in October, but during the summer." He pulled up in front of the Colombe d'Or. "Here we are, Monsieur. They do not allow cars inside the town."

A porter came out of the old inn and took his bag while Paul paid the driver. It had been raining and there were still mud puddles on the cobblestone streets.

He followed the porter across the courtyard to the small lobby and registered.

"How long do you expect to be here, Mr. Sanderson?" the girl behind the desk asked, as she took his passport.

"I'm not quite sure yet. Two or three days possibly."

She handed him the key and the porter took his bag. They went outside again past a swimming pool and up a path to a bougainvillea-covered cottage. It was a large room with white walls and rustic beams, antique furniture and paintings. The porter hung Paul's raincoat in the closet and opened the shutters.

"Is there anything you'd like, Monsieur?"

"No, thank you." Paul tipped him and he left, closing the door behind him.

Paul sat down on the large double bed. Liz would like it here, he thought. It was too bad she hadn't wanted to come with him but had taken the train to Paris instead.

He heard doves cooing outside and there was the smell of woodsmoke in the late afternoon air. He opened the door and walked down the steps and along the path back through the lobby.

"Will you be dining with us tonight?" the girl at the desk asked. "I ask so that we may save a place for you in the dining room."

He had no idea. It all depended. "I don't know yet," he said. "I will let you know later."

"Very well, Monsieur."

Across the street in front of the Café de la Place some old men were playing boules. There was laughter and shouting and the clicking sound of metal balls being knocked around on the grass.

Paul stopped and watched them for a few minutes and then walked on.

The houses had heavy carved oak doors and some had black wrought-iron balconies with trailing geraniums. Red and green vines clung to the ancient stone walls and everywhere he saw splashing fountains and white doves.

Suddenly a shuttered window opened and an old woman wearing a gray shawl put a pair of men's shoes on the sill to dry.

Tourists were strolling about looking in the shops. Three plump, middle-aged women were speaking German. A young French couple passed him, arms wound around each other, lost to everything but each other.

Was I ever that young? Paul asked himself.

A harsh Brooklyn accent jarred his thoughts. "Honey,

stand in front of that fountain so I can take a picture."

The man had gray hair and was dressed in sport clothes, his wife wore slacks, a gaudy print blouse and a lot of jewelry. Paul could imagine him showing the snapshot later to friends at home and saying, "This is when we were in—honey, what was the name of that little French town?"

What was the mania of all tourists to take pictures? he wondered, pictures that no one else wants to look at, and that we ourselves usually shove in a drawer to be forgotten until years later when someone finds them and asks, "Who's that in the silly hat?" or "Is that really Grandmother riding the camel?" Do we take them in an attempt to freeze immortality, to capture the elusive? For the camera lies, it only shows the exterior, never the true picture. The true picture is hidden deep inside where no one can see it.

He continued to walk. There was a shop selling ceramic doves filled with straw flowers and several art galleries and a *pâtisserie* with strawberry tarts in the window. He had not eaten much on the train and he was almost tempted to go in and buy one until he saw yellowjackets crawling all over them.

He went down a few steps and there was another fountain, this one larger than the others.

I must be near the boutique where Anne-Marie works, Paul thought, looking at the name Germaine had written on a small piece of paper.

Then he saw it.

There was a white wicker cage in the window with two doves and some small black and white etchings of Saint Paul de Vence. And arranging some blouses he saw a girl with long golden hair. She looked up and smiled at him. Anne-Marie? Yes, it must be. He felt his heart beating faster as he went in the shop.

"*Bonjour, monsieur.*"

"*Bonjour.*"

She was wearing tight French jeans and a hand-painted blouse and her eyes were very blue. He tried not to stare.

"*Oui, monsieur?*" She switched to English. "What can I show you?"

Her voice had a musical lilt with just a trace of a French accent when she spoke English. It was Noela's voice.

"I'm looking for a present for my wife," he said.

She pointed to some silk blouses and skirts "You would like perhaps a beautiful blouse?" She took one from a hanger and held it up in front of her. "This one I like especially. The water-lilies are very pale, blue and mauve. It is flattering to all colorings. What is the color of your wife's hair, Monsieur?"

She has no idea who I am, Paul thought, and he wondered how long he should wait before telling her. She was taller than Noela, with a sprinkling of freckles across her nose, the same kind he always got when he was in the sun.

"Oh yes," he said. "It is—" Liz's hair was normally dark brown, but now that she had started frosting it he wasn't sure what shade to call it. "Brown with a touch of silver, I guess."

"Then this one should be very becoming. You see, it ties at the waist—"

Just then a young man dashed in, a dark and handsome Mediterranean type in jeans and a shirt smeared with paint. He called her Anne-Marie and they spoke in Italian. Then he gave her a quick kiss. "*Ciao, tesora,*" he said and left.

"Excuse me," she said.

"Your husband?" Paul asked. Germaine had not mentioned that she was married.

"Luciano? No." She paused a moment. "He is a good friend."

A very good friend with whom she was evidently living, Paul thought, from what he had been able to understand of their Italian. I am sounding like a father. What right have I to approve or disapprove?

"There is something wrong, Monsieur? You are staring at me as if—"

"You remind me very much of someone." He wondered how often she'd heard that line from men and whether her boyfriend had popped in like that to discourage any advances.

She smiled. "Let me show you some other blouses." She brought out several more.

"They're all lovely," Paul said. "It is hard to decide."

"I am glad you like them. They are all hand-painted on silk and each one is different. I do them myself."

"You are very talented."

"Thank you, Monsieur."

"I think I will take the one with the water-lilies."

"You have made a good choice. I am sure your wife will be happy with this blouse."

Paul took out some francs and started to count them. How should he go about telling her? He wondered. Should he just come out with it? And how would she react when she discovered who he was? What if Liz was right? He might just be stirring up things that were better left in the past.

"The lady of whom I remind you—was she American or French?"

"She was French. It was a long time ago. Twenty-six years ago."

"And you still remember her after all this time? She must have been someone very special."

"She was. Very special."

"I can tell that you loved her very much. What happened to her?"

"She died."

"Oh. I am sorry. That is a sad story, Monsieur."

Should I tell her or not? He waited a moment and then

he said, carefully watching her face as he spoke, "Her name was Noela. Noela Fornay."

She looked stunned. "But that is very odd. It was my mother's name."

"Yes."

"Then you—" She stopped and shook her head. "No, it is not possible."

"Do you know who I am, Anne-Marie?"

"I—they told me that—"

"That your father was dead?"

"Yes. How do you know?"

"Because I have been to Saint-Gingolph. I have talked with your grandmother."

She looked at him, disbelieving.

"What were you told about your father?"

"My father was an American pilot who was killed before I was born. That is why he did not come back to marry my mother." She recited like a small girl something she had memorized out of a book. "My father is dead."

"Do you believe that now?"

"I am not sure what to believe. If you really are my father why did you not come back before?" The voice was accusing now. "You never intended to marry my mother, did you?"

"You have asked me questions that are very difficult for me to answer. They are ones I have asked myself."

"I think that my mother was a dreamer, that she lived in a fantasy world. Me, I am a realist. I see the world the way that it is."

"And how do you see the world?"

"As a place that is polluted, over populated. You see, I do not intend to marry and have children. I want a career."

Did Jennifer feel the same way? he wondered. He had never really discussed it with her, he just assumed that she would go to college, meet the right man, and then get married and raise a family.

"So Women's Lib has reached France as well?" He smiled.

"And why not? Do not women have an equal right to do the things that men do?"

"I suppose so. And your friend, how does he feel about all this?"

"Luciano?"

"Yes."

Anne-Marie shrugged. "Like all Italians, that a woman should stay in the home and have many babies."

"And you?"

"I do not intend to be a housewife and spend my life cooking and taking care of children, to live in the shadow of a man. I want to be an important designer."

"I am sure that you will be."

To live in the shadow of a man, is that how most women regarded marriage? Was that the reason for Liz's discontent, that she had no life except as a wife and mother, no identity of her own? He had never thought of it that way before. Now he remembered that Liz had mentioned wanting to take a course in real estate and he had discouraged her. "That's fine for widows and divorcees who have to make a living," he had told her, "but you have enough to keep you busy."

Just then two women came in the shop and asked Anne-Marie if she spoke German. She answered them in German and they looked at some blouses, decided that they were too expensive and left.

"Could you have dinner with me tonight?" Paul asked. "I am staying at the Colombe d'Or. And bring Luciano," he added, hoping that she would not.

"I am not sure what time Luciano will be back. He had

to go to Nice to deliver a painting. But I would like very much to have dinner with you."

"At eight o'clock at the Colombe d'Or?"

"Eight o'clock would be fine."

He would have to let them know at the hotel. Anne-Marie handed him his package.

"Then I will see you later," he said.

There was a message for him at the Colombe d'Or. Liz had called from Paris.

He went to his room and gave the operator the number of the Hotel Meurice. In a few minutes the telephone rang.

"Your call to Paris, sir," the operator said. "I have Madame Sanderson on the line."

"Liz," he said. "It's so good to hear your voice. I was going to call you this evening."

"Darling, I'm sorry about everything. I was unreasonable and—"

"No, you weren't. It was perfectly natural and I don't blame you."

"Have you. . . ." She paused. "Did you find Anne-Marie?"

"Yes."

"What's she like?"

"A very attractive young lady, quite independent. She's coming to the hotel for dinner."

"I see."

"And how is Paris?"

"Lonely."

"I miss you too," he said. "Look, I have a wonderful idea. Why don't you ask the concierge if he can get you a ticket on the night train to Nice? You'd love it here. Then we can rent a car and drive back to Paris."

"Well. . . ."

"I love you. I need you here with me."

"You're sure?"

"Quite sure."

"All right. I'll speak to the concierge and call you back as soon as I find out. But don't you have to be back at the office next week?"

"I've decided to take an extra week off. I've got a competent staff. They ought to be able to handle things. You've always told me that I should let my partners handle more of the work."

"That's right. But you never listened to me."

He thought suddenly of Anne-Marie's statements about marriage. "I want to ask you something. Do you feel that you're living in the shadow of a man, that you have no life of your own?"

"I never said that."

"No, you didn't. Then you don't feel that you've thrown away your life, that you should have had a career instead?"

"Of course not."

"Good."

"What gave you such an idea?"

"Something Anne-Marie said this afternoon." He glanced at the package on the bed. "I bought something for you that I think you'll like."

"What is it?"

"I'm not going to tell you. You'll have to come and get it."

She laughed. "All right."

"I do miss you," he said.

"I'm glad."

"You get on that train. I'll meet you at the station in the morning."

❧ 21 ❧

HE WAITED IN THE LOBBY
of the Colombe d'Or for Anne-Marie. It had started to rain
again and the drops were falling on the flowers in the walled
courtyard. He thought how significant rain had been in his
life. It had been raining the first time he made love to Noela
and the night that he left her. . . .

"Hello. I hope I have not kept you waiting."

It was Anne-Marie. She had on an emerald green
raincoat with a hood and black leather boots.

"No, I just came down. Let me take your coat."

She unfastened her raincoat and handed it to him.
Underneath it was a dress of lilac silk and she wore a small
gold cross on a chain around her neck.

Noela's.

She is more sentimental than she pretends, Paul
thought. He noticed the girl at the desk watching them and
then when she caught his eye she looked away. No doubt she
thought he was with his mistress. He walked over to the desk.

"Could we check this raincoat, please?"

A sly smile. "Certainly, Monsieur."

He turned to Anne-Marie. "Shall we go in to dinner
now?"

The maître d'hôtel led them to a table for two in the
corner and handed them the menus, then withdrew.

"Luciano hasn't come home yet," she said. "I left a note
for him where I was going."

"And with whom?"

"I said that I was having dinner with someone whom I would like him to meet. I did not tell him that it was my father."

How strange it seemed to hear her say that word. "Is Luciano jealous?" he asked.

"Like all Italians." She smiled. "But I can handle him."

"How long have you known him?"

"We have been together for three years. He is a painter, a very good one. We met in Paris."

"You lived there?"

"For a while. I was studying art at the Sorbonne."

He looked at the gold cross around her neck. "That was your mother's," he said. "She wore it all the time."

She seemed pleased that he recognized it. "Yes. My grandmother kept it for me and gave it to me when I made my first communion."

The maître d'hôtel came back and they ordered dinner and wine. They talked about Noela, about the years in between, and then suddenly Luciano appeared.

Anne-Marie beckoned him over.

"Did you sell the painting?" she asked.

"Yes," he said. "I sold it." He was glaring sullenly at Paul.

"I wanted you to meet someone," she said. "Someone who is very important to me. Someone I thought was dead." She paused. "Luciano, I want to introduce you to my father."

That night, for the first time in years, he slept without tossing and turning, and when he awoke the rain had stopped and sunshine streamed in through the half-open shutters and there was the scent of mimosa and the sound of doves cooing.

How good it was to be alive!

Others had not survived. He had survived. He did not know why he should be alive when others far more worthy had died, he would never know, but he did know what he must do.

What had happened in Saint-Gingolph could not be changed, but the terrible things that had happened there and in so many other places must never be forgotten. History repeats, and once more the world was on the brink of blowing itself up.

Would we, too, end like other civilizations, a pile of stone and buried rubble?

No, that must not happen, he told himself.

People had become bitter and given up hope. There still was hope among the many voices of despair.

Suddenly he felt a new strength.

He had been given extra time and from now on he had a purpose, an obligation in life. He must help others and work for a better world, for peace and understanding.

Yes, he had been given extra time. But he must use it well.

For no one has unlimited time.

While he waited in the Nice station for the Blue Train from Paris, he observed the panorama of life around him. An old woman in a gray coat walked by with a large black-and-white dog, on the next bench a young dark-haired man and his very pregnant wife were speaking French, two small children ran by laughing. He appeared to be the only American in the train station. Near a cart piled with luggage a porter was telling a group of Italians that on Thursday there was going to be a general strike all over France.

He was glad now he had rented a car. They could drive back to Paris, stopping at charming little inns on the way, sample the food and the wine, have a second honeymoon.

The lights of an engine appeared coming around the bend, followed by a long train. The porter started to walk along the platform pushing his cart.

"*C'est le train bleu?*" Paul asked him.

"*Oui, monsieur.*"

The express came roaring down the tracks. It would stop for exactly three minutes. People were looking out the windows and others were standing in the doors with suitcases ready to jump off. He ran along beside the train looking in the compartments for Liz.

He saw her before she saw him. Then she smiled and waved.

When he reached her, they kissed as if they had been separated for a long time. Finally she said, tears of happiness shining in her eyes, "I'm back."

So am I, he thought, holding her close. So am I.

THAT MAN IN RIO

PROLOGUE

NATALIE

"ALL MY CHILDREN HAVE BEEN divorced. Some more than once."

"Now, Mother, let's not get started on that again. We came to La Jolla to celebrate your eightieth birthday and have a happy time together."

Happy time? A poor choice of words. How did I ever think that a visit with Mother could be called a happy time? I threw Johanna a desperate look across the table. All the years of carefully built-up veneer crumbled whenever I saw Mother, instead of the successful designer whose clothes are worn by famous women, I was again the homely little girl in Rio with the red birthmark hidden by bangs that came to the bridge of my nose, shy, unloved. Had my father loved me? Perhaps, but he never told me so. He was a silent, remote man, in love with the sea and ships.

"Natalie's right, Mother," Johanna said, pausing while Pauline passed the roast lamb with browned potatoes and peas, the favorite Sunday dinner of my childhood. "Not in front of the servants" was a phrase I remembered well, though after more than twenty years of working for Mother, I'm sure there were few family secrets Pauline didn't know.

"In my day, if you got a divorce you were an outcast socially," Mother continued, putting mint sauce on her lamb. "Now, no one thinks anything of it."

Only three more days, I thought. If I can just get through the next three days without some kind of a terrible scene. ...

"I always liked Skipper's first wife. If he hadn't divorced her—"

"She was an alcoholic, Mother. Everyone knew that." And she was sleeping with half his friends, but I decided not to add that. What Mother didn't know at this stage of her life wouldn't hurt her.

"Still, divorce is far too easy these days. Every marriage has its problems and you just have to work them out. When we were in Rio. . . ." Mother paused and looked around the table of Brazilian jacarandá set with écru lace placemats, heavy antique silver and Waterford crystal, as if considering whether to continue.

Rio. If I close my eyes I can see it all the way it was, our house on Avenida Atlantica, my room with its balcony and view out over the bay. "You were too young to remember Rio," people tell me, but they are wrong. It is all there, the smells, the sights, the sounds, as if by pushing the right button it could all come back to life. No, it is not all there quite. Some things are buried, perhaps they are too painful to recall, I do not know, and I wonder if hypnosis would bring them out, those dark hidden places I cannot reach in my memory, that torment me still.

"What happened in Rio?" Johanna asked.

"When we lived in Rio," Mother said, "I fell in love with another man."

Johanna and I looked at her in amazement. "Another man?" I asked. "Who was he?"

"It doesn't matter now," Mother said. "And it was all a very long time ago. But I couldn't leave your father because he was such a fine person."

"Well, that was certainly a bombshell Mother dropped at dinner, wasn't it?" Johanna said, when we were lying in the twin beds in the guest room unable to sleep. "It explains a lot. The way she treated him, the separate bedrooms. . . ."

To have lived without love all those years, playing the role of the respectable Navy wife—how bitter she must have felt!

"Do you have any idea who he was?" Johanna asked.

"No. I'm as surprised as you were."

"But you were in Rio. You and Skipper. I wasn't born then."

"I was five years old when we left Rio. And Skipper was four."

Skipper. The family always called him that instead of Donald Junior, the little boy in his sailor suit, even when he was a grown man. Maybe that was why things turned out for him the way they did.

"But you must remember something?" Johanna insisted.

Yes, I remember. Or at least there is something I am trying to remember about Rio. But what?

A bed. I am lying in a four-poster bed of carved jacarandá covered with mosquito netting. I always have to get undressed and put on my nightgown to take my nap. The sunlight filters through the slats of the shutters and dances across the Oriental rug, from downstairs I hear piano music, "Song of India," haunting and sad. Today whenever I hear it I cry and don't know why.

Then, suddenly a shot rings out, a woman screams, the music stops. And there is the sound of a woman sobbing.

That is all I remember. . . .

Rio de Janeiro,

1932

1 ⊚

LILA DRESSED CAREFULLY, THEN combed her newly-bobbed blonde hair and dabbed perfume behind her ears and at her throat and wrists. She stood back to admire her reflection in the tall baroque mirror. Yes, the new dress of aquamarine chiffon had turned out perfectly, it fell in drifts around her slim figure to her ankles and brought out the blue in her eyes. No one would be able to tell that it was not a Paris original but a copy run up by a Russian seamstress she had discovered on a narrow little street off Avenida Rio Branco.

"You look smashing," Donald said, his favorite expression lately, one he had picked up from a British diplomat. "All the other Navy wives will be jealous."

"I hope so." Her voice still had a trace of North Carolina, no matter how hard she worked on it, but people told her they found it charming. Men, that is. She'd never had many women friends. Except for the one who invited her to the Annapolis hop for a blind date with her beau's roommate from Oklahoma, who turned out to be Donald.

She loved living in Rio de Janeiro. At first it had seemed strange having the seasons reversed and that what she thought of as summer was the middle of the Brazilian winter, but after a year here she was used to it. And not only was Rio a beautiful and exciting city, but they had a life style they never would have back home, where President Hoover was desperately trying to cope with failing banks and long lines of unemployed. Here in their rented house on Avenida Atlantica they had three Brazilian servants and a German governess for the children, and all on Donald's salary as a lieutenant commander.

"We'd better get going," Donald said.

"I just want to tell Bertha something first about Skipper," Lila said. "It won't take a minute."

She walked quickly down the hall, passing Natalie's door with scarcely a glance, and went in Skipper's room. He lay curled up with his teddy bear, his eyes closed. When she leaned over his bed, his eyes opened.

"Where are you going?" he asked sleepily.

"Daddy and I are going to a party," she said, kissing him. How sweet and warm he felt, his cheek like velvet, his tousled blond curls like strands of silk.

"No, I don't want you to go." He sat up, clinging to her.

"But Bertha will be here with you." Behind her she heard the rustling of a starched uniform and turned. Bertha looked displeased about something.

"I just wanted to check on him before we left," Lila said. Why did the German woman always make her feel guilty? "I thought he looked feverish earlier."

Bertha glared. "I took his temperature and it was normal. What he needs is sleep."

"Yes, of course. You have the phone number where we can be reached if anything. . . ."

"I am sure that will not be necessary. Have a nice evening, Madam."

"That woman makes me feel as if I'm interfering with my own son," Lila told Donald, as they got in the car.

Donald shrugged. "But she's efficient and capable. The last nurse we had—"

"Yes, she was hopeless. And it's so hard to find

someone good. I guess you can't have everything, but I wish she had a pleasanter disposition. You don't think she's ever mean to the children, do you?"

"No, I just think she has a very brusque manner that's typically German. Did you check on Natalie?"

"Yes," she lied. "She was asleep."

Natalie lay in the large four-poster bed with its high canopy covered with mosquito netting, her doll Anastasia on the pillow beside her. She heard the click of her mother's high heels on the polished wood floor as she passed her room on the way to Skipper's. She could always tell her mother's walk because she had quick light steps, unlike Bertha, who clumped in her heavy nurse's shoes like someone marching. She hated Bertha. The nurse before her, the one who came down on the ship with them from the United States, had been much nicer. She was young and pretty and not nearly as strict as Bertha.

Natalie hugged her doll. "You love me, even if I have a birthmark, don't you, Anastasia?"

Her father had given her Anastasia and told her he got her from a White Russian. She was named after a little Russian princess, the daughter of the czar, who was like a king, her father explained, but in Russia they were called czars. That was until the Bolsheviks took over and killed all the royal family. When she heard that she started to cry, but her father said that a soldier took pity on Anastasia and helped her escape. That made her feel better.

She snuggled under the covers, holding Anastasia tighter. She couldn't remember much of her life before they came to Rio, except visiting her grandparents in Raleigh and having a vaccination for smallpox by the doctor who told her it wouldn't hurt. He lied to her. It did hurt when the needle went in her arm and she screamed. The doctor just laughed.

And then they took the train to New York and got on a big white ship, her mother, Skipper, and the pretty young nurse, for her father had already gone on ahead. The voyage took two weeks and the ship pitched in the rough seas and the pretty nurse got seasick and spent most of the time in her berth moaning, "Oh, why won't this boat stop rocking?"

They were the only children on the ship, the *Southern Cross*, and everyone was nice to them. The captain took them up on the bridge, and the engineer showed them the engine room, and one of the sailors had a talking parrot. The only thing she didn't like about the trip was when they threw her mother in the pool with all her clothes on. She cried because she thought they were trying to drown her mother, but they explained that this was a special ceremony about Neptune and everyone who had not crossed the equator before had to be dunked in the water, like a christening. They didn't do it to her or Skipper because they were children, and the pretty young nurse escaped because she was in the cabin seasick.

She heard the clump-clump of Bertha's feet coming down the hall and then the door opened and a crack of light came in the room. Natalie closed her eyes tight and pretended she was asleep. Bertha walked closer to the bed and she could feel Bertha's heavy breathing as she pulled back the mosquito netting and roughly snatched Anastasia.

Natalie opened her eyes and sat up. "Give me Anastasia!"

"You are too old to sleep with a doll. Shame on you! A big girl four years old and acting like a baby."

"Where are you taking Anastasia?"

"I will put her on this chair. See? Now go to sleep. And if you are not good, the bogeyman will come during the night."

You are a wicked witch and I hate you, Bertha! I hope they bogeyman comes and carries you away, Natalie thought, but she was too scared of Bertha to say it aloud. She waited until Bertha was gone and then she got out of bed, picked up her doll, and tucked her under the covers beside her.

"Sleep well, Anastasia," she said, kissing her.

2 ⑥

"GALINHA! GALINHA!"

Natalie stirred in her bed as she heard the familiar cry of the chicken man beneath her window. She always had trouble sleeping when Bertha put her to bed for her nap. Bertha made her get completely undressed and put on her nightgown and lie down for two hours every day after lunch.

"Galinha! Galinha!"

Pushing aside the mosquito netting, she got out of bed and tiptoed to the window overlooking the street. The chicken man had his live chickens in a large straw basket slung over his back. She wondered if their cook would buy one from him today. Once she had come out the back door to the walled garden by the kitchen and seen Ana with a hatchet chasing a terrified chicken. Bertha had discovered her and quickly pulled her inside. There were awful squawks and then silence.

That evening there was chicken for supper and she refused to eat it.

"Eat your chicken!" ordered Bertha, glaring at her.

"Isn't this the chicken that I saw Ana chasing?"

"Never mind, just eat it."

"I won't."

"Then straight to bed without any dessert. And when your parents come home I will tell them that you have been a bad girl." Bertha grabbed her by the back of the neck and marched her up the stairs.

"I want dessert." She bit her lip, determined not to cry.

"No ice cream for you," Bertha snorted. "Why in Germany, after the war, we were happy to eat anything. Even sawdust," she said bitterly. "We were starving."

Natalie looked up at her, frightened by the expression on Bertha's face. "What is a war, Bertha?"

"Perhaps one day you will see. And the next time, Germany will win."

There were so many things she didn't understand, Natalie thought. She felt so lonely and she wished her mother would spend more time with her. Why did she and Skipper always have to be with Bertha? And her father was busy too. Sometimes they met other children on their promenades with Bertha and played with them in the park, but not often. It would be nice to have a friend, a special friend, or even a dog to play with.

She walked over to the dressing table with its carved mirror of dark wood and pushed back her blonde bangs and stared at the red birthmark that ran from the top of her forehead to where her nose started. "How unfortunate for a girl," she once overheard a friend of her mother's say when she thought she had left the room. "Yes, I know," her mother replied. "And she's so shy as well."

Would the red mark fade when she grew up or would she have to wear bangs for the rest of her life? She rubbed it with her finger trying to erase it but it only made it redder.

Suddenly she heard footsteps coming down the hall and she quickly scampered back to bed.

Bertha opened the door. She was actually smiling and seemed to be in a good mood for a change. "Time to get up from your nap," she said. "I am going to take you and Skipper to the park." She selected a blue smocked dress with a lace collar and a matching blue bonnet. "And if you are good I will buy you each a balloon. Come, let us get dressed."

"*Sorvete?*"

"*Bom dia, Senhorita.*" Ana beamed at Natalie. "*Sim,*" she nodded. "*Sorvete.*"

Every Sunday morning Natalie sneaked down the back stairs to the kitchen where Ana was making ice cream for dinner. Sometimes she would even let her turn the crank of the wooden mixer with the salted ice. Ana was fat and jolly and she laughed a lot and it was fun being in the kitchen. Ice cream was one of the three Portuguese words Natalie knew, the others being chicken and streetcar. Her father spoke Portuguese fluently and her mother spoke what she laughingly called "kitchen Portuguese." She was able to tell Ana what to cook and that was about it.

When I am grown up, Natalie promised herself, I am going to learn lots of different languages so that people won't be able to say things around me that I can't understand. Sometimes Bertha would mutter things in German under her breath and when Natalie asked her what it meant she would reply, "Never mind." She was sure it was not anything very nice.

She wished she could say more to Ana, who seemed to like children, unlike Bertha, or even her mother, who was sleeping now and wouldn't be up until noon.

"Natalie!" It was Bertha calling her.

She smiled at Ana and ran up the stairs two at a time, almost colliding with Bertha in the hall.

"Bad girl! Where have you been?"

"Talking to Ana."

"You know your mother doesn't like you in the kitchen with the servants."

Skipper was with her, holding his pail and shovel and

dressed in a blue sunsuit with a red sailboat on the front.

"We're going to the beach," he said happily.

"And we are late," Bertha said. "I looked for you in your room and you were not there." Bertha took out a sundress and bonnet and a pair of sandals from the armoire. "Get dressed quickly. We are going to the beach in front of the Copacabana Hotel."

"I'm going to build a sand castle," Skipper said. "Bertha is going to show me how."

"*Ja*. We have many castles in Germany. Beautiful ones."

"Like the castles in Grimm's *Fairy Tales*?" Natalie asked. "I would like to see them."

"One day perhaps you will," Bertha said. "You will see how beautiful a country is my Germany."

"Then why did you leave?" Natalie asked.

"That is a long story." Bertha's lips pinched into a narrow line. "Now hurry up."

"Are we going to take the streetcar?" Skipper asked.

"No, we are going to walk. The exercise is good for you."

They walked along the wide promenade of Avenida Atlantica to the Copacabana Palace Hotel. Flame acacias spilled their scarlet flowers over garden walls, green mountains rising behind them, and on the other side of the boulevard was the harbor lined by palm trees, the ocean a pastel blue with islands that appeared to float in a milky-bluish vapor. Far out Natalie could see a ship, its bow rising and falling in a white glitter of spray, so small it looked almost like a toy.

The beach with its striped umbrellas was almost full when they arrived in front of the hotel.

"We are going to look for a little boy called Michael who is with my friend Ilse," Bertha announced. "Michael is just your age, Skipper." Bertha scanned the beach and then she saw a tall thin woman in a white uniform with a little boy waving to her. "*Ach*, there they are. Come."

Michael was very blond with pale skin and spoke in a very clipped British accent.

"He talks funny," Skipper said.

"Skipper!" Bertha scowled. "That is very rude. Michael is English. His father works at the British Embassy. Now, you children go play on the sand. Ilse and I want to talk." She waved them off and Natalie heard the two nurses speaking German together.

I wish Michael had a sister, Natalie thought, or someone I could play with. She looked out at the ocean to see if the ship was still there but it had already put out to sea. She started to walk down the beach with her pail and shovel and then she saw a little black-and-white spotted dog following her. She stopped and the dog came up to her and licked her hand. Then it looked at her with pleading brown eyes and whimpered.

"Hello, doggie." Natalie looked around to see who the dog belonged to, but it seemed to be all alone. Like me, she thought. She bent down and stroked it. "Nice doggie. Where's your master?" The dog wagged its tail. "Are you lost?"

"Natalie!" Bertha shouted. "Come back here."

Natalie started to walk back and the little dog followed. "Go home, doggie," she said, but the dog wouldn't leave her.

"What is that you have with you?" Bertha asked. "A stray dog. Dirty." She tried to shoo the dog away.

"It doesn't belong to anyone, Bertha," Natalie said. The dog's sad eyes looked up at her hopefully. "I think it's hungry."

"Dogs are always hungry," Bertha said. "And they have fleas."

"They also bite," Ilse added.

Just then Michael came running over in tears.

"What is it, Michael?" Ilse asked.

"He won't let me play with his toys." Michael pointed to Skipper.

"Of course he will," Bertha said. "Come with me." She marched over to Skipper. "You must share your toys with Michael."

"No!" Skipper picked up a handful of sand and threw it at Michael.

"Skipper!" Bertha gave him a quick slap on the bottom. "You are being a bad boy. You must play nicely with Michael."

"I don't want to."

Now both boys were crying. Bertha said something to Ilse in German and shrugged.

Natalie sat down and the dog crawled into her lap.

"If you are not going to play nicely," Bertha told Skipper, "we will go home."

There was no reply.

"So. That is your answer. We will leave now. Come."

"I don't want to leave," Natalie said, stroking the dog. "I like it here."

"Get that filthy dog off your lap."

"Don't hurt it, Bertha."

"We are going home now." Bertha turned to Ilse. "*Auf Wiedersehen.*"

They started back, the dog trotting behind them. Natalie was hoping Bertha wouldn't notice, but she did. Bertha turned, looking for a stone to throw at the dog. "Go away, dirty dog!"

"If you hurt it, I'll tell Daddy and he will fire you!" Natalie was amazed at her boldness. For a minute she thought that Bertha was going to hit her. She held her breath.

"You are both bad children," said Bertha. "Very bad."

They walked to the house in silence, the little dog still following at a safe distance.

They always went in the back way with Bertha through the gate and the kitchen garden. The green wooden gate had a bell at the top on a long rope that you pulled to open. They went through it, leaving the dog sitting forlornly outside. I'll get Ana to give it some food, Natalie thought, and maybe Daddy will let me keep it. The idea of having a dog made her happy. She had never had one. Once she had asked her mother for a puppy. "It's too difficult when we are always moving around," her mother said, dismissing the subject.

The minute Bertha was out of sight Natalie went down to the kitchen. Ana had a kind heart. She would take pity on the little dog and give it some scraps. Natalie motioned to Ana to come to the back gate. There sat the dog waiting patiently. Natalie made motions of eating. Ana smiled and nodded. "*Sim, Senhorita.*"

"Just a minute, doggie," Natalie said. "We're going to give you some food.

Ana came back with some left-over meat and a bowl of water and the dog ate hungrily, then licked Natalie's hand.

She was sure her father would let her keep the dog if she asked him nicely and she had already picked out a name for it.

"You have a new home, Spotty," she said.

"A dog," said Lila, frowning. "No, it's out of the question, Donald. She can't have one. Remember that time she saw the puppy in the pet shop in Coronado? We settled all that then."

"But this is a homeless little dog who followed them home from the beach."

"What happens when you get transferred? We're not going to be in Rio forever."

"True, but that won't be for another year. And she's so attached to this dog."

Lila sighed. "All right. But the dog can't sleep in her room. Be sure you make that quite clear to Natalie."

"Be quiet, Spotty," Natalie said. "You mustn't bark or make any noise. Here's a nice place for you under my bed. See, I've given you my bathrobe to lie on." Spotty wagged his tail happily. "Now lie down and go to sleep. I'll let you out the first thing in the morning before Bertha comes to get me up." She hugged the dog one more time. "I love you, Spotty. I'll give you a good home and take care of you. And no one is going to take you away from me. Ever."

3 ૬

BEHIND IPANEMA LIES A
picturesque lagoon, Lagoa Rodrigo de Freitas, and on the
west side are the Jockey Club and Gavea Racecourse, where
on the first Sunday in August the most important race of the
year is held, the Grand Prix of Brazil. All Brazilian society
attends this event, dressed in the latest couture fashions.

"May I borrow your binoculars?" Lila asked Donald.

He handed them over and Lila looked around the
racetrack, more at the spectators than at the horses. The
Spanish ambassador and his wife had several guests in their
box, among them a very handsome man she had never seen
before. His blondness stood out among the many Latin types
and she did not recall meeting him at any of the parties.

"The horses are over there," Donald said. "Do you want
me to adjust the binoculars for you?"

"No." She handed them back. Lately everything Donald
did or said irritated her, but of course she couldn't show it,
especially in public, and nothing could be more public than
the Grand Prix. "I was just wondering who that man is sitting
in the Alfaros' box."

Donald glanced over. "Which man?"

"Next to Pilar."

"He's a new attaché at the German Embassy. Quite a
good polo player, so they say."

"Oh?" She held on to her large-brimmed hat as a chill
breeze swept across the lagoon. The crowd shouted and

cheered, calling encouragement to their favorites as the horses galloped down the racetrack. She pretended to concentrate on the race. I can make some excuse to go by the Alfaros' box on the way out, she thought. No, that would be too obvious and Donald might notice. Just then the German turned around and she saw him looking at her, then he said something to Pilar and Carlos. Donald muttered something under his breath and tore up his ticket as the race ended.

"Are you going to bet on the next race?" she asked.

"I think I'll skip it. I'm not lucky today."

Lila started to get up.

"Where are you going?"

"I have a hunch about the next race."

"I'll place the bet for you," Donald said.

"No, I'll do it. I want to stop in the ladies' room on the way."

She walked down the aisle and passed the Spanish ambassador's box, nodding to Carlos and Pilar as she went by, but deliberately did not stop. The German was standing up now and she saw that he was tall, towering above the others. She felt his eyes following her. I'll meet him another time, she thought. In the meantime, let him wonder who I am. She was suddenly filled with a delicious sense of intrigue.

And a feeling of danger.

The following Sunday they were invited to the polo matches by some Navy friends who had a box. Donald didn't want to go and she tried to persuade him in vain. Finally he said, "If you want to go so much, why don't you go with them?"

"Without you?"

Donald smiled. "It's not as if you're going off to some clandestine meeting. I trust you."

What did he mean by that? "You're sure you don't mind?"

"I give you my permission. Besides, I have some reports I have to work on."

"Then I'll call the Harrisons and say that you have to work but I'd love to come," Lila said.

He was galloping down the field swinging his polo mallet and leaning so far over the side of his pony that Lila thought he surely would fall off, but he expertly hit the ball just as a member of the opposing team tried to head him off.

"That's Count von Jaeger," Fletcher Harrison said. "The number three player in the green shirt on the black pony. He's a new attaché at the German embassy."

"He's really good," Lila said. Now she knew who he was without having to ask. His white polo helmet with the chin strap hid most of his face as he raced down to the other end of the field and made a goal.

"He and Pilar Alfaro are rumored to be having an intrigue," Aline Harrison whispered to Lila. "But they're very discreet."

"Then how do you know?" Lila asked.

"It's what people say," Aline said, somewhat defensively. "You know how they like to gossip."

"Then perhaps that's just what it is," Lila said, as the sounding of a horn announced the end of the first chukker.

She looked around to see where the Alfaros were sitting and then she saw them. Count von Jaeger had ridden over and was talking to them.

"Pilar has always had her little flings," Aline said. "But Carlos just looks the other way."

The second chukker started and the eight players, now on fresh ponies, raced and swung their mallets wildly, but Lila was watching only one: Count von Jaeger in the green shirt, number three.

I'll meet him after the match, she thought, and then I can tell him how much I admired his game. Or does everyone tell him that? She was glad that Donald wasn't with her. This way everything was perfectly proper yet she could talk to whomever she chose.

A whistle blew shrilly and the umpire, in a red-and-blue striped shirt with his ball carrier and pick-up stick, rode into the center of the field.

"What's the matter?" Lila asked. Several of the players were shouting.

"A foul," Fletcher said. "Against von Jaeger's team. He crossed in front of another player."

"What happens now?" Lila leaned forward in her seat. Von Jaeger and the umpire were having an argument.

"The other team gets a free shot," Fletcher said.

The opposing team scored a goal and the play resumed.

"I don't see how someone doesn't get killed playing polo," Aline said, as a mallet just missed a player's head.

"Sometimes they do," Fletcher said. "It's not a game for sissies."

Danger, thought Lila, is that what I am attracted to? Her body tingled, her face was flushed, she felt alive. Our destinies are entwined in some way, she thought as she watched von Jaeger. I don't know how, but I know.

It will happen.

But it did not happen that day. The Harrisons had to leave right after the match and she couldn't stay for the festivities at the clubhouse without them.

"Give my best to Donald and tell him I hope you both can join us another time," Fletcher said, as they dropped her off at the house on Avenida Atlantica.

"Yes, I'll tell him. Thank you for taking me. I had a marvelous time," Lila said.

The children were in the dining room having their supper with Bertha.

"Hello, Mommy," Skipper said. "Natalie won't eat her rhubarb."

"I don't like it," Natalie said, pushing her plate away. "Do I have to eat it, Mommy?"

"You must eat everything on your plate," Bertha ordered.

"Where is Commander Townsend?" Lila asked, ignoring Natalie's pleading look.

"Commander Townsend telephoned to say that he will be home in an hour and that you are going out to dinner."

"Oh, yes, I'd forgotten." She would have to bathe and change. Almost every evening there was some social event they had to go to and they seldom had a quiet evening at home together, not that they had much to say to each other when they did. Donald usually buried himself in some technical book and she read a romantic novel or looked at the latest copy of *Vogue* sent from the United States. Then to bed. They made love about twice a week, and if Donald's love-making did not make the earth move for her, well, maybe she expected too much. Donald was a good man and he loved her. He was not tall or handsome, but he was nice-looking and considerate and he was well liked by other officers and everyone told her that he had a brilliant naval career ahead of him. One day, if they played their cards right, she would be an admiral's wife.

Was that what she wanted? My whole life is mapped out for me, she thought, and suddenly she wanted to break free, to run barefoot on the beach, to do what she chose without eyes watching her all the time and people gossiping. Was it true about Count von Jaeger and Pilar Alfaro, were they having an affair? These intrigues went on all the time, she knew, there were rumors about Lady Mountbatten and other

men, and English houseparties at country homes were well
known for musical beds, the British who always appeared so
proper and stuffy. But let one get a divorce and disgrace
followed, you could no longer be presented at court or sit in
the royal box at Ascot. It seemed a very strange morality to
her, but it was the way things were.

She ran her tub and poured rose bath salts in the water.
And then she heard Donald's voice.

"I'm home," he called up the stairs.

Her clothes were laid out on the bed. He walked in the
bedroom and saw that she was in the bath. "You'd better
hurry," he said. "We're due at the French Embassy at eight."

"I'll be out in a few minutes."

"How was the polo match?"

"Marvelous. The Harrisons sent their best. They've
invited us to come another time."

"Maybe I can make it then." He sounded uninterested.
"I'm glad you enjoyed yourself."

Oh, I did, she thought, as she rubbed scented French
soap over her body, examining it carefully as she did so and
wondering how it would look to another man. Donald was
the only man who had ever seen her nude, except for her
doctor, of course, when she had the children, and luckily that
unpleasant process hadn't damaged her figure. She stepped
out of the tub and patted herself dry with a towel, then
dusted herself with bath powder. She wondered if Count von
Jaeger would be at the party tonight. Life was suddenly much
more interesting and filled with a delicious sense of
adventure.

"How beautiful you look tonight, Lila."

"Thank you."

"You should always wear that color. It makes your eyes
look like aquamarines. I am mesmerized."

"Oh, Jorge!" She threw her head back and laughed. At parties she felt truly alive, like a flower that has been starved for water, and now she drank in the compliments as she whirled around the dancefloor with different partners, her body pulsing to the samba rhythms. Brazilian men were adept at flattering women and what did it matter if they meant it only for the moment? She liked to be told that she was beautiful, desirable, to feel like a femme fatale.

Another man cut in and then she saw Donald approaching. He tapped her partner on the shoulder.

"I want you to meet someone," Donald said, leading her off the dancefloor.

"Who's that?" she asked. Someone who could advance his career, no doubt, because that was a large part of Navy life, apple-polishing the higher brass and being nice to their boring wives.

"He was my commanding officer on the *Memphis*," Donald said. "He and his wife have just arrived in Rio. I'm sure you'll like them."

"I was having such a good time dancing. You should learn the samba. It's fun."

"I can fake it. When I have to."

She noticed a man and woman watching them.

"Captain and Mrs. Bell, may I present my wife Lila?"

"How do you do." Lila smiled and held out her hand.

"So this is the beautiful wife I've heard so much about," Captain Bell said.

Captain Bell was trim and good-looking but Mrs. Bell was overweight and her face had the puffiness of someone who drank too much. Her speech was slightly slurred when she spoke.

"Donald tells me you're a Southerner too," Mrs. Bell said. "I was born and raised in Atlanta."

"I grew up in Raleigh," Lila said.

"Then I'm sure you know Pinehurst? My father used to go there every winter to play golf."

"Yes, it's not too far from Raleigh."

"How do you like Rio?" Captain Bell asked.

"It's a fascinating city," Lila said.

"I've been here before," Captain Bell said. "When I was a bachelor. But this is the first time for Mary Lou."

"You'll have to tell me the best places to shop," Mrs. Bell said. "I've been admiring your dress."

"Thank you."

"I wish I had the figure to wear something like that, but I just love food too much."

"My wife is a terrific Southern cook. Every night I dine like a king," said Captain Bell.

"Oh, Gerald, you flatter me!" She beamed happily.

Her mother's favorite saying that the way to a man's heart was through his stomach certainly applied in the case of the Bells, Lila thought. She'd always found cooking boring, but thank God servants were so cheap in Rio that she didn't have to spend any time in the kitchen except to tell Ana what to prepare.

"Would you care to dance, Lila?" asked Captain Bell.

"I'd love to," Lila said, glancing at Donald, who quickly invited Mrs. Bell to dance.

"You made a big hit with the Bells," Donald said on the drive home from the party. "It's important to have the wives like you."

"Yes, you've told me," Lila said, looking out at the lights twinkling around the bay, disappointed that Count von Jaeger hadn't been at the party.

"The Navy is a small club," Donald said, turning the car onto Avenida Atlantica. "You run into the same people over and over again, and a wife can do a lot to advance her husband's career."

"Is that why you married me?"

"I married you because I fell in love with you. As you very well know."

"I was just joking." She opened her cigarette case and lit a cigarette. Donald was so serious sometimes.

"I wish you wouldn't smoke," Donald said.

"You smoke."

"That's different. I'm a man."

"Most women smoke today."

"Not all. Mary Lou Bell doesn't."

"It relaxes me to smoke," Lila said, taking a deep drag of her cigarette. "And besides, I enjoy it."

4 ⊚

PRINCE VASSILY KOUMANOFF
was enjoying court balls in Saint Petersburg when the
pleasant world of his youth was swept away in the Bolshevik
Revolution, his father shot, and his family estates confiscated.
He escaped from Russia via the Black Sea to Turkey. From
there he went to Paris, where he found that émigré White
Russian aristocrats were working as doormen, cab drivers,
and seamstresses. A Brazilian he met in Paris persuaded him
to come to Rio, and he became extremely successful in the
import-export business. Tall, charming and distinguished, he
gave many parties and liked to surround himself with
beautiful women.

Lila Townsend was one of them.

And it was at the home of Prince Vassily Koumanoff, on
an evening in late September, that her path crossed with that
of Count Kurt von Jaeger.

The garden was lit with Japanese paper lanterns, casting
lavender, green and blue lights on the teahouse and goldfish
pond. A small orchestra was playing "Dark Eyes."

"Isn't it beautiful, Donald?" Lila exclaimed.

Just then Vassily saw them arriving and came through
the crowd to greet them.

"Good evening. I'm so happy you're here." He kissed
Lila's hand. "The party would not be complete without the
most beautiful woman in Rio."

"Vassily, you say that to every woman," Lila said, as

Donald looked annoyed, his eyes searching for the bar.

"Only when it's true," Vassily said. "Please, do have a drink and some caviar." He motioned to a buffet table spread with Russian delicacies, then moved on to welcome other guests.

"The bar looks crowded," Donald said. "I'll go get us some drinks. "Wait here."

Lila glanced around and then she saw a man watching her. It was Count von Jaeger. Their eyes met and he smiled and walked over.

"May I get you something to drink? The champagne is very good. And of course the vodka."

"Thank you, but my husband has already gone to the bar."

"I do not think we have been properly introduced. I'm Kurt von Jaeger."

"Lila Townsend."

He kissed her hand. "I have seen you at the races and also at the polo matches."

"Yes. I enjoyed watching you play."

He looked pleased. "I wish I had more time to play, but official duties prevent it." He shrugged. "So, how long have you been living in Rio?"

"A little over a year."

"And do you like it?"

"I love it."

"It is my first time here. Before that I was posted in Shanghai. Vassily I knew in Paris. He is an old friend."

Paris. Shanghai. How casually he tossed off the names. She had never been to those cities, but she longed to see them, be part of that sophisticated world. She saw Donald across the room holding two drinks and chatting with a Navy couple. Don't rush back, she thought, take your time. "Are you from Berlin?" she asked.

"No, I was born in Schleswig-Holstein. Near the Danish border. My father is German but my mother was Danish."

She wondered why there was no wife in the picture. Had he been married or was there a sweetheart who had died? Or like his friend Vassily, did he not want to be tied down to any one woman? The most attractive men were always complex—and elusive. Perhaps that was part of their charm, she thought, and again that restless feeling swept over her. She decided to be bold. "Your wife didn't come with you to Rio?"

"I have no wife," he said. "I've never met the right woman."

"I find that hard to believe."

"It is true." He smiled. "The ones I am attracted to are always married."

Did he mean Pilar Alfaro? She had not noticed her here tonight. She was about to say something else when Donald appeared with the drinks.

"This is my husband, Commander Townsend, Count von Jaeger."

"I have been enjoying talking to your lovely wife. You are a very lucky man, Commander Townsend."

"I think so," Donald said.

"It has been a pleasure meeting you both. I will see you again, I hope."

"Yes, I hope so," Lila said, as Donald handed her the drink.

"Let's get some caviar," Donald said, and they made their way to the buffet table. Out of the corner of her eye Lila noticed that Kurt von Jaeger was now absorbed in a conversation with an attractive Brazilian woman. How nice it must be to be a man, she thought, to be able to move like a bee from one flower to another, picking what you choose, instead of being a woman who has to wait to be chosen, and then possibly discarded. And a man did not have to worry about his reputation either. No scandal was attached to him, but the woman who was involved was destroyed. It wasn't fair. She saw Kurt von Jaeger smiling at her. So what happens now? she wondered. Nothing. What could happen?

Later in the evening he asked her to dance. A tango was playing and when he held her in his arms it was as if an electric current went through her. She was sure he felt it too.

"You're a good dancer," he said. "Not many American women can do the tango."

She threw back her head. "I love to dance. Unfortunately my husband doesn't care much about it."

After she said it she felt slightly disloyal to Donald, who had many other good qualities, she reminded herself. But it was true. Their interests weren't the same. Had they ever been, or was it just because she was bored?

Kurt had a strong lead, it was fun dancing with him, and she was sorry when the music stopped and he led her back to the table where Donald was engrossed with some people in a discussion about the Brazilian political scene. But she would see Kurt at other parties. It was something to look forward to. A harmless flirtation, that was all it was, who could be hurt?

Liar! a voice inside her said, but she paid no attention.

"Thank you very much," Kurt said, kissing her hand.

She gave him a dazzling smile. "I enjoyed it."

"I can't stand these phony, hand-kissing foreigners," Donald remarked on the drive home.

"Which one are you referring to?" she asked innocently, knowing perfectly well. "Vassily?"

"And the German you were dancing with. I don't trust him. Maybe I should learn to tango."

Lila laughed. "I do believe you're jealous. Good! Don't take me for granted."

"I never have. It's just that it's hard for me to express my feelings. But you know that I love you. I always will."

Yes, she thought, trying to imagine always in her mind, like a silver ribbon of lights stretching into eternity. Devoted Donald. He had waited for her and finally won her. But now she felt herself teetering on the edge of a volcano, drawn to the flames, wanting to be consumed by them.

She looked out the window. To the right was Sugarloaf and the city climbing the hills, glittering with myriad lights, and the moon, like a golden torch casting a shimmering path over the dark harbor. Rio de Janeiro. Was there any city more beautiful?

She did not know that it was to be the city of her destiny—and her downfall.

5 &

FROM THEN ON HER LIFE revolved around the next meeting with Kurt von Jaeger. It gave a delicious anticipation to each day. When she awoke she asked herself: Will it be tonight that I will see him at a party? Tomorrow? Next week? Playing mah-jongg with other Navy wives, listening to the red-breasted sabiás singing in the evening twilight, she waited and wondered. Soon, let it be soon.

October turned into November and the woods on Corcovado were full of lovely fragrance, and here and there, above the billows of forest that tumbled down the hillside, rose the golden-yellow domes of the acacias. Soon many Cariocas would move to their summer homes at Petrópolis to escape the searing heat. The polo season was over.

A letter came from her mother in Raleigh telling her news of neighbors and people she barely remembered and cared less about. Franklin Delano Roosevelt was elected President in a Democratic landslide. All of that world seemed far away and unreal to her.

"Let's go to the Yacht Club for dinner," Donald said. "It should be cool there."

"That's a good idea," Lila said, fanning herself with a bamboo fan. Her linen dress was sticking to her and her hair was damp with perspiration. "I'll have a bath and change my clothes."

&

On a rocky point looking out over Guanabara Bay
stands a large white house with arcaded verandas and
terraced gardens. Narrow stone steps lead down to the sea
wall where the waves break with a gentle splashing and
sailboats lie at rest on the blue tide. This is the Brazilian
Yacht Club, many of whose members are German.

So it was not surprising that when Lila and Donald
walked out on the veranda, Kurt von Jaeger was sitting there
having a drink with some German friends.

Lila saw him immediately and her heart skipped a beat.
He looked over and smiled. "Good evening," he said. He got
up and walked across to them. "Commander and Mrs.
Townsend. How nice to see you again," he said, kissing Lila's
hand. "Won't you join us for a drink before dinner?"

"That would be very nice," Lila said. "Wouldn't it,
Donald?"

"Yes, of course."

Kurt introduced them to his German friends. They had
been living in Rio for some time and were members of the
Yacht Club. They also had a house in Petrópolis.

"Have you been to Petrópolis?" Kurt asked. "It reminds
me very much of Baden-Baden. A charming little town."

"Donald and I drove up there one weekend," Lila said.

"In November Petrópolis is a symphony in blue," Herta
Neumeier said. "The gardens are blooming with hortensia
shrubs—"

"I believe in English you call them hydrangeas," said
her husband Gustav.

"Yes, the lawns are so gay with blue hydrangea
blossoms and also blue trumpet-shaped lilies. It is a really
beautiful sight."

"I should like to see it," Lila said.

"You would enjoy it, I am sure," Kurt said. "I am going

up there next weekend with the Neumeiers. They have been gracious enough to invite me to be their houseguest."

"But perhaps Commander Townsend is not interested in all this talk about flowers," Gustav said. "I understand that you have elected a new President. Are you happy about the choice of Roosevelt?"

"I don't know much about him yet," Donald said warily. "But whoever is the President, he is my commander-in-chief."

"Of course," Gustav said. "In Germany we also expect changes in the government. I think Adolph Hitler will do much for our country. Kurt does not agree with me. He does not like him."

"I believe that if Hitler becomes chancellor it will be a disaster for Germany," Kurt said. "But it has not happened yet."

"We shall see," Gustav said, finishing his beer.

Kurt turned to Donald. "When I return from Petrópolis I am going to give a small dinner party. The Neumeiers are coming and our mutual friend Vassily Koumanoff. I would like to invite you and Mrs. Townsend to join us, if you would do me the honor?"

"That sounds lovely, doesn't it, Donald?" Lila said.

Kurt took out a small leather notebook with a crest on the cover and a gold pen. "I will telephone you with the details," he said. "May I have your number?"

"*Ipanema nove sete zero*," Lila said.

"*Ipanema nove sete zero*," Kurt repeated, writing it down in his book.

Now he knows how to get in touch with me, Lila thought, and then she felt suddenly guilty. I am a married woman with two children, I should not be feeling like a young girl again with her first love, waiting for him to call, counting the minutes till I see him again. But that was the way she felt. She caught Kurt looking at her intently across the table and she blushed. He acts as if he can read my thoughts, as if he knows a secret about me that no one else does.

Kurt ordered another round of drinks. The sun had set over the bay and the lights were coming on around Botafoga. Then on Corcovado the huge statue of Christ the Redeemer with arms outstretched over the city of Rio was illuminated. It was a sight that always made her gasp.

"Beautiful, is it not?" Kurt said, noticing her reaction.

"And a great feat of engineering," Gustav added. "The monument is designed to stand winds up to one hundred and sixty kilometers an hour."

"Gustav is an engineer," Herta said. "He looks at the practical side of everything."

"That is important," Donald said.

"We arrived in Rio last year just after the statue was completed," Lila said. "I never get tired of looking at it, no matter how many times I see it."

"I am a friend of the architect Heitor da Silva Costa," Gustav said. "It took five years to construct. You can imagine what a task it was, having to take everything up to the top of the mountain by funicular."

"The Brazilians believe that the Redeemer statue protects the city from harm and looks out for them," Herta said.

Kurt raised his glass. "*Prosit*. To old friends and new."

He tried his best to satisfy Lila and make her happy, Donald thought, but there was an elusive core that he could not penetrate. Tonight when they made love she seemed to be somewhere else. Now she lay beside him dreaming, her lips moving slightly, her breath coming in a gentle musical rhythm with a faint scent of jasmine mingled with wine.

He could not sleep. He pushed back the mosquito

netting and walked barefoot across the parquet floor, careful
to avoid any cockroaches that might have slipped in the
windows. Brazilian houses had no screens, but instead
wooden shutters with diagonal slats, and in the tropical
climate insects flew all year round. One night a bat had flown
in and he had to chase it out, accompanied by Lila's terrified
screams which had awoken the children. She was lucky that
she had not had to share duty with him in Panama, but that
was before they were married, when he was still trying to
persuade her by letters to marry him.

He opened a box covered with iridescent butterfly
wings and took out a cigarette and lit it. He inhaled several
deep puffs and then he saw something staring at him, its dark
eyes in the moonlight like vertical slits, its body a yellowish
color so transparent that he could see the blood pulsating in
its arteries. It was a gecko, a Brazilian lizard, its outspread
spatulate fingers clinging to the wall. As he moved toward it,
the tiny creature ran upside down across the ceiling and
down the wall again, disappearing behind the picture frame.

Lila stirred restlessly in her sleep, mumbling something
he could not make out. She had looked beautiful tonight at
the Yacht Club, but then she always did. He could not get
over his good fortune in winning her to be his wife. She was
like a white orchid, the one the Brazilians called the Espirito
Santo, fragile, delicate, exquisite. But he could never say
these things to her, he would feel foolish. Yet he adored her,
she meant everything to him. He did not know what he
would do if he ever lost her. He knew she liked to flirt at
parties, but it meant nothing, and like all beautiful women,
she craved admiration.

Suddenly he heard someone crying. He went to the
door and opened it. The sobs were coming from Natalie's
room, she must be having a nightmare. Closing the door so
as not to awaken Lila, he walked quietly down the hall and

opened the door to Natalie's room. Then he almost tripped over something on the floor and caught himself on the four-poster bed to keep from falling. He turned on the light. It was Spotty.

So she was letting the dog sleep in her room after all, when she had promised him that she would not. If Lila found out. . . .

He bent over his weeping daughter. She was hot and perspiring.

"Natalie, it's Daddy. Wake up. You were having a bad dream."

She opened her eyes and he put his arms around her and stroked her hair. "Everything's all right. Daddy's here with you."

She continued to sob. "Oh, Daddy, I had the worst dream, and it was so real!"

"What was it? Tell me about it."

She saw Spotty on the floor. "I dreamed that someone took Spotty. And I never saw him again."

"It was just a bad dream," he said, kissing her. "And bad dreams never come true. Only good ones."

Did he really believe that? Or was it what he wanted to believe?

"Go back to sleep, Natalie," he said.

6 🌀

KURT VON JAEGER'S HOUSE WAS
tucked away at the end of a winding road in the hills above
Rio. French doors opened onto a bougainvillea-covered
terrace with a breath-taking view of the bay and the city
below twinkling with lights. The dinner table was set with
antique Bohemian crystal and Limoges china and instead of
flowers the centerpiece was a gemstone arrangement in a
brass basket. The base was of turquoise enamel cloisonné
decorated with flying cranes and blue lace agate and lapis
lazuli. Attached to the brass handle were bunches of green
and white jade grapes. Lila thought it was the most delicate
and beautiful thing she had ever seen.

"I bought it in China," Kurt said.

"I've always wanted to see the Orient," Lila said.

"Shanghai is a fascinating city," Kurt said. "Also Peking."

There were eight of them for dinner. Herta and Gustav
Neumeier, Vassily Koumanoff with an elderly Russian
countess, and a German widow named Monika. Was she
another of Kurt's ladies? Lila wondered. Apparently Monika
and Herta had known each other in Berlin. Monika was
seated next to Donald and the Russian countess was on
Kurt's right with Lila on his left.

"After my husband and I escaped from Russia, we lived
in Shanghai for several years," the countess said. "But it was
very difficult. My husband became extremely ill and I was
forced to sell my jewels to survive. But one does what one

has to do." She said something in Russian to Vassily.

"Irina quoted an old Russian proverb," Vassily said. "Unfortunately it does not translate very well."

Looking around the table, Lila realized that she and Donald were the only Americans present. It was an interesting group. At the large parties she and Donald usually attended, one never got a chance to know anyone, it was just light social chitchat with no substance. She wanted to know more about the old countess with her elegantly structured face and white hair and narrow aristocratic hands with transparent blue veins. And Monika—had her husband been killed in the war? These people had all gone through so much, did they resent them as Americans sitting here, citizens of a country that had never been conquered in a war, their possessions stripped from them?

"What part of America do you come from, Commander?" the countess asked Donald.

"Oklahoma."

"Ah, yes." She nodded. "Where there are Indians."

Donald smiled. "That's right. But they live on reservations now."

"I would like to visit the United States one day," said the old countess. "I have heard so much about it and I should like to see it for myself before it is too late. My friend Alexandra Tolstoy, the youngest daughter of our great writer, lives in New York."

"I have read *Anna Karenina* twice," Lila said. "It is one of my favorite novels."

The countess looked interested. "So you like *Anna Karenina*?" She quoted Tolstoy's opening line. "'Happy families are all alike; every unhappy family is unhappy in its own way.' Often I have wondered if that is true."

"Saint Petersburg must have been a very beautiful city," Donald remarked.

"It was," said Vassily. "Before the Bolsheviks. We remember, don't we, Irini Petrovna? Winter nights with moonlight on the Neva, riding through the snow in a sleigh with silver bells ringing. . . ."

"But those days are gone, Vassily Nikolayevich," the countess said. "They live only in our memories now."

"How lucky you were to find this charming house, Kurt," Monika interrupted, attempting to get on a more cheerful subject. "Especially since Brazilians do not rent their homes readily."

"Pilar Alfaro knew the owner. He had gone to France for two years, so I was most fortunate."

I wonder why the Alfaros aren't here tonight? Lila thought, and again she was conscious of Kurt's eyes on her.

"Will you play the piano for us after dinner?" Herta asked Kurt. "It is always such a treat."

"Oh yes, please," Monika begged, as Kurt seemed hesitant.

"If you like. Let us have our coffee and brandy in the living room."

He sat down at the Steinway piano and played a Liszt étude, then a Beethoven sonata and another piece that Lila did not recognize. It was haunting and sad with an Oriental quality.

Afterward he joined Lila on the loveseat.

"You play beautifully," she said.

"I'm glad you enjoyed it. Do you play the piano?"

"I took lessons as a child, but I never liked to practice. Tell me, the piece you played after 'The Moonlight Sonata'— what was it? I don't think I've ever heard it before."

"It's called 'Song of India.' From the opera *Sadko* by Rimsky-Korsakov."

"It's lovely."

"So are you." He glanced over to where Donald and

Gustav were having a discussion. "Would you like me to show you the garden? This is the first time you have been to my house and nature has cooperated with a full moon."

She smiled. "I'm sure you planned it that way."

"Of course."

They walked out onto the moonlit terrace and down a path bordered by lilies and night-blooming jasmine. He plays the piano, polo, he is handsome, and dangerous, Lila thought.

"Now, tell me about yourself," he said. "I know very little. Except that you are beautiful and that you admire *Anna Karenina*, the story of an unhappily married woman who falls in love with another man. Is that also your story?"

"Not at all. Donald and I are very happy. And we have two children, a boy and a girl." He was too sure of himself, this Count von Jaeger, he thought he had only to look at a woman and she would throw herself at his feet. Well she was different.

"The perfect family," he said. "So. But something tells me that you and your husband do not have many interests in common. That you are restless, searching for something."

"And what would that be?"

"I am not sure."

Below them lay the harbor of Rio and the moon a golden path across the dark water.

"I would like to know you better," he said. "Perhaps we could have lunch one day at the Yacht Club. Just to talk."

The women I am attracted to are always married, he had said. Did that make him feel safe, free of permanent ties? "My husband has to take a trip up the Amazon in two weeks," she said.

"And are you going with him?"

"No."

"Possibly then?"

"Possibly."

"I will telephone you. *Ipanema nove sete zero.*"

"You know my number by heart?"

"I could not forget it. Nor you." He leaned closer.

"Tell me about some of the people I've met this evening," she said quickly. "The Russian countess, for instance. She seems like a fascinating woman."

"She is. Irina Oblonsky is from an aristocratic Russian family and was a great beauty in her youth, so they tell me. Vassily knew her in Saint Petersburg and used to attend balls at her home. They lost everything in the revolution and they escaped to China, where her husband died. They had no children and Irina is very fond of young people. I thought you would like her."

"I do. And Monika?"

"Monika and Herta were friends in Berlin. She is a very nice woman but not my type. Is that what you were wondering?" He smiled.

"I think we had better get back to the house and join the others."

"Very well. Careful." He took her arm. "There is a broken step here. I don't want you to fall."

"Von Jaeger is in German Intelligence," Donald remarked on the drive home.

"How do you know?" Lila asked.

"I did some checking through our sources. The attaché part is just a cover."

"Are you sure?"

"Quite sure. That may explain his interest in us."

"And I thought he was interested in me," she said with a laugh. "How disappointing!"

"I'm sure he finds you attractive. Most men do. You didn't tell him that I was in intelligence, did you?"

"Of course not. I don't mention that to anyone."

"Good. Well if we run into von Jaeger again, just be on your guard."

7 ☙

"WHY IS NATALIE CRYING?"
Donald asked Lila, hearing broken-hearted sobbing coming
from his daughter's room.

"It's the dog. He's been missing since yesterday." Lila
started to buff her nails. "And good riddance if you ask me.
Bertha told me that she found fleas on Natalie's bed and I
specifically told Natalie that she was not to allow Spotty to
sleep in her room."

Donald went down the hall and opened Natalie's door.
She was lying on the bed and her pillow was soaked with tears,
her small thin body shaking and her eyes red and swollen.

"Natalie?"

"Oh, Daddy!" She threw herself into his arms. "Spotty's
gone. Someone left the gate open and he ran away and he
hasn't come back. I'm so afraid something awful has
happened to him."

"Now, now. He'll probably come home as soon as he
gets hungry enough."

"But he didn't come back last night."

"Give him another day." He wasn't too hopeful but he
didn't want to upset Natalie.

"I love him so much, Daddy. Help me look for him."

Finding a stray dog on the streets of Rio wasn't very
promising, but he had to try. He had never seen Natalie so
upset. "Very well," he said. "Let's go look for Spotty."

☙

Holding his daughter's hand, they walked along the back streets with high walled gardens calling Spotty's name.

"He could have followed the chicken man," Natalie said.

"Was he here yesterday?"

"Yes, he always comes while I'm taking my nap."

They turned onto Avenida Atlantica. Let's hope he didn't get out here, Donald thought, the crazy way these Brazilians drive. Cars raced past honking horns loudly, a truck loaded with workers singing and shouting. There was no sign of Spotty. He held Natalie's hand tighter.

"Where could he be, Daddy?"

She looked up at him with such faith and trust. "I don't know," he said. "We'll just have to hope that he gets hungry and remembers where his home is."

A week went by and Spotty did not return. Natalie was desolate. She refused to eat.

"If you do not eat you will get very sick and they will take you to the hospital," Bertha said ominously. "They will put a tube in you and force you to eat."

"I don't care. I want Spotty."

Another week passed

"See, he was just a stray dog," Bertha said. "He's probably followed someone else home."

"No! He was my dog and he loved me."

"So now he loves someone else. That is the way life is."

"Natalie, maybe Daddy will get us another dog when he comes back from the Amazon," Skipper said. He was wearing a new sailor suit. "But I'd rather have a crocodile."

Natalie kicked him.

Skipper hit her back.

"Children!" Bertha grabbed them both. "Behave. It is time for our promenade. We will take the ferry to Niteroi and you can see the dolphins. Won't that be fun?"

"I don't care," Natalie said. "I just want Spotty back."

"*Ipanema nove sete zero*," he said to the operator.

The phone rang by her bed and Lila picked it up. "Hello."

"Good evening. This is Kurt von Jaeger."

"Oh." She had been wondering when he was going to call. "How are you?"

"Excellent. I was hoping you had time free this week to have luncheon with me. Would Wednesday be possible?"

She paused a moment, pretending to consult her engagement book, but any date she had she would have broken. "Yes, that would be fine."

"Shall we say one o'clock at the Yacht Club?"

"Perfect. See you then."

"I will be looking forward to it," Kurt said. "Goodby."

"I'm going out to luncheon," Lila told Bertha. "And I may do some shopping afterward, so don't expect me back before five."

"Certainly, Madam," Bertha said. "Then will you have dinner with the children since Commander Townsend is away?"

"Yes, that would be nice. Ask Ana to fix something simple."

"Of course."

Lila glanced at her reflection again in the mirror in the entrance hall. Yes, it was just right, the mauve linen with a white hat and pearls, ladylike yet seductive. Donald seldom noticed what she wore. Or did all marriages settle into a certain routine after a time, so that there were no surprises, nothing new? My life doesn't have enough ups and downs, she thought, as she headed out the door, and that was the very reason I wanted to get away from North Carolina.

"You look beautiful," Kurt said, kissing her hand.

"Thank you."

"What will you have to drink?"

"A Daiquiri, please." She studied him sitting across from her. He's with German Intelligence, Donald had said. Be careful. A ceiling fan turned slowly overhead creating a slight breeze.

"I like your perfume," he said. "Most Brazilian women wear such heavy overpowering scents."

And Spanish ones too? she wondered. Had he stopped seeing Pilar Alfaro, or was she just one of many on his list? "I have not seen Carlos and Pilar Alfaro lately," she said. "Have they gone back to Spain?"

"Only for a month," he said. "They are old friends," he added, as if reading her thoughts. "We knew each other in Paris."

"I would love to go to Paris. Is it as beautiful as I have heard?"

"There is no city quite like Paris. Except of course Rio." He leaned across the table and lit her cigarette. "So tell me more about yourself and what it is you are seeking."

"You know much more about me than I know about you," she said, looking at him sideways.

"What is it you would like to know?"

"About your life. Our worlds are so different. You said you were not from Berlin but from a place near the Danish border—"

"Schleswig-Holstein. It is to me the most beautiful part of Germany with lakes and canals and dairy farms. My family has lived there for many generations and I grew up on our country estate near the town of Flensburg."

"Did you have brothers or sisters?"

"An older sister, Gabriele."

"And you had a happy childhood?"

"Very. It was a most pleasant life with riding and sailing and fishing and other things boys like to do. And the region of Schleswig-Holstein has always been rich in history and musical tradition. My mother played the piano and we attended all the music festivals. I had ambitions at one time to become a musician."

"What happened?"

"When I was in my third year at the University of Heidelberg, the war started. So, like the sons of most wealthy Prussian families, I joined the Ninth Potsdam Infantry Regiment." He paused. "Unlike many of them who were killed or seriously wounded, I came home from the war unscathed, but with the guilt of the survivor, wondering for what reason I had been spared. I finished my last year at Heidelberg and then went into the diplomatic service."

"Instead of becoming a musician."

"I decided I was not good enough to make it my profession. And also, my father objected."

"Are your parents still alive?"

"My father is. My mother died two years ago. While I was in Shanghai." He took a quick sip of his drink. "My sister Gabriele lives in Hamburg with her husband and three daughters."

"And where will you go when you leave Rio?" she asked.

"I have no idea."

"Like the Navy, where they send you?"

He laughed. "Exactly. In that way, we are alike."

"And like your sister Gabriele, have you never wanted to settle down with a family?"

"Oh, I would like children. That is the one thing I regret about my life. And of course, my father would like a grandson to carry on the family name."

She tried to picture his father and imagined a tall, stiff man with a monocle. Kurt must resemble his Danish mother. Obviously they had been close from the way he looked when he spoke about her.

"I was afraid you might cancel our luncheon at the last minute," he said.

"Why would I do that?"

"Several possibilities. Your husband returning earlier than expected. Or fear of gossip."

She looked at her drink and said nothing.

Kurt smiled. "If you always think about the consequences of something before you do it, you will never do it. One has to take chances in life."

"The way you play polo?"

"Exactly."

"I'm not afraid of taking chances," she said and her eyes met his. She waited. Now the next move was up to him. Like a game of chess.

"I am going to drive up to Petrópolis on Saturday. Perhaps you would like to accompany me?"

Was he suggesting a weekend together? She was not quite prepared for that. At least not yet. "When are you returning?" she asked cautiously.

"Later the same day."

Then he did not plan to stay overnight. "That sounds very pleasant," she said.

"Then you accept?"

"With pleasure, Count von Jaeger."

"My friends call me Kurt."

"Kurt." She smiled.

"That's better. I hope we shall become very good friends."

Or lovers? A warning bell sounded and then receded. I can control the situation, she told herself, feeling like a swimmer who has gone out beyond her depths. She had never had an affair. Donald was her first lover and she had been faithful to him throughout the six years of their marriage.

"You are very beautiful," Kurt said. "And very complex. You need a man who understands and appreciates you."

He drove a car the same way he played polo, fast and recklessly, and several times on the road to Petrópolis climbing high into the hills, Lila held her breath as she looked over the side. At its highest point the road was one way.

"Does my driving worry you?" Kurt asked.

"No. I'm just glad there are not any cars coming the other way."

Already she could feel the difference in temperature and she understood why so many wealthy Brazilians came to Petrópolis to escape the stifling summers of Rio. With its tree-shaded streets and streams lined with hydrangeas, the town had a restful charm.

"I thought we'd have luncheon at the Quintadinha," Kurt said, pulling up in front of the luxury hotel. "Then we'll walk around and see some of the sights. The cathedral is very beautiful, also the yellow palace. Do you know the history of Petrópolis?"

"Just a little bit."

"Then I will fill you in. I'm a very good tour guide."

"I'm sure you are."

"I told you that the town reminds me of Baden-Baden, not only because it has a spa and a gambling casino, but because one hears German spoken often. You wonder why?" he asked, as he noticed her look of surprise. "In 1845, during the reign of Pedro the Second, a settlement of over two thousand German immigrants was established in Corrego

Seco, which at that time was just a hamlet built around a farmhouse. The Germans were very industrious and the hamlet grew and became a town. Pedro chose it as his summer residence and it was renamed Petrópolis in his honor."

"I didn't know all that."

"History lesson for today." He took her arm. "Now, let's have luncheon. I hope you're as hungry as I am."

"Tell me more about yourself," he said during luncheon. "Where did you grow up?"

"In North Carolina."

"What is it like, North Carolina?"

"It's a very pretty state. There are tall pine trees everywhere and holly bushes and in the spring flowering dogwood with pink and white blossoms. We lived in Raleigh. My father is a doctor." A slight lie, but doctor sounded better than dentist. "It gets very hot in Raleigh during the summer so then we would visit my grandparents in Asheville in the mountains."

"It sounds nice."

"It was." Except that I knew what I wanted wasn't in North Carolina, she thought. I didn't want a life like my mother's, the church socials, the bridge club, the dull routine month after month, year after year. "I lived in Raleigh most of my life," she said. "Until I met Donald."

"Your husband? How did you meet?"

"A girl I went to school with fixed me up with a blind date for an Annapolis hop. The date was Donald."

"And you fell in love. A romantic story. Forgive me for saying so, but from the little I have seen of your husband, he does not seem like the type of man who would attract you."

She did not feel like discussing Donald with him. "And what type of man do you think would attract me?"

"Someone more daring, adventurous."

Like you? she wondered. But he was right. Kurt was her type, not Donald. If only she had met him first. But there was no way that would have been possible. Somewhere she had read that you meet the great love of your life only when it is too late and your lives cannot be changed without causing disaster.

And she realized how trapped women were with the man they chose to marry. For life. Yet there was no other life for a woman. Spinsters were pitied and widows also who were forced to work after their husbands died and left them with not enough to live on. There was a friend of her mother's like that in Raleigh. Her mother tried to include her in things and help her out whenever possible. To be able to say "my husband" gave a woman respectability. She did not know what she would do if she ever had to support herself. She had no special talents, she knew nothing about business. She was a typical Southern woman, brought up to charm men and to run a comfortable home and entertain her husband's friends.

"You are lucky being born a man," she told Kurt. "I wish. . . ."

"You wish what?"

"Well, I can't change what I am, so I guess I should be satisfied."

"I would say that you are a very lucky woman. And I am fortunate to have met you." He paused a moment. "You remind me very much of someone I used to know."

"Was she German?"

He nodded. "We were engaged to be married." His voice seemed strained, his eyes veiled with memories.

So there was someone else, a woman he loved enough to want to marry. Yet he did not. "What happened to her?"

"She died."

She should not have asked. "I'm sorry," she said.

"It was a long time ago and I was very young. But, that is life. It does not always work out the way you expect." He pushed back his chair brusquely and signaled for the waiter to bring the check. "Let us go now and walk around the town."

It was dark when they returned to Rio, the necklace of golden lights shimmering around the bay, the sky full of stars. A warm breeze rustled the palm fronds.

Tomorrow Donald would be home.

In a few weeks it would be Christmas, the most special of family holidays, and here she was with a romantic stranger, entertaining thoughts that should never enter her mind.

Yet why did she feel like throwing all caution to the winds?

"Would you care to come in for a drink?" she said as they pulled up in front of the house.

"Yes, I'd like that."

The house was dark except for the entrance hall and a light at the top of the stairs. The children and Bertha were probably asleep. Lila turned on the living room lamps with their silk shades, just enough to cast a soft glow on the white brocade sofa, the dark carved jacarandá furniture and vases of white flowers, the Oriental carpet.

"Ah, you have a piano." Kurt walked over to the Steinway and ran his fingers along the keys.

"I must have it tuned," Lila said. She picked up the heavy crystal decanter and poured brandy into two glasses, then handed him one.

"*Prosit.*" He raised his glass and clicked it with hers, then took a sip. "Very good."

Donald kept all the liquor locked up, except for the brandy decanter, so that the servants would not drink it, and when he went away he took the key with him. She remembered this suddenly after she invited Kurt in for a drink. Kurt sat down beside her on the sofa.

"You attract me very much," he said, leaning toward her. "But I am sure that you know that."

Those were the words she wanted him to say. But was attraction the same as love? She only knew that she felt an excitement being with Kurt that she had never felt with Donald.

"And I find you very charming," she replied lightly. She must keep the situation under control without letting him think she was swept away by him.

He drew her hands to his lips and kissed her fingertips one by one. "My beautiful Lila," he said.

I love you, she thought. He leaned closer and then she was in his arms, he was kissing her face and her lips and murmuring her name over and over. She responded passionately, her body pressed against his. His hand touched her knee and then went higher under her dress. She moaned slightly, then suddenly she pulled away.

"What's the matter?"

"Nothing. It's just that. . . ."

"You're afraid?"

"Possibly."

"Of where this might lead?"

"I don't want to hurt anyone. And I don't want to be something casual in your life."

"You're not someone casual in my life. Whatever gave you that idea?"

The many married women with whom you have had affairs, Pilar Alfaro and the others, she thought.

As if reading her mind he said, "You must not listen to gossip. But I will not force you to do anything you do not want to do."

Just then she heard footsteps on the stairs. Bertha.

"Is that you, Madam?"

"Yes, Bertha. Go back to bed. I'll be up shortly."

Kurt finished his brandy and stood up. "I'd better leave. Thank you for good companionship. It was a lovely day."

"Yes, it was." Have I frightened him away now? she wondered. But surely he didn't expect to seduce me on the sofa.

He kissed her hand. "I'll call you."

She walked with him to the front door and watched him get in his car and drive off. Then she turned out the lights and went up the stairs.

She undressed slowly, then took off her make-up and put on a chiffon nightgown. But she could not sleep. I want Kurt to make love to me, she thought, I want to feel his hands caressing me all over, I want to feel him inside me, I want. . . .

She sighed. What good was it? She was married to Donald, she would be married forever to Donald. What she was thinking of was sinful. She got out of bed and walked to the window looking out over the garden. A sabiá was singing a plaintive song in the moonlight.

Tomorrow evening at this time Donald would be home.

8 ⑥

"DON'T PLAY WITH YOURSELF," Bertha said. "It's not nice."

"Do girls have a pee-pee?" Skipper asked.

"Of course." Bertha took the soapy sponge and scrubbed his back briskly.

"Daddy has a big one," Skipper said, noticing how his pee-pee stood straight up in the water like one of his toy soldiers. He touched it again, and the next thing he knew Bertha had smacked his hand and soapy water flew into his eyes and made them sting. He started to scream.

The door opened and his mother stood there. She was dressed to go to a party.

"What's the matter?"

"It is nothing, Madam. Skipper got soap in his eyes, that is all."

"Bertha hit me!"

Bertha looked flustered. "He was doing something very naughty."

His eyes were still smarting but he could see that his mother looked worried. "My eyes hurt," he said. "I want you to give me a bath instead of Bertha."

"I can't tonight," his mother said. "You be a good boy and mind Bertha. Daddy and I are going out to a party. We'll be home soon."

"You're always going out," Skipper sobbed. "I want you to stay here with me."

"Lila, we're late. Come on." He heard his father's voice and then his father appeared at the door. He was in his uniform with all his decorations.

"What's all this crying about?" his father said. "Sailors don't cry."

"I don't want to be a sailor."

"Donald, he's only a little boy," his mother said.

"He's not too young to learn. Stiff upper lip, son. And if you're a good boy, I'll bring you home something from the party."

He stopped crying. "What, Daddy?"

His father smiled. "Just wait and see. Come, Lila."

And he watched them go out the door together. Now he was left with Bertha.

He was always left with Bertha.

"You're too severe with him, Donald," Lila said, walking to the car. "After all, he's only three."

"He's got to learn some discipline. He can't cry for his mother all the time. When he goes to the Naval Academy he'll thank me."

"And suppose he doesn't want to go in the Navy?"

Donald looked amazed, as if the idea had never occurred to him. "Why wouldn't he?"

"Well, he might want to do something else."

"Like what?"

"Anything. Perhaps an artist. Who knows?"

"An artist! That's a hobby, not a profession."

"It's a long ways off, Donald. And besides, Skipper should decide what he wants to be, not us." Skipper. Donald had chosen the nickname. "Hey, Skipper," he used to say when he was a baby, chucking him under the chin. "Up you go, Skipper," tossing him in the air. Skipper would scream in terror. "I've heard that's bad for babies," she told him. "You never did that to Natalie." "Got to toughen him up," Donald replied. "Don't want a sissy for a son."

They got in the car and started off. Tonight the party was at Admiral Callahan's.

"We should have a small dinner party," Lila said. "You're going to be here for a while now, aren't you?"

"Yes. I have to go away the week after next. Just for a few days," he added.

"Then why don't we have some people over next week? Say Wednesday?"

"That's fine with me."

"I thought the Harrisons and Vassily Koumanoff—we owe them—and Kurt von Jaeger and Countess Oblonsky."

"Countess Oblonsky?"

"You remember the fascinating old Russian countess we met at Count von Jaeger's dinner party?" She had been about to say Kurt, but stopped herself in time. She wondered what Donald's reaction would be if he found out that she had gone to Petrópolis with Kurt. Well they hadn't done anything wrong, just had luncheon together, and she could always say that the Neumeiers were supposed to join them but had to cancel at the last minute. "I think that sounds like a good group. That makes seven, counting us. We need one more to make eight."

"You arrange it," Donald said. "That's your department."

Natalie peeked in the dining room. Her mother was putting place cards around the table, which was set for a party with a lace tablecloth and silverware and delicate crystal glasses and an arrangement of white flowers in a silver bowl. Her mother looked at the cards, frowned then changed two of them. Natalie watched her in fascination. When I am grown up, she thought, I will give dinner parties and wear pretty dresses. Her mother looked like a fairy princess in a dress of pale green with panels of silver beads and a short skirt that flared out in a lot of little points like petals. Everyone said that her mother had pretty legs and she wore silver sandals with spike heels. Natalie wondered how she could walk in them.

Her mother looked up, startled. "Oh, Natalie. I didn't see you there. Tell Bertha to get you ready for bed."

Her face fell. "But it's not time yet."

Her mother seemed flustered. "It must be. I want you children in bed before the guests come." She looked at the table, then changed the place cards again. "Bertha!"

Natalie planted her feet firmly. "Daddy said we could stay up and see the people."

"Oh Daddy did, did he? Where is Daddy?"

"Upstairs."

"Then let's go find him. Donald!"

Natalie followed her mother up the stairs.

"Donald, did you tell the children that they could stay up?"

Natalie watched her father. Would he change his mind now and say they had to go to bed? These must be very special guests that her mother was so nervous.

"Yes, Lila, I did. I want them to meet our friends," her father said. "And then they can go to bed. Bertha can give them one of those little iced cakes as a special treat."

"The *petits fours*?"

"Yes, why not?"

"Aren't they too rich? You know Skipper has a delicate stomach."

"Nonsense! You baby him too much."

"Then we can have a little cake? Oh, thank you, Daddy!" Natalie jumped up and down. "I want one with pink icing."

"If you're going to meet the guests, tell Bertha to

change your dress," her mother said, looking her over and frowning. "The one you have on makes your skin look sallow."

Natalie fled to her room, holding back tears. I know I'm not pretty, she thought. But why did her mother always have to bring it up?

"What delightful children," Irina Oblonsky remarked, as Natalie curtsied and Skipper bowed to each guest. "And so well-mannered."

"Thank you," Lila said. Perhaps Donald had been right. The children did make a good impression, especially Skipper in his sailor suit. She watched Kurt out of the corner of her eye, but it was impossible to tell what he was thinking.

"Now, children, off to bed with you," Donald told them. "And ask Bertha to give you your special treat."

Natalie and Skipper dashed upstairs.

"A charming family," Kurt said.

Was that Donald's intention in showing off the children? So that seeing them all together as a family Kurt would realize . . . but of course she was imagining things. Donald didn't suspect anything between Kurt and herself. And nothing had happened. Yet. Donald was watching her, she must be very careful that her eyes did not reveal her true feelings when she looked at Kurt.

How difficult it was playing this charade!

"I think the dinner party was a great success," Donald said as he got into bed beside her. "We should have them more often."

"Yes, I thought it went very well." I hope he doesn't want to make love to me, Lila thought nervously. I'll have to fake it and I'm just not in the mood. She sighed. "I'm so exhausted I think I could drop right off to sleep."

Donald moved closer and she could feel his erection pressing into her side. With one hand he pulled her nightgown up above her waist.

"How would you feel about having another child?" he asked.

"Another child?" She pushed him away. "Don't you think two are enough?" The thought of another pregnancy, her body bloated and stretched out of shape, filled her with horror. And then the months of nursing . . . no, it was unthinkable! She would not go through that again. And besides, I'm in love with another man, she wanted to tell him, but she knew she could not.

"It was just an idea," he said, hurt at her rejection. "I thought it might be nice for Skipper to have a brother."

"We have a boy and a girl. That's a nice family."

Oh, Kurt, Kurt, she thought with anguish, I want you, I want you so much. But what can I do? I am trapped in this marriage and there is no way out. I must try to make the best of things. She held out her arms to Donald. "I'm sorry," she said. "I didn't mean to be so abrupt. It's just that I was so ill when Skipper was born—"

"I was being inconsiderate," Donald said. "You're right. I don't want to put you through that again."

And they made love and she tried to pretend that it was Kurt, not Donald inside her, and she wondered how much longer she could go on like this.

Kurt telephoned the next day. "I just wanted to say how much I enjoyed your delightful dinner party," he said.

Was that all he was calling about? She waited. She must see him, and soon. Aline had mentioned last night that Pilar Alfaro was back from Spain. "I am so glad you could come," she said, trying to keep the anxiety out of her voice.

"You looked beautiful, as usual. I hope we can see each

other again before too long."

"I would like that."

"I will call you. Thank you again."

She was swept by a sense of desolation after she hung
up the phone. But what did I expect? she thought. He was
obviously seeing Pilar again and he did not need
involvements with two married women. And he had not said
that he was in love with her, only that he was very much
attracted to her. She should forget him and stop flirting with
fire.

I'll go shopping, she thought. Buy something new and
I'll feel better. And she'd have to get a Christmas present for
Donald and toys for the children and make preparations for
the holidays. There would be lots of parties and she needed
new dresses. And she would surely be running into Kurt at
the different parties, then they could take it from there.

Donald had mentioned getting a puppy for Natalie to
replace Spotty, but she planned to talk him out of that. After
all, they would probably only be in Rio another year and
then. . . .

Then when would she see Kurt again? He would go his
way and she would go hers. With Donald.

She did not notice Skipper walk in the room.

"Mommy, I don't feel well."

He didn't look well either. "What is it, darling?" she
asked, feeling his forehead. It was damp and clammy.

"My tummy hurts." Suddenly he threw up pieces of
stringy orange fruit and curdled milk on the Oriental rug.

Mangoes! Had he been eating mangoes with milk? Fear
gripped her. The combination was deadly. "Bertha!" she
screamed. "Bertha, come quickly!" She rushed to the
bathroom and grabbed a towel.

Bertha came running down the hall, followed by
Natalie. "What is it, Madam?"

"Has Skipper been eating mangoes?"

"Yes, I gave each of the children one. There were some nice ripe ones on the tree."

"And milk with it?"

"I didn't drink any milk, Mommy," Natalie said. "I know better than to drink milk with mangoes. Daddy warned me."

"I'll call the doctor," Lila said. That fool nurse! She should have known better. Her voice trembled as she repeated the number twice in Portuguese to the telephone operator. If anything happened to Skipper. . . .

"Hurry up!" she said. "*Apresse-sé!*"

Bertha was cleaning up the mess on the rug and Skipper was holding his stomach and moaning. Then he threw up again, a pale orangish liquid.

"Oh, my God!" Where was the doctor? Doctor Bowen was the only American doctor in Rio and all the Navy families used him. Please let him be in, she prayed.

"Is Skipper going to die?" Natalie asked.

"Of course not!" Lila snapped. "Don't say such stupid things." What was wrong with the telephone service in Rio when you needed it? "*Senhorita?* It's an emergency!"

After what seemed an eternity she reached Doctor Bowen and hysterically told him what had happened.

"Bring him to the hospital right away," he said. "I'll meet you there."

She paced the terrazzo floors of the hospital, wringing her hands nervously and saying half-forgotten prayers from her childhood under her breath. Skipper. Her darling little boy. Nothing must happen to him, he must be all right, please, God, make him all right, I'll do anything you want, but don't let my baby die. She was scarcely aware of Brazilians with worried faces waiting in the corridors or nurses rushing past her.

Finally she saw Doctor Bowen walking toward her.

"He's going to be fine," he said. "You can take him home in a little while." He reached out his arm to steady her as she swayed. "There, there."

"I was so worried." Tears ran down her cheeks. "I don't know what I'd do if—"

"I know. But it's all right now. We were lucky."

9 ⑥

CHRISTMAS IN RIO. STEAM RISING from mosaic pavements, palm trees swaying in a tropical breeze, the sweltering heat of the Brazilian summer. They opened their presents early in the morning and then Donald said, "Let's go for a swim at Copacabana Beach."

Skipper brought along his sand toys from Santa Claus and Natalie carried her new Chinese doll.

"I'm going to build a pagoda for her," she announced.

Lila stretched out lazily on the sand. "It seems so strange to go swimming on Christmas," she remarked. Lying in the warm sun made her feel sexy and she wondered what Kurt was doing today. She had not seen him for several weeks except briefly at parties and then he had avoided dancing with her.

"Take advantage of it," Donald told her. "Next year at this time we could be back in the snow and ice."

"Daddy, help me build a castle," Skipper said.

"I'll build you a big ship with two smokestacks. How would you like that?"

Skipper pouted. "I'd rather have a castle."

"You keep trying to make a sailor out of him," Lila said, adjusting her large-brimmed hat to keep the sun off her face. She had heard that sun aged your skin and she had managed to avoid getting a tan, but both children were a pale nutmeg and their normally ash blond hair was bleached flaxen. Donald had the kind of skin that didn't tan but turned red and blistered and then peeled in unattractive strips.

Next year at this time . . . she didn't want to think about it. And yet she knew that they couldn't stay in Rio forever. Donald was transferred every two or three years depending on his assignment.

"Do you have any idea where you'll be ordered next?" she asked, making circles in the sand with her forefinger.

"Why? Are you getting tired of Rio?"

"No, I love it here." She mustn't arouse his suspicions. "I just wondered."

"I have no idea where I'll be assigned," Donald said. "But I'm due for sea duty. In fact I need a command to advance my career. Possibly a cruiser."

When Donald spoke about ships his whole face lit up, like Skipper's opening his toys on Christmas morning. Sometimes she thought he loved the sea more than he did her, even his children. And when he was at sea it was her duty to sit at home and wait, like other Navy wives. But I'm not like other Navy wives, she thought. She stood up. "I think I'll walk along the beach. Will you watch the children?"

"Can I come with you, Mommy?" Natalie asked.

Lila frowned. She wanted to be alone with her thoughts, not have Natalie tagging along asking questions. "You stay here with Daddy. I won't be long."

Several Brazilian men turned and made comments in Portuguese as she walked by and one even spoke directly to her but she ignored him. She walked along the wet sand and let the small waves roll over her bare feet. Sailboats from the Yacht Club bobbed on the horizon and she thought again of Kurt. Perhaps he was out on one of them. Or spending the day with one of his friends, the Neumeiers possibly at their home in Petrópolis.

She glanced over her shoulder and Donald and the

children were like small specks in the distance. I want . . . I want so many things, she thought. I know I should be happy, but I feel trapped, like an animal in a cage yearning for freedom. Yet marriage was what every woman wanted, wasn't it? And she had that, a marriage and children, but she wanted more.

A Brazilian man whistled appreciatively as she passed. I'd better turn around and start back, she thought. Brazilian women didn't stroll around by themselves, at least nice ones didn't.

Oh, Kurt, Kurt, where are you now?

"There's a party at the Casino in Petrópolis on New Year's Eve," Donald said the next day. "Would you like to go?"

She thought of her day in Petrópolis with Kurt. Maybe he might be there. "Yes," she said. "That sounds like fun."

"I'll book a room at the Quintadinha. We can drive back New Year's Day."

Natalie was cutting out paper dolls from a book her grandmother had sent her from the United States. She loved all the different pretty dresses and she liked to imagine herself all grown up and wearing beautiful gowns. Sometimes her mother let her have her old dresses, the ones she was going to give away, to play dress-up in and some of her hats and even a pair of her shoes, but those had such high heels she couldn't walk across her room without wobbling and falling down. She couldn't understand how her mother could wear those spike heels all the time.

Just then her mother and father came in her room. Her mother was wearing a beautiful black-and-gold dress with a matching filmy cape and long dangling earrings that glittered.

"We're going to a New Year's Eve party in Petrópolis,"

her father said, giving her a kiss. "I want you and Skipper to be good and mind Bertha."

"When will you be back?"

"Late tomorrow," her mother said. "We'll bring you back some favors from the party. Then we can all have a New Year's celebration together."

"May I look at your fashion magazines while you're gone, Mommy?"

"Of course. If you're careful with them." She bent down and kissed her and Natalie could smell a scent of roses and jasmine. "Be good."

"I will be."

And they were gone but her mother's perfume lingered in the room.

Hundreds of green lights from fireflies illuminated the gardens of Petrópolis in the fragrant summer night of New Year's Eve. They pulled up in front of the Casino and an attendant took their car. Balloons and streamers of confetti were everywhere and trays of champagne were being passed. Lila glanced quickly around the ballroom but saw no signs of Kurt.

"Shall we dance?" Donald asked.

He pulled her close to him as they danced and then she saw a woman watching her with interest. It was Pilar Alfaro. A moment later she saw Kurt walk across the room bringing her a drink. She stiffened in Donald's arms, then forced herself to relax as she nodded casually to them. So he was here after all. Had he come with the Alfaros?

Other men invited her to dance and Donald wandered off. Then suddenly someone tapped her partner on the shoulder as a tango started. It was Kurt.

"I've missed seeing you," he whispered into her ear, as they went into a low dip. "When can we get together?"

Donald was leaving for the Amazon again in a few days. "I'm not sure," she said.

"I must see you. Next week? Try and arrange something."

So he had missed her after all. "Call me," she said, as someone else cut in.

Kurt did not dance with her again and she tried not to show that she could hardly keep her eyes off him. Then it was midnight and all the lights went out. Donald kissed her as the orchestra played "Olde Lang Syne."

"Happy New Year, my dearest," he said. "To 1933. May it be a wonderful year for us."

"Yes," Lila said. "To 1933."

10 ꙮ

"YOU KNEW I'D COME, DIDN'T you?" she asked Kurt. They were in his house, standing on the terrace looking out over the harbor of Rio.

"I hoped so." He took her in his arms and pressed her to him, kissing her deeply again and again. "Ah, Lila, I have wanted you so much. You cannot imagine."

"Do you love me?" she asked.

"Of course."

"You have never said so." She needed to hear the words, to know that she was not just another conquest. And yet she knew at the same time that she would do whatever he wanted.

"My beautiful Lila, I love you, I desire you. What are we waiting for?" He drew her inside, continuing to kiss her as he led her toward the bedroom. Slowly he undressed her, kissing her all over, and then he took off his clothes and lay down on the bed beside her.

She had never imagined such rapture. If this is sin, she thought, then I will pay whatever price is demanded of me.

"Kurt, Kurt, my love," she murmured, and the intensity of her passion overwhelmed her. She felt that she could never get enough of feeling him moving inside her, she clung to him, they were one.

Drenched with perspiration, finally he withdrew and rolled over on his back.

"Was it good for you, darling?" he asked.

"Wonderful." She had never known anything like this with Donald, it was something she had only read about in books, and now she realized what love could be like and she was spoiled forever. I want him all the time, she thought, again and again and again. She stretched our luxuriously, lying nude beside him, satiated. He lit a cigarette and handed it to her, then lit another for himself. She felt wicked and wanton in his bed and she never wanted to leave. She wanted him to hold her and caress her, but instead he got up from the bed and walked over to the window.

"It's going to rain," he said. "I'd better get you back before it does. Sometimes this road becomes impassable after a heavy downpour."

"Then we'd be marooned," she said, laughing lightly. "I'd just have to stay here." And why not? The children were safe with Bertha and Donald wouldn't be back for several days.

Just then the telephone rang but he did not answer it.

"If you'd like to take a shower, the bathroom is in there," he said.

She went in and noticed how neat it was with large fluffy bathtowels and perfumed soap. Did he have all this for his lady visitors? She turned on the shower and lathered herself with the soap. It was scented with jasmine.

He was smoking another cigarette when she came out. She combed her hair and put on fresh lipstick while he showered. On the bureau she noticed a photograph of a woman in a silver frame, an aristocratic-looking woman with fair hair piled on top of her head. His Danish mother? Next to it was another photograph of a Prussian officer with a mustache and a stern expression. That must be his father. There was a man's silver dressing set, two military brushes and a comb and a shoehorn. The brushes had the same crest that she had observed on his gold cigarette lighter.

On the wall was a framed picture of a beautiful Alsatian dog. She was looking at it when he came out of the bathroom.

"That was the dog I had as a boy," he said.

"What was his name?"

"Bismarck. He was a good companion. I still miss him, even after all these years."

They could hear the rain now coming down in torrents, as if the skies had suddenly opened up. He took her in his arms and kissed her once more. "We'd better run for it. Ready?"

"Yes." She picked up her purse.

"I'll follow you in my car just to Avenida Atlantica to make sure you get home all right."

He opened the front door and they dashed through the rain to her car. Quickly he opened the door and helped her in, then got into his.

Now I am going back to my real life, she thought, as she drove carefully down the road from Kurt's house, his car following her. Back to her home and children and her husband who would be home in a few days.

That night a terrifying dream tortured her sleep.

She was walking along Avenida Atlantica, when out of nowhere a *resaca* rose in a wall of water as high as a house. She tried to run away but it was no use. The sea water engulfed her, filled her mouth and lungs and dragged her under, she thrashed around, flinging out her arms and legs, she couldn't catch her breath, she was drowning. . . .

When she awoke the sheets were tangled, her hair was wet, her breath coming in short gasps.

The rain had stopped and sunlight was coming through the shutters. Then the telephone rang. It was Kurt.

"Good morning, darling," he said. "How are you?"

She was startled, still trying to shake off the effects of the dream. "Fine," she said, but her voice trembled.

"Did I wake you up? I wanted to get you before I left for the embassy. Can you have dinner with me tonight?"

"Yes, I'd love to."

"I'll pick you up at eight-thirty," he said.

After he hung up she stretched out on the bed, recalling their passionate love-making of the night before and her body tingled with anticipation and desire. I am playing a dangerous game, she thought, but I don't care!

She heard the children's voices in the hall and Bertha admonishing them to be quiet.

"I want to see Mommy," Skipper whined.

"No, your mother is asleep," Bertha said.

"It's all right," Lila called. "Come on in and see me, children. I'm awake."

Natalie and Skipper ran into the room and climbed up on the bed, one on each side of her.

"Can't you play with us, Mommy?" Skipper asked.

"Yes, please, Mommy," Natalie pleaded. "We don't like being with Bertha all the time."

"Now, now, you mustn't say things like that. You'll hurt Bertha's feelings."

"She doesn't like us anyway," Natalie said.

"Let me get dressed first and have some breakfast and then we'll do something together."

"Really truly?" Natalie asked.

"I want to go to the park and see the bat-fish in the aquarium," Skipper said.

"All right," Lila said. "We'll do whatever you like." Suddenly she felt like the unfaithful husband who buys his wife an expensive piece of jewelry to assuage his guilt. "We'll have fun together this morning. Now run along and let me get dressed."

Natalie turned at the door. "When is Daddy coming back?"

"The day after tomorrow," Lila said.

"Look, Mommy, there's the bat-fish!" Skipper pointed to a fish whose shoulders protruded right and left like a couple of pointed stakes, bearing on their tips two fins like little banners.

"Oh, yes, I see," Lila said.

"I think he's ugly," said Natalie.

"He is not!" Skipper said.

"He is! I like this one." Natalie indicated an orange-and-green fish with a fan tail swimming around in the aquarium. "Don't you like my fish better, Mommy?"

"It has beautiful colors, Natalie. But the bat-fish is very unusual-looking."

Skipper stuck out his tongue at Natalie. "See, Mommy likes the bat-fish better."

"Now, children, let's not quarrel," Lila said. "Oh, look at that big turtle."

"I want a turtle," Skipper said. "Can I have a turtle, Mommy?"

"Perhaps a little one. We'll ask Daddy when he comes home."

"You always want something," Natalie said. "You wanted an alligator."

"But I didn't get one."

"Of course not," Lila said. "We couldn't have an alligator crawling around the garden."

"If Skipper gets a turtle, I want a dog," Natalie said. "Daddy promised me after Spotty ran away that he'd get me another dog."

"We'll see," Lila said.

"When you say that it always means no," said Natalie.

"Now let's continue our walk," Lila said. How did some women spend all their time with small children? she wondered. It would drive her crazy. She was beginning to appreciate Bertha's job. No wonder she got cross at times. And Donald wanted to have another child. No way.

Not if she could prevent it.

11 ⌾

LILA LAY IN KURT'S ARMS IN HER
carved canopy bed draped with mosquito netting, drowsy
after making love. In the garden a sabiá was singing a
plaintive song and the air was heavy with the scent of jasmine
and carnations. Kurt reached over her for a cigarette in his
gold case with the von Jaeger coat of arms.

Suddenly she gave a startled gasp and in the moonlight
coming through the open shutters, Kurt saw terror on her
face. "What is it?" he asked.

"The doorknob just turned." Quickly she pulled the
sheet over them. "Someone's there," she whispered.

"You locked the door, didn't you?"

"I think so." They had been foolish to come up to her
bedroom, but when they returned from having dinner it was
late and she was sure Bertha and the children were asleep.
Could Donald be back? But he wasn't due until the day after
tomorrow and he was very precise and always did what he
said he was going to do. Unless his plans had changed
unexpectedly.

Then the door opened. Skipper was standing there in
his pajamas and bare feet, staring at the bed.

"Mommy, I'm sick."

"Go back to your room. I'll be right there," Lila said.

"I want to get in bed with you and Daddy." He came
closer, his eyes focusing on Kurt. "Who's that?"

"A houseguest."

"What's he doing in Daddy's bed? I have to go to the bathroom again," he said and ran out.

She grabbed a robe and followed Skipper to the bathroom. She took a thermometer from the medicine cabinet and shook it, then took his temperature. It was 104 degrees. A deathly fear gripped her. Diarrhea and a high fever. What could it be? There were so many strange tropical diseases here. That was one of the problems of living in a primitive country like Brazil with small children. The milk wasn't pasteurized and canned milk had to be imported from the United States, there were poisonous insects and cockroaches as large as rats. . . .

"My tummy hurts." Skipper started to cry.

"There, there, sweetheart. You're going to be all right." She washed his hands and led him back to his room.

"I'll get Bertha," she said, opening the bureau drawer and taking out fresh pajamas.

"I don't want Bertha!"

"I'll be right back."

She dashed down the hall to her room. Kurt was already dressed.

"You can go down the stairs before anyone sees you," she said.

"I'll call you tomorrow."

"Yes." Her thoughts were disconnected, fragmented with worry and anguish.

He kissed her quickly and left.

She went to Bertha's room and knocked on the door. The German woman was snoring loudly. Lila knocked again.

"What do you want?" the voice said angrily.

"Bertha, I need you. At once."

The voice changed. "Oh, it's you, Mrs. Townsend."

Is this how she acts with the children when I'm not here? Lila wondered.

Bertha had on a tan flannel robe over her nightgown, her long gray hair in a braid hanging down her back. Without her glasses she looked like a near-sighted owl. "Something is wrong?"

"Yes, it's Skipper. I'm afraid he's extremely ill."

Skipper was huddled up on his bed moaning and looking deathly pale.

"I got out fresh pajamas for him. His were soaking wet." Lila handed them to Bertha. "I'll go call Doctor Bowen." Her voice was shaking. Was this punishment for her affair with Kurt? All that mattered now was that Skipper get well. He couldn't die, he couldn't!

"It's better that we take care of him here at the house," Doctor Bowen said, after examining Skipper. "Keep him quiet and give him boiled water. He must have liquids to replace what he's lost so he doesn't become dehydrated."

"What does he have?" Lila asked nervously.

"I'm not sure yet. Some form of dysentery. I'll look in on him tomorrow. If he gets any worse, call me."

"What should I watch out for?"

"If his fever goes higher, or convulsions—"

"Convulsions?"

"Sponge him off with cool water. That will help to keep the fever down."

If only Donald were here with her. She felt so alone and frightened. And just a few hours ago her thoughts had been only of Kurt. But Donald was Skipper's father, he was always calm and controlled during a crisis, while she went all to pieces.

"Sometimes these things look worse than they are," Doctor Bowen said. "Try not to worry too much."

Natalie got out of bed and opened the door of her

room. All the sounds in the hallway, feet scurrying back and forth, had woken her up. She heard voices coming from Skipper's room and she wondered if he was sick. Skipper was always getting sick and when he was he got so much attention that everyone forgot about her. She thought she would pretend to be sick so she could have milk toast and Jell-O brought to her on a tray and have her mother fuss over her and be worried the way she always was about Skipper.

She saw Bertha coming out of Skipper's room carrying a wet towel.

"What's the matter, Bertha?" she asked. "Is Skipper sick?"

"Yes. Now go back to bed. We are all busy." Bertha disappeared into the bathroom and Natalie could hear water running in the bathtub. Then she heard her mother's voice calling anxiously for Bertha.

"Yes, Madam. I am coming." Bertha raced down the hall with more towels, water dripping on the parquet floor.

Doctor Bowen's expression was grave. "When will your husband be back?" he asked Lila.

"The day after tomorrow."

"Good."

"What's the matter?" Her face had drained of all color. "Skipper's worse, isn't he?"

"Let's say he's not getting any better. Usually these intestinal upsets run their course in forty-eight hours."

"What can we do?"

"There's a new Japanese serum I'd like to try. They've had some good results from it." Doctor Bowen hesitated. "It's not very pleasant and there can be side effects."

"You mean it's painful?"

He nodded.

Once as a child she had been bitten by a rabid dog and

she would never forget the pain of the shots she had to take afterward. They had to hold her down while they gave them to her and she had screamed and screamed.

"I hate to put Skipper through all that," she said, her eyes filling with tears.

"We have no choice," Doctor Bowen said. "Better that than flowers."

"Daddy, Daddy, you're home!" Natalie came running down the stairs and threw herself into her father's arms.

"Hello, Natalie." He kissed her absent-mindedly and then turned to her mother. "What does Doctor Bowen think it is?"

"Some kind of tropical dysentery. He's given Skipper a new serum," she said, as they went up the stairs together leaving Natalie standing at the bottom. "He seems a little better today."

Natalie sat down on the steps and picked at a scab on her knee. She heard her parents go into Skipper's room and then her father's booming voice saying, "How's my sailor boy?"

Skipper opened his eyes. "Daddy," he said weakly.

Donald kissed him. "What's this about you being sick? We can't have any of that. You've got to get well."

Skipper stared at his father. "Are you really here?"

"Of course I'm here."

"I thought you were home before. I went in your room, but it wasn't you."

My God! Was he going to tell Donald about the strange man in her bed? "Skipper was delirious with a high fever and he imagined he heard your voice," Lila said quickly.

"Well I'm home now, son, and I'm not going away again. At least not for a long time."

"Good. I'm glad, Daddy." Skipper closed his eyes.

"You get some sleep, son," Donald said.

Lila patted Skipper's damp blond curls. I will give up Kurt, she vowed, consumed with guilt. I will never see him again if only Skipper gets well. My precious little boy, my darling baby. For every moment of joy there is a price and this is it. But it is too high. Dear God, it is too high. I could not bear to lose Skipper. But the idea of never seeing Kurt again, of never making love again . . . I couldn't bear that either. Oh, what am I to do?

"Don't look so worried, darling," Donald said, putting his arms around her. "Skipper's going to be just fine."

12 ⑥

"WE HAVE A NEW CHANCELLOR,"
Bertha said, as they took their afternoon promenade, Natalie
and Skipper dressed in matching brother-sister outfits.
"Adolph Hitler will make Germany great again."

"What's a chancellor?" Natalie asked.

"Like your President," Bertha said.

"Oh." She didn't quite understand but Bertha certainly
seemed happy about it. "Can we take a cable car to Sugarloaf
today?"

"Not today. We are meeting Ilse and Michael in the
park."

Natalie's face fell.

"I don't like Michael," Skipper said.

"Now, now," Bertha said. "Michael is a very nice little
boy. And besides, I have something to discuss with Ilse."

"I want to go on the cable car," Skipper said.

"We will go tomorrow," said Bertha. "But today we are
going to the park."

Lila drove up the winding road to Kurt's house and as
she pulled in the driveway she heard piano music coming
through the open windows. She rang the bell several times
before he heard her and came to the door.

"Ah, you are here." He took her in his arms. "I did not
hear the doorbell. Forgive me. Were you waiting long?"

"Only a few minutes. What was that you were playing?

It was beautiful, and wild and passionate."

"It was a Liszt étude, *Wilde Jagd*. Wild Hunt."

"I can't stay very long," she said. "Bertha has taken the children for their afternoon promenade."

After Skipper recovered from his near fatal illness she had vowed never to see Kurt again, but then she ran into him at a party and when she saw him she knew she was lost. I want him, her whole being cried out. Now. I cannot live without him. The next day their affair resumed and they met at his house in the afternoons.

"I may be transferred back to Berlin," he said, as they walked into the bedroom.

Her body stiffened. "But I thought that you were going to be here for a year or two?"

"I had hoped so, but since Adolph Hitler is now chancellor, there will be some changes."

"When would you leave?"

"I'm not sure. Probably soon."

Then I wouldn't see him again, he would be gone from my life. No, I couldn't stand that. "Oh, Kurt," she cried, throwing her arms around him.

"There, there, my love. There is a solution, you know."

"What is that?"

"Leave Donald and come with me."

"You mean get a divorce?"

"Would that be so impossible?"

"I don't know. There are the children—"

"We don't have to decide right this minute. Come, my darling, let us not waste any time." He pulled her over to the bed and started to undress her.

Divorce, what a hideous word, she thought, as she drove down the winding road from Kurt's house. But of course, that was the only way. Yet Donald was such a good man, he loved her, he trusted her completely, she was his whole life, well not his whole life because she had often thought that the sea and ships meant more to him than anything, but a divorce would destroy him, and his naval career. And what about the children? Donald would fight for them. There would be ugly accusations, a terrible scandal. Could she face all that?

She gripped the steering wheel tightly as she rounded a sharp curve. Oh, Kurt, Kurt, what am I to do? The idea of losing him forever, that was not bearable either. Why did life demand such impossible choices?

In the beginning their love affair was like a fantasy and the secrecy made it exciting, but now that it was about to come out into the open and people would be hurt. . . .

No, I can't go through with it, I can't face Donald and tell him—what? That I no longer love him, that I want to marry someone else? But Kurt had not mentioned marriage, though that was what he meant, wasn't it?

She swerved suddenly to avoid another car coming rapidly around a blind curve. Why he was way over on her side, he had almost hit her! Then she would be out of all this mess, to sleep peacefully forever under a shady tree with flowers heaped on her grave. "She was so young," people would say. "Such a tragic accident."

Now I'm being morbid, she thought. I must figure out what to do. But whatever I do, I will hurt someone.

As she turned onto Avenida Atlantica she saw Bertha and the children walking toward the house. How sweet Skipper and Natalie looked in their matching brother-sister outfits. No, I can't do it to them, she thought, I can't turn their world upside down. Tears filled her eyes and her throat felt tight. She must get control of herself before the children sensed that something was wrong and started asking questions, questions that she couldn't answer because she did not know herself what the answers were.

"Look, Bertha, there's Mommy's car!" Skipper pointed.

"No, it isn't. She said she was going to take a nap," Natalie said.

"It is too. And I see Mommy driving it."

"I believe Skipper is right," Bertha said, as the yellow Pierce-Arrow slowed down in front of the house.

"Mommy! Mommy!" Skipper started to run.

"She can't hear you," Natalie said.

"Come back here," Bertha said sharply. "Don't you dare cross the street without me."

The car stopped and Lila got out and walked up the front steps to the house.

"Mommy!" Natalie called.

Lila turned around and waved. Bertha grabbed Skipper's hand but he slipped away from her and ran toward his mother with Natalie skipping after him.

"Hello, children. Did you have a nice walk?"

"We saw some beautiful butterflies in the park," Natalie said.

"And I saw a snake," Skipper announced. "Mommy, can I have a snake?"

"Now, Skipper," Lila said. "You know how I feel about snakes."

"I hate them," said Natalie, making a face at Skipper. "Snakes are slimy and ugly."

"I'll ask Daddy if I can have a snake," Skipper said. "I bet he'll let me have one."

"Let us go in now and get cleaned up before dinner," Bertha said.

"That's a good idea," Lila said, unlocking the front door. "You go have your baths."

"I don't want a bath," Skipper said. "I want you to play with us, Mommy."

"Now, children, I have things I have to do. You run along with Bertha." Bertha was looking at her oddly, Lila thought, and she wondered if she suspected anything. "I'll see you later."

She took a scented bath and sponged herself off carefully, but she could still smell Kurt's tobacco on her skin. She lit a cigarette and paced the room nervously, trying to figure out what to say to Donald when he came home, which should be any minute. How complicated her life had become! Like wandering among those hedges that are cut in a maze and you keep going back again and again to the same place without being able to find the way out.

I may be transferred back to Berlin.

Kurt's words went through her like a winter chill and she felt herself shivering. If only she had the courage to leave her husband and join her lover, to take happiness when it was offered to her, to fly with winged feet where it led and not think of the consequences. But how could she face Donald or her children, or herself, if she did?

"I'm home, dearest." She heard Donald's voice on the staircase. He came in the room and embraced her. "How was your day?"

"Oh, fine. The same as usual." She couldn't say it, she couldn't. I'll wait and see what happens, she thought.

She dreamt that she and Kurt were in a cable car coming down from Sugarloaf. Behind the mountains the sun was slowly sinking, turning the green ranges into dark corridors. Then, in a flash, it disappeared and an orange-red plume of color flamed to heaven. The car swayed in the wind and for a moment she felt afraid and she gripped Kurt's hand tightly, but the fear vanished as the lights around the harbor came on one after another, like lighting a huge birthday cake.

They seemed to be floating in the pure ether of space as they descended, with a sky full of stars and the glittering lights of the city below.

Suddenly there was a sound, a horrible creaking sound of metal braking, the car broke free from its cable and hurled itself downward, there were terrified screams as they fell, faster and faster. . . .

"No, no, I don't want to die! Not yet!"

She awoke shaking and Donald was holding her and trying to comfort her.

"It's all right," he said. "You were having a bad dream."

13 ☙

"HAPPY BIRTHDAY TO YOU, HAPPY birthday to you, happy birthday, dear Natalie, happy birthday to you!"

Natalie took a deep breath and blew out the five pink candles. "I did it!" she said. "I get my wish."

"What did you wish for?" Skipper asked.

"I won't tell. If I tell anyone, I won't get it."

"Whatever it is, I hope it comes true," Lila said. "Now let's cut the cake."

Bertha handed Lila a knife.

"I want to cut the cake myself," Natalie said.

"All right," Lila said. "But be careful. The knife is very sharp."

"When do we open the presents?" Skipper asked.

"In a few minutes," Lila said.

"I wish Daddy could be here," Natalie said.

"So do I," said Skipper.

"He'll be home tomorrow," Lila said.

"But tomorrow's not my birthday. It's today."

"Daddy has a special surprise for you," Lila said. "A present you'll really like."

A puppy, that's what it must be, thought Natalie. Daddy had promised, hadn't he? "Where is it?" she asked.

"Wait and see. Now you have the first piece of cake for yourself, Natalie." Lila handed Natalie a large slice with white frosting and a pink rose. "And here's one for Michael."

"I want that one," said Skipper.

"Guests first," Lila said. "There you are, Michael."

"Thank you," Michael said.

"You may serve the ice cream now, Maria," Lila said in Portuguese to the pretty Brazilian maid.

"*Sim, Senhora.*"

"I want chocolate," Skipper said.

"What kind would you like, Laura?" Lila asked. Laura was the Harrisons' daughter and Natalie hadn't wanted to invite her. It was embarrassing when children didn't care for the children of your friends, Lila thought. Laura seemed like a nice child.

"I'd like strawberry, please," Laura said.

Skipper had smeared his face with icing.

"Skipper, use your napkin," Bertha said. She wiped his face, throwing a hopeless glance at Ilse behind Lila's back. "See what good manners Michael has."

"I don't care," Skipper said.

Natalie could hardly wait to finish her ice cream and cake so she could see what her special present was.

"Now, let's go out in the garden and open the presents," Lila said. The sooner she got them outside the better, she thought. Skipper had already spilled ice cream and cake on the Oriental carpet and had gotten down from his chair and was challenging Michael to a race around the dining room table. Maybe they should have eaten outside as well, but Natalie had wanted to have the ice cream and cake in the dining room "like grown-ups." Well, for Skipper's birthday next month she was going to have the whole party outside, or else take them to the beach. "I'll get the presents," she said. "You children go on outside with Bertha and Ilse."

"May I help you carry something, Mrs. Townsend?" Ilse asked.

"Why yes, that would be a help. Thank you, Ilse."

Lila and Ilse carried the gaily-wrapped gifts out to the

walled garden back of the house and Natalie started to open them. Unlike most children, who ripped the paper to shreds in their eagerness to get to the present, Natalie carefully took off the ribbons and papers and put them in a neat pile, and on a rainy day she would get them out and make dresses for her paper dolls with them.

She opened the gifts and politely thanked each person, waiting to get to the special present. Skipper had something too so he wouldn't feel left out, a toy ferry with tiny cars that he could use in the bathtub. Her grandmother in Oklahoma had sent a dress and her grandfather had sent a book called *Pinocchio* with pop-up pictures. Skipper liked that, especially when the whale opened his mouth. Her other grandparents in North Carolina had sent a big box of crayons of all different colors and a drawing pad and a fairy princess costume to wear for Carnival. They must be keeping the special present in a closet somewhere so he wouldn't bark, she thought, when she had unwrapped everything.

"Now I'll get Daddy's present," Lila said. She went in her house and came back with a big box.

Could a puppy be in that? Natalie wondered. But nothing barked or moved inside the box. She opened it eagerly and took out a large doll with short blonde curls all over her head and wearing a blue-and-white polka-dot dress.

"A Shirley Temple doll!" exclaimed Laura. "Oh, let me see her."

Natalie handed her over, trying not to show her disappointment.

"She even has a blue bow in her hair and matching blue socks," Laura said. "And look, two dimples, just like Shirley Temple."

"Isn't that something special?" Lila asked. "Daddy had quite a time finding a Shirley Temple doll. They're all the rage back home."

But I wanted a puppy. Daddy knew I wanted a puppy.

"Don't you love your doll?" Lila asked.

"Yes, she's very nice," Natalie said.

Lila smiled. "Daddy thought you'd like her."

"I don't think she really likes the doll," Donald said.

"Of course she does. She's crazy about it," Lila said.

"I did promise to get her another dog after Spotty."

"But that would be impossible the way we move around."

"I know. But I think she's disappointed."

"You don't get everything you want in life," Lila said. "And Natalie might as well start learning it now."

Donald looked at her sharply. What did Lila mean by that? Was she referring to herself? She had been evasive lately, there was something about her he couldn't put his finger on, in fact if he didn't know her better he would swear she was having an affair with someone. But that was ridiculous, he assured himself. He reached out his arms to her. "Let's go to bed."

"I'll be up in a few minutes."

Last night, after Natalie's birthday party, she had driven to Kurt's house and they had made passionate love in the desperate fashion of shipboard lovers at the end of the voyage, wondering when, if ever, they would see each other again. She did not ask if he had received his orders from Berlin because she did not want to know. And now Donald was waiting for her, waiting for her to come to bed with him. She was living a lie and she did not know what to do.

"Lila!" Donald was calling her.

"I'm coming," she said.

◈

Crystal prisms exploded in her head and then jagged streaks of amber lightning. Lila pressed the pillow against her left temple but the migraine pain continued, throbbing fiercely, she clenched her hands and cried out, "Stop! Oh, God, I can't stand it any longer! Please make it stop!"

But no relief came.

The sounds of the crowd celebrating Carnival came closer, the beat-beat of drums and samba music and a smell that was sickening sweet drifted into her room. I want quiet, she thought, holding the lace-edged pillow over her head, but nothing would block out the sound.

Kurt had received his orders. He was returning to Berlin in two weeks.

Was that what had triggered the migraine? He had pleaded with her to speak to Donald, to tell him she wanted a divorce, but she could not. It was too cruel. Yet every part of her being longed for Kurt.

Oh, make the music stop! I want to lie in this room in silence and darkness until I forget everything, until the pain goes away and I am at peace again.

Peace, she thought. Will I ever know it again? Odd when the one thing I longed for in life was excitement, and now I want above all peace. Snowflakes falling on pine trees, holly growing wild along the sandy paths of my Carolina childhood, soft Southern voices, all the things I fled from and now want again.

For every moment of happiness we pay a price. "Oh, Kurt, Kurt!" she moaned, pressing her face against the pillow, as if she could blot out the pain that would not stop, the pain that would be with her forever.

Natalie stood on the balcony overlooking Avenida Atlantica watching the parade with Skipper and Bertha. She was wearing her fairy princess costume and had a rolled-up streamer of confetti in her hand. People were throwing confetti streamers from cars and they looked like brightly colored ribbons hanging on the lampposts and scattered in the street.

"Can I throw it now?" she asked.

"Go ahead," said Bertha, and Natalie tossed the purple streamer into the crowd below.

"I want one too," Skipper said, and Bertha handed him a green one.

Large floats passed with dancers twirling and shaking to the samba rhythms, bands playing loudly, everyone joining in the merriment.

"Let's go down there, Bertha," Natalie said.

"Are you crazy? Everyone is drunk, it is not safe. It is worse than Octoberfest in Munich."

"I want Mommy to come and watch the parade with us," Skipper said.

"Your mother is not feeling well," Bertha said sharply. "She has a migraine. Do not bother her."

"What's a migraine, Bertha?" Natalie asked.

"A very severe headache. Just hope that you never get them."

"When Daddy comes home he'll take me down to see the parade," Skipper said. "I want to ride on one of the floats."

"I like all the pretty costumes," Natalie said. "When I'm grown up I'm going to be a dress designer."

"And I want to be an acrobat," Skipper said. "Look!"

A black man dressed in a tiger costume was turning somersaults.

"See what I can do." Skipper started to climb up on the balcony railing.

Bertha grabbed him. "Be careful. That is dangerous."

"I won't fall," Skipper said.

They heard footsteps behind them and Bertha turned around.

"Daddy!" Natalie said.

"Can we go down on the street and watch the parade, Daddy?" Skipper asked. "Bertha won't let us."

"Yes, Daddy, please," Natalie pleaded.

Donald hesitated. "You can see it better from here."

"That's what I told the children," Bertha said.

Natalie looked crestfallen, Bertha smug.

"Well, if you'll each hold my hand tightly—"

Natalie jumped up and down. "Oh, thank you, Daddy."

"You'll have to be very good and stay right with me. No dashing out in the crowd. It would be very easy to get separated."

"We'll be good," Skipper said.

"You promise?"

"Promise and cross my heart," Natalie said.

14 ⑥

LILA FELT LIGHT-HEADED, GIDDY, the way she always did after a migraine attack, but at least the awful pain was gone.

"Do you feel better?" Donald asked.

"Yes." It was like coming back from the dead and with each one she thought she couldn't bear another. Her mother had suffered from migraines too but that was when she was going through the menopause and after that they stopped.

"Maybe you should see a neurologist about those headaches," Donald said. "You're having them more often than you used to."

"What could he do? They'll go away eventually." Dear Donald, he was so sweet and concerned and he knew nothing of the turmoil going on within her.

"I hate to see you suffer so," he said. "There must be something—"

"There's nothing." Nothing, she thought. Donald, I don't love you anymore. I'm in love with another man. I want to leave you, to go away with him, to be with him forever.

"I love you so much," Donald said. "I can't bear to see you in pain."

"It's over now." She avoided looking at him. "I'm fine.

"I have a present for you," Kurt said on the phone. "Something you've admired. I want you to have it."

"What is it?" Lila asked, wondering what it could possibly be. "Tell me."

"Wait and see. Are you going to be home? I'll bring it by."

She felt all her firm resolve melting at the sound of his voice, the thought of seeing him again. "Yes, I'll be here."

What did it matter if Donald made a fuss? Kurt was leaving, there was nothing wrong with him giving her a gift if he wanted to, she rationalized.

She opened the large box packed carefully with tissue paper and unwrapped the brass basket of gemstone flowers.

"Oh, Kurt! It's too much, I can't accept. This is yours, you brought it from China, you love it."

"I love you and I want you to have it. Then whenever you look at it you'll remember me."

I'll always remember you, she thought, and then she burst into tears. How unfair life was!

He put his arms around her. "There is still time for you to change your mind and come with me."

And leave a note on the pillow for Donald, slip out in the middle of the night? "I want to be with you," she said. "You know that."

"Then speak to Donald."

Only ten days left and then Kurt would be gone. The days that remained to them were slipping away like sand through a sieve. "I have to wait for the right moment," she said, knowing that there was never a right moment to tell a husband you want to leave him, that you want your freedom so you can marry another man.

"And when will be the right moment? We haven't much time left."

"I know. But there are the children to consider—"

"Let Donald have custody."

She pulled away from him. "You mean give up my children?"

"Not exactly—"

"What do you mean then?"

"They could visit you. And we could have a child. I would like a son with you."

"You are making it a very difficult choice for me."

"In life there are no easy choices. Either you love me and want to be with me, or you don't."

"I do love you. I love you and I wish I didn't!" she burst out.

"I'm sorry you feel that way. I'd better go now."

"Yes, Bertha will be back any minute with the children." The children. Could any other man be expected to love your children the way you did? Or their own father? And Donald did love them? To Kurt they were just something in the way, something to tolerate because of her. "Oh, Kurt, you are making it so hard for me."

He took her in his arms and pulled her close. "I do not mean to, my darling. I have known many women in my life, but you are the one I want, the woman I wish to be with me always, to be my wife."

"I can't think clearly now. Call me later. No, I'd better call you. Donald might be home."

"And you'll speak to him?"

"Yes," she said.

After Kurt left she walked over to the French windows facing Avenida Atlantica and watched his car drive away. And then she saw another car come out of a side street and start to follow him.

Was it just her imagination? No, the car was definitely following him. Had Donald suspected something and hired a detective? Or if it was true that Kurt was in intelligence, as Donald had told her shortly after they met, could there be a reason that he was being tailed?

The cars were now out of sight, lost in heavy traffic.

She turned away from the window and as she did she heard the children's voices. They were returning from their promenade with Bertha.

"Hello, Mommy." Natalie ran into the room, followed by Skipper.

"Will you play with us?" Skipper asked.

Lila kissed them both. "Did you have a nice walk?"

"It was all right," Natalie said. "Oh, what's that? It's pretty." She went over to the gemstone arrangement on the table beside the box.

"Is it a present?" Skipper asked.

"Yes, a friend gave it to me," Lila said. She had meant to put it away but now it was too late.

"Can I eat the grapes?" Skipper asked, reaching out to touch them.

"They're not real, silly," Natalie told him.

"They're made of jade," Lila said, "and very delicate, so you must be careful or they could break."

"I like the flowers," Natalie said. "Especially the lavender ones."

"Those are amethysts," Lila said.

"Where are you going to put it, Mommy?" Natalie asked.

"Where do you think it would look nice? Perhaps on this console?" She wanted it high enough out of reach so that small fingers could not play with it or knock it over. Not waiting for them to answer and possibly disagree she set the brass basket on the carved jacarandá console. "There, it's perfect." She saw Bertha hovering in the hallway. "Now run along with Bertha and get your baths and then I'll come up and read you a story."

"I want Daddy to read me a story," Natalie said.

"Oh, fine." She tried not to show that she was hurt by Natalie's remark. Perhaps the children wouldn't miss her so much after all. No, Skipper would. Skipper was her baby, he needed her. Oh, what am I to do? she thought. As Kurt had said, in life there are no easy choices.

"I hear your tango partner is being transferred back to Berlin," Donald remarked when he came home that evening.

"Which one is that?" she asked nervously.

"Count von Jaeger. I'm sure all the ladies will miss him, especially Pilar Alfaro."

"You don't like him, do you?"

Donald considered a moment. "I don't like or dislike him. He makes a good extra man for dinner parties and women apparently find him attractive, but that's his stock in trade. He never stays with any woman very long, so I'm told."

How little you know him, she thought, and wondered how she should begin.

"Anyway, I'm sure he'll find available ladies in Berlin," Donald said. "He doesn't seem to be the marrying kind, so that may be part of his charm."

But he wants to marry me. He wants to marry me, Donald, and I want to marry him. She took a deep breath. "I—" She stopped, unable to plunge in the knife. If only Donald had done something despicable, something that justified her leaving him, it would make it easier.

"Yes? You were about to say something?"

"I think you're wrong about Kurt von Jaeger."

"Oh, I've noticed that you seem intrigued by him. But I also know that you have too much sense to take him seriously. Women are a game to von Jaeger."

How much did Donald really know? She recalled the car pulling out of the side street and following Kurt's car.

"There are men like that, you know," Donald continued. "Men whose only interest is the chase and collecting notches in their belt. One of my roommates at Annapolis was like that."

Was that Donald's ploy, trying to cast doubt on Kurt's faithfulness, making her seem like a fool for being taken in? Suddenly she felt weary and filled with doubts. Suppose she did divorce Donald, lost custody of her children, and then Kurt walked out on her, refused to marry her? What would she do then? She would be left with nothing.

No, now was not the moment to ask Donald for a divorce, to tell him that she wanted to marry Kurt von Jaeger. She would have to wait for another time.

Later, lying in the darkness beside Donald, yearning to be with Kurt, she wrestled again with the decision that would turn all of their lives upside down. If Donald suspected a flirtation, she was sure he had no idea how far things had gone, or perhaps he had decided to act like a woman who knows her husband is having an affair but chooses to ignore it in the hope that if nothing is said it will break up of its own accord. But somehow that didn't seem like Donald. He was so disciplined, he had his emotions so under control, that if he thought he had been betrayed . . . she did not like to think of the consequences.

And she lay there most of the night listening to the sabiá singing in the garden, unable to sleep, until dawn and weariness claimed her.

15 ❧

"YOU DIDN'T ASK HIM FOR A divorce, did you?" Kurt said.

"I meant to," Lila said. They were at his house the following afternoon during siesta time lying on his bed, the shutters closed, the ceiling fan turning slowly overhead. "I tried, but I just couldn't bring myself—"

"Putting it off won't make it any easier. You just have to plunge in, like jumping into cold water."

How easy it is for you to say that, she thought. You don't have children who will be hurt, and Donald as well, a man who loves me and has never done me any harm. You have nothing to lose, I have. "I'll speak to Donald tonight," she said.

"What a wonderful life we will have together, my darling. You would like Berlin. It is one of the most sophisticated cities in the world with the best symphony orchestra, museums, theatres, cabarets, important literary figures. How good it will be to see each other openly, have tea at a café on Unter den Linden with violin music playing, travel together to Paris, London, Rome. You would love all those places."

"I know." She imagined signing Countess von Jaeger in a flowing script, Count and Countess von Jaeger being announced at balls. . . .

"And we will have a child together. A fine son to carry on the family name."

"Suppose it's a girl?"

"Then we will try again."

She tried to picture herself living in Germany with Kurt, but the scene was unfocused, blurred, as if the camera had been jarred suddenly just at the moment the shutter clicked. "Some people believe that Hitler is planning a war," she said. "That he will re-arm the Germans."

"Rumors only. There will be changes in Germany of course, but Hitler cannot change what is basically German. And none of my friends in Germany takes Hitler seriously. I believe the people will get tired of him soon and throw him out."

That was not what Donald thought but she did not say so. Was Kurt just saying that to reassure her?

"I'll have to learn German," she said.

"I will help you. It is not difficult."

How simple he made it sound, to change her whole life, for that is what she would have to do. A new country, a new language, leaving everything she had known behind.

"You will see, my darling, how happy we will be," he said, taking her in his arms.

She snuggled close against him. "Yes." But could happiness be built on the wreckage of others' lives?

"Now it is up to you," Kurt said. "You must make the decision. Life with me, or to continue as you are."

A life with Donald, the different Navy stations, apple polishing, always saying and doing the right thing until he became an admiral, all the while dreaming of Kurt, her lost love. Or to abandon her husband and children and go off with Kurt, choosing lust over honor, guilt her constant companion through the years. I want everything, she thought, and it is not possible.

"Oh, Kurt," she said. "I cannot live without you."

⑥

"You must be out of your mind," Donald said. "I had no idea it had gone this far."

"I tried to fight it. I didn't want to hurt you." She kept twisting the strand of pearls at her neck as she watched his face contorted with anger and pain.

"It's a little late for that, isn't it?" he said sarcastically.

"I didn't want it to happen."

"But it did. My wife, whom I trusted implicitly."

"Please, Donald, I know how you must feel—"

"You can have no idea how I feel."

"I would have given anything if I could have—"

"Spare me your pity. But if you think I'm going to give you a divorce, you're wrong."

The pearl necklace suddenly broke and pearls scattered across the parquet floor and rolled under the bed and bureau. Lila got down on her knees and started to pick them up.

"And what about the children? What did you propose to do about them?"

"I thought . . . we could share custody."

"Never! But that won't come up, because there will be no divorce."

And if I were to just run away with Kurt, what would you do then? she wondered. But she knew she could never face the scandal of that. Oh, Kurt, help me, help me!

"Von Jaeger is leaving shortly," Donald said. "In a week, I believe. So we will put all this behind us and go on as before." He seemed to be struggling with his emotions. "Maybe I am partly to blame. I have taken you too much for granted, not been as attentive as I should have. But all that will change. We will start over. Every marriage has a crisis and this is ours, but it is not the end."

You are wrong, she thought, it is the end, and she put the broken pearls on the bureau in a china bon-bon dish that was decorated with roses and violets and listened to the sound of the pearls as they clinked against the china. They are pieces of my heart breaking, she thought, and I will never be able to put it together again.

"So you can tell von Jaeger that there will be no divorce," Donald said. "The matter is finished and I will never bring it up to you again."

How magnanimous, she thought, staring at him with hatred. How smug you are in your righteousness. Forgive the sinner. But how had she expected him to act? To say, "Go off with your lover and *bon voyage*." No, he had behaved the way any husband would under the circumstances, possibly better than most.

"You will realize that I am right," Donald said. "In time.

That night she dreamed she was living with Kurt in a castle in Germany on the Baltic Sea. All of a sudden dark storm clouds appeared and she saw soldiers marching, they were doing the goosestep in black uniforms with red swastikas. Germany had declared war. Planes flew overhead and bombs started to fall, everything was going up in flames.

Then far out at sea she saw a speck coming closer, it was an American destroyer and as it approached she saw that Donald was on the bridge. He had come to rescue her.

"You are my wife now," Kurt was saying in German, "and Germany is at war with America."

"No, no, I want to go home," she heard herself replying in German, she was crying, saying more things in German, she had no idea she could speak it so fluently, it rolled off her tongue. "I am not German!" she screamed. "Let me go!"

But Bertha appeared, Bertha was in a military uniform and she had a whip. "Here I am in control, not you," she sneered. "*Heil Hitler!*"

"Where are the children? I want my children!" she cried.

"You will not see them again," Bertha said. "Ever." She raised the whip. "Repeat after me, *Heil Hitler*."

"I won't! I am an American and—"

The whip came down on her back, again and again, while Kurt stood there watching. She screamed in pain and tried to get away but there was no escape. . . .

She awoke with a start. Donald was lying in bed beside her, snoring softly, in a deep sleep.

Later, after Donald had left for work, she telephoned Kurt.

"Can you come by this afternoon?" she asked.

"Did you speak to him?"

"Yes."

"And?"

"I'll tell you when I see you. Around two?"

"Very good."

No, it's not very good, she thought when she hung up the phone. There is no way for us to be together. Tears came to her eyes and she wiped them away. She had her love affair and now it was over. She had no choice but to remain with Donald, and in time, perhaps, the pain would dull and she would be left with the memory of love, a love that she would keep hidden in her heart. Forever.

16 ☺

LATER WHAT HAPPENED ON THAT
terrible day would blur in her memory like paint colors
running into each other, so at the inquest that followed Lila
had trouble remembering the exact sequence of events.

The living room filled with white flowers, "Song of
India" playing on the piano, the new music roll that had just
arrived from New York, and she sat at the piano watching the
keys play, as if by a mysterious ghost, the haunting sad
melody that she had first heard Kurt play, and it seemed
fitting that it should be their final song.

Any moment he would be here and she must tell him
that it was over, finished, that there was no way they could be
married, and tears filled her eyes as she rehearsed her
speech. Then he arrived, looking so handsome that her heart
broke at the sight of him and she knew that she could not
give him up, that she would love him forever.

And suddenly, like a scene in a nightmare, Pilar Alfaro
facing them with a gun, why did Maria let her in, but it is
already too late, the gun goes off, a strange pop-pop sound
like a toy gun of Skipper's, but this is real and Kurt clutches
his chest and falls to the floor.

Screams, sobs, blood seeping onto the Oriental carpet,
"Song of India" playing, she had put it on repeat, please
someone turn it off! Kurt's face ashen, his breath coming in
short gasps, call an ambulance, he is dying.

Kurt's body covered with white flowers, they could not save him, he had lost too much blood, he told them it was an accident and then he died.

How do I go on living without him, how do I stand the years ahead?

The inquest, the questions, endless questions, will they never stop, I can't take any more. Over and over the same territory, probing, dissecting, until I feel like something under a microscope. Donald, stiff-lipped, standing beside me, wiping away my tears. Pilar, hysterical, remorseful, wringing her hands. Diplomatic immunity. An unfortunate accident. It is finished. Everyone go home.

Home to the children, faces blurring around me as I sink into a drugged sleep. Voices fainted and fainter, dissolving into a black cloak of grief. . . .

17 ☉

THE TUGBOATS WERE SLOWLY pulling them out to sea. Lila stood on the deck of the white ocean liner, Natalie and Skipper beside her, watching the harbor of Rio disappear from view.

"Why couldn't Daddy come with us?" Skipper asked.

"Daddy's going to join us in Washington in a couple of weeks," Lila said. "He had some business in Rio to finish up first."

"Are we going to live in Washington now?" Natalie asked.

"Yes, for a while. We have to find a house to rent there."

"Then can I have a dog?"

"We'll see, Natalie. But first we're going to visit your grandparents in North Carolina. Won't that be fun?"

Farewell, Rio, she thought. The shoreline was getting farther and farther away, the city enveloped in a blue-gray mist, and rising above it the green mountain range with Sugarloaf and Corcovado, now smaller and smaller in the distance. Farewell Rio and samba music and orchids and white beaches and lazy afternoons of love.

Does time passing fade the greatest passions until there is left only a dim memory? Is my life changing so slowly that I do not notice? Will I want something different tomorrow?

The tugs cast off their cables and the ship gave three long blasts of its horn, long mournful wails as it headed out to sea.

Natalie put her hands over her ears.

"Why are you crying, Mommy?" Skipper asked.

Natalie looked up at her mother. Tears were running down her cheeks. "She's sad about leaving Daddy, silly," she told Skipper.

"But we'll see him soon," Skipper said.

The tugs had now headed back toward the harbor and the sea was beginning to get rough. Lila felt suddenly queasy. She had always prided herself that she never got seasick, even in the roughest weather, and now she had no one with her to take charge of the children.

"Let's go back to the cabin," she said.

"I want to explore the ship," Skipper announced, starting to walk away.

"Come back here," Lila called. "Natalie, go get him. I want to lie down in the cabin. I'm not feeling well."

Natalie ran after Skipper.

They just made it down to the cabin when Lila was violently sick. If only Bertha were with them to take the children so she could lie down and rest, she thought, as she vomited into the toilet again and again. Finally she collapsed on the narrow berth, a cold cloth on her forehead.

"Can I get you anything, Mommy?" Natalie asked, worried at her mother's pallor. "Shall I ring for the cabin steward?"

"No, I'll be all right. I just want to rest quietly for a little while." And she was over three weeks late for her period, she remembered, in fact she was almost due for a second period, or had she counted incorrectly? No, she was sure she was right. It couldn't be that she was pregnant? Oh, no! And if she were pregnant, and it certainly appeared so, was the baby Kurt's or Donald's? She held her head and moaned.

"Does something hurt, Mommy?" Skipper asked.

"No, sweetheart. It's nothing, don't worry. You and

Natalie look at some of your books or color some pictures or something." How could she stand two weeks on this ship feeling the way she did? Maybe she could give the cabin steward some extra money to watch the children part of the time. She closed her eyes wearily and drifted off into a half-sleep.

Suddenly there was a scream and she sat up with a start.

"Skipper took my *Pinocchio* book," Natalie yelled.

"I only wanted to look at it for a minute," Skipper said. "I like the picture of the whale."

"No, you can't have it. It's mine!" Natalie tried to snatch the book away and the cover ripped off. Natalie burst into tears. "Look what you did. You've ruined it!"

"You did it yourself," Skipper said, sticking out his tongue at Natalie. "So there."

"Children, please, I can't stand this fighting. Can't you be good?"

"I'm being good, Mommy," Skipper said.

"You are not!" retorted Natalie.

"Natalie, will you call the steward and ask him to bring me some tea?"

"Yes, Mommy." Natalie pushed the buzzer by the bed.

"And perhaps you children would like something. Ginger ale or some ice cream?"

"I want chocolate ice cream," Skipper said.

"And I want ginger ale and vanilla ice cream."

"I bet you get seasick," Skipper told her.

"I won't," Natalie said.

"Have whatever you want," Lila said. She pressed her face against the pillow. Oh, God, how do I bear two weeks of this? And the voyage had just begun. . . .

EPILOGUE

NATALIE

After we left Rio everything seemed to go faster, seasons turned all around and tumbled upside down, days gray instead of golden. Washington was gloomy and the apartment on Connecticut Avenue filled with the heavy Brazilian furniture from the house on Avenida Atlantica was dark and depressing. And it was here, on a cold January morning, that Skipper and I were introduced to our new baby sister Johanna.

Mother was lying in bed and the nurse, Mrs. Myers, was holding something with a red face wrapped in a blanket.

"Here's your big brother and sister," Mrs. Myers said, holding out the baby for our inspection.

"She's ugly," Skipper said.

"She's a very pretty little girl," cooed Mrs. Myers.

I stared at Johanna. How tiny her hands were. Had I been that small once? Mother was looking proudly at her accomplishment. Already she loved her more than she did me, I thought, and I wondered if my father, when he returned from sea, would feel the same way. He had been sent a cable about her birth and would be home in a month. I would rather have had a dog than a baby sister, but maybe when she got bigger we could play together. "Can I hold her?" I asked.

"If you sit down in this chair," Mrs. Myers said, "I'll put her in your lap."

Mother watched as she placed the baby in my arms.

She smelled of talcum powder and sour milk. "Isn't she a beautiful baby?" Mother said. She had never said that about me. I rocked Johanna gently like a large doll.

"I want to hold her too," Skipper said.

"You might drop her," I said.

"I won't." Skipper tried to grab Johanna from me.

"Children, stop fighting," Mother said. "You'll turn my milk sour."

"I'll take the baby," Mrs. Myers said, removing her from my arms.

"Tell Caladonia to give you your luncheon now," Mother said to me and Skipper. "It's time for me to nurse the baby."

We were ushered out of the room by Mrs. Myers.

"Why does Mommy have to nurse the baby when she has Mrs. Myers as a nurse?" I asked Caladonia as she served us our lunch.

A grin spread over Caladonia's black face. "I reckon you'll know all about that when you have your own babies some day, Miss Natalie," she said mysteriously, leaving me more in the dark than before. "Now eat your Brussels sprouts."

"I don't like them," I said, pushing them to one side of my plate. Caladonia had been hired to take care of us after Bertha left and she was much nicer, but she still tried to make me eat everything on my plate.

"I have something real good for dessert," Caladonia said.

"Oh, all right." I put one of the Brussels sprouts in my mouth and chewed it. What an awful taste it had! "That's all I can eat."

"Two more," Caladonia said. "Then you can have dessert."

⑥

Years blending into years, gray ships, new schools. . . .

It was the summer we were supposed to go to Europe and didn't, the summer of 1939. At the last minute Mother became ill and had to be rushed to the hospital for a hysterectomy. I was eleven. I wasn't quite sure what a hysterectomy was, only that it was something about not being able to have any more babies. "That's the only good thing about it," Mother said when it was over. What did she mean by that? Was it that she didn't want any of us? Ironic that I, who wanted children so much, was never able to have them. I think that I would have been a good mother, but perhaps not. Anyway, it was not to be.

But to get back to that summer. My father was already in the Mediterranean in command of a cruiser. We were to stay in a hotel at Cap d'Antibes and I had looked forward to it ever since school finished in May. We had booked passage on the *Ile de France* and our car had already been shipped to New York to be loaded on the ship, when everything was suddenly canceled. A cable was sent to my father and we spent the summer instead with my grandparents in the mountains of North Carolina.

I remember the day Mother came home from the hospital with a trained nurse. She took me aside and said to me, "Your mother is very upset because she thinks you are disappointed about the trip, so I want you to go into her room and tell her that you really don't care anything about going to Europe." I complied.

It was years before I went to Europe and then the first place I headed for was the south of France. I stayed at Cap d'Antibes.

Philippe worked for *Paris Match*. He was not handsome, but very intelligent, with a Gallic charm that swept me off my feet. Shortly after we were married, when I discovered he was being unfaithful, I was devastated. It brought back all the early rejection of my childhood in Rio, the feeling that no one, no one really loved me or ever had.

"Did you really expect a Frenchman to be faithful?" friends asked me after the divorce. I did not have the sophistication of European women who took such things in their stride, I wanted Philippe to love me and only me.

"But it meant nothing, *chérie*," Philippe told me when caught. "You are the one who matters."

How was I to know that? I didn't. I couldn't live with lies.

When I think of my father I remember a favorite saying of his: "You can't have two sets of manners." When I was about eight I did something at the dinner table that he reprimanded me for. "You wouldn't do that if you were eating at the Merrills' house, would you?"

"Of course not," I replied. "But I'm not at the Merrills', I'm at home."

"You can't have two sets of manners, one for home and another when you go out," he said sternly. "Or else when you go out you might slip."

I used to think he was just referring to table manners, but I came to realize that it applied to all of life.

When he died in late September of 1964 I had no idea he was ill until Mother telephoned. "I'm afraid I have bad news," she said. "Your father died this morning. Of pneumonia." I was stunned, the breath knocked out of me. "It was very sudden," Mother said. "He didn't want to go to the hospital. He insisted he was fine. You know how he is."

Yes, I knew.

I remember a scene in Newport. "There's nothing wrong with me," I heard him shouting at Mother. "I'm going back to my ship." Then he collapsed. An ambulance came and two medical orderlies lifted him onto a stretcher and took him to the Newport Naval Hospital where he remained three weeks with double pneumonia.

But that time he recovered. This time he didn't.

The funeral was at Arlington National Cemetery and there were crowds of tourists gaping at President Kennedy's grave nearby. My father had a full military funeral, his wish, and six white horses slowly pulled the ancient caisson with his flag-draped coffin, while a naval officer led a riderless black horse with the boots turned backwards.

I bit my lip hard as they played taps and his body was lowered into the grave, and I was able to control my tears until the moment when an officer handed the folded flag from his coffin to my mother.

"Did you know my husband?" Mother asked him.

"No," he replied. "I did not have the honor to serve with Admiral Townsend."

You can't have two sets of manners.

I sometimes used to wonder what happened to Bertha after we left her in Rio. And then, when my designs became known and were shown in magazines all over the world, I received a letter posted from Munich. It was from Bertha. She wanted to see me.

I figured she had probably returned to Germany, as she spoke of it so often during the days in Rio, and I imagined her as a matron in a concentration camp, swinging whips at terrified inmates with that fierce expression I knew so well.

I do not know what prompted me to look her up one time when I was in Munich. Perhaps I thought I could capture some of what eluded me in Rio, something that was missing in my life, possibly lost forever. Anyway I found her, a frail old woman in a nursing home. Had I made her seem more awful than she really was? No, I don't think so.

She did not know about Skipper's death. I had to tell her and I was surprised to see her weep. I did not know it was in her to feel for anyone. Maybe I should not have said anything, but she asked me about Skipper and I didn't know how I could avoid it. My father had died two years before, but she wanted to know about Mother. And she seemed to know something she was not telling me.

"So, it is no longer there," she said, looking at my forehead. "The birthmark."

Oh yes, it is still there, Bertha, only I have managed to hide it. And it has faded somewhat over the years. But whenever I get angry it shows fiery red, as if to remind me to keep my emotions under control.

But it is still there, it will always be there, just as Rio will always be part of me.

It took me a long time to come to terms with Skipper's death. Even though we fought a lot as children, and I guess all brothers and sisters do, I was not prepared for his terrible and tragic ending.

After Skipper's divorce he seemed to lose interest in women. I guess he was bitter. I still don't believe some of the things that the newspapers implied, and I know Mother didn't because she threatened to sue them for libel. Anyway, Skipper moved to Los Angeles and opened an antique shop on Melrose Avenue with another man. Then they bought a house together in the Hollywood Hills. They gave a lot of parties and they had very interesting friends and they traveled to Europe frequently. One time they took a South American cruise that stopped in Rio and Skipper said our old house there had been torn down and in its place was a tall apartment building.

I tried to picture it and couldn't. I can still see in my

mind the house in Rio and walk through every room.

I know it was a big disappointment to Dad that Skipper didn't want to go to Annapolis and had no interest in the Navy as a career, though he did serve on a destroyer escort during the war as an enlisted man and that was rough duty. But when the war ended he couldn't wait to get out.

I remember him at Dad's funeral at Arlington. Johanna and I were crying but he showed little emotion, or perhaps he was better at hiding it than we were.

"I know this will be harder on you girls," he said to Johanna and me after the funeral. "You were both close to him, but I never understood the old man. And I know he never understood me," he added as an afterthought.

I did not know that two years later we would be attending Skipper's funeral.

He was found bludgeoned to death in his home in the Hollywood Hills, his car stolen and his wallet and Rolex watch missing. He was living there alone at the time, as he and his friend had had a quarrel, according to friends. Several weeks later the police arrested a young man in Massachusetts who was driving Skipper's car and had been using his credit cards. He was a transient, who told the police that Skipper had picked him up on the Sunset Strip and invited him to his home for a party. He said there was no one else there and that they consumed a lot of liquor and then Skipper made advances to him. After that he said he couldn't remember anything. It was a messy trial and I was amazed at Mother's strength in holding up through it. But I was thankful that Dad was not still alive.

There was not enough evidence to prove anything, so the young man was released when the jury couldn't agree.

From then on Mother blamed Skipper's troubles on his divorce, as if it was the reason for everything that happened. But I never did. Because I think that whatever went wrong with Skipper's life started long before that.

It started in Rio.

I lay awake a long time in the guest bed, going over in my memory those long ago days in Rio, trying to imagine who the man could have been that Mother fell in love with, because even before her revelation at dinner tonight, I knew that she never really loved my father.

How lonely she must have been all this time and suddenly I felt more compassion for her.

Poor Mother. We never really know what goes on in anyone else's life, do we? Least of all our parents.

A frantic knocking on the door awoke me in the morning. Johanna stirred sleepily in the other bed.

"Miss Natalie, Miss Johanna, come quickly. It's your mother."

I threw on my robe and opened the door. Pauline was standing there in a state of shock, tears running down her cheeks.

"I brought your mother her breakfast tray, at eight o'clock the way I always do, and when I looked at her. . . ." She was unable to go on.

Johanna and I hurried down the hall to Mother's room. She lay back on her pillow, a faint smile on her face.

"Mother?" I bent over her. She was absolutely still. I felt for her heartbeat and there was none.

"Maybe she's in a coma," Johanna said. "Did you call an ambulance?" she asked Pauline.

"One's on the way, ma'am."

I knew that it was too late. Mother was gone. "It won't do any good," I said.

Johanna started to cry.

"At least she didn't have some awful, drawn-out illness,"

I said. "We can be grateful for that. She went the way she always wanted to, peacefully in her sleep."

Johanna wiped away her tears. "Yes, that's true."

"I'll make some more coffee," Pauline said, tactfully leaving us alone.

"She must have had some premonition," Johanna said. "I keep thinking about what she said last night at dinner, how she kept it to herself all these years, and on her eightieth birthday. . . ." She paused, remembering. "Now, we'll never know who he was."

I was thinking of all the things we had to do now, the funeral arrangements, notifying friends, the obituary. "Who?" I asked absentmindedly.

"Why the man she told us about last night at dinner," Johanna said. "That man in Rio."